MW01258406

Suicide in Modern Catholic Literature

Suicide in Modern Catholic Literature

————————— Martin Lockerd —————————

CASCADE *Books* · Eugene, Oregon

Cascade Books
An Imprint of Wipf and Stock Publishers
199 W. 8th Ave., Suite 3
Eugene, OR 97401

www.wipfandstock.com

PAPERBACK ISBN: 978-1-6667-8601-9
HARDCOVER ISBN: 978-1-6667-8602-6
EBOOK ISBN: 978-1-6667-8603-3

Cataloguing-in-Publication data:

Names: Lockerd, Martin, author.

Title: Suicide in modern Catholic literature / by Martin Lockerd.

Description: Eugene, OR: Cascade Books, 2025 | Includes bibliographical references and index.

Identifiers: ISBN 978-1-6667-8601-9 (paperback) | ISBN 978-1-6667-8602-6 (hardcover) | ISBN 978-1-6667-8603-3 (ebook)

Subjects: LCSH: Suicide in literature. | Suicide—Religious aspects—Christianity. | Christianity and literature. | English literature—19th and 20th centuries—History and criticism. | American literature—20th century—History and criticism.

Classification: PS153.C3 L60 2025 (paperback) | PS153.C3 (ebook)

VERSION NUMBER 06/06/25

Parts of chapters two and four of this book appeared respectively in the journals *Christianity and Literature* and *Mythlore*. Thanks to the editors for allowing reprinting of that material. I also owe thanks to Penguin Random House LLC for permitting me to quote small selections from Michel Houellebecq's novels *The Elementary Particles* and *The Map and the Territory*. The cover image, Gustave Doré's illustration of Dante's encounter with Pier della Vigna in *The Divine Comedy*, was provided by Art Resource, New York.

For my parents

Contents

Acknowledgments

THIS BOOK IS DEDICATED to my parents, Benjamin and Micheline Lockerd, who gave to me the gift of faith. Like most children who receive a gift they cannot immediately eat, play with, or understand, I often treated it with less care and gratitude than it deserved, but they patiently waited for me to know it for what it was and consistently modeled what it was for. Thank you.

I must also thank my father for reading and providing feedback on nearly everything in this book in its earliest and least polished form—not an enviable job. Others also did their best to turn this little book into something better than its maker could conjure on his own. Ellis Hanson and Richard Russell separately helped to improve the chapter on decadence and antinatalism. Sr. Maria Frassati Jakupcak greatly enriched my analysis of Benson's *Lord of the World* with her insights. Joshua Hren, who encouraged me to tackle this project at a crucial time, provided invaluable feedback on the chapter dealing with Tolkien. Tim Furlan helped me to refine my chapter on Walker Percy. Any residual bad philosophizing in that chapter is entirely my fault. Alan Friedman provided much needed input on the Graham Greene chapter, a very generous act. Many other friends and colleagues assisted greatly by discussing the ideas in this book. Among them are Liz Cullingford, Lee Oser, Brian Carl, Tom Harmon, Clark Elliston, Grant Kaplan, Patrick Lockerd, Anna Skinner, and Andrea Thomaz.

My thanks are also due to my colleagues and students at the University of St. Thomas, Houston, from whom I have drawn much inspiration. UST is one of the few schools to have bucked the more nihilistic intellectual trends of our age and insisted on giving its students a true vision of purpose and hope in an all-too-often despairing and seemingly meaningless modernity. We need more institutions like it, and I am proud to have served as a member of its faculty.

This book was difficult to write at times. Those who stare too deeply into the realm of despair risk something. Luckily, my wife, Jacqui, kept me thoroughly grounded and well loved during its composition. She also made many sacrifices to provide me with the time to write the darn thing. My daughters—Mary Thérèse, Madeleine, Cecilia, Aibhin, Bridget, and Léonie—and their new brother, Patrick, have kept my mind on those things that really matter. They evangelize me daily and remind me that this life is only the beginning. We are all together on a long journey, led through a maze of joy and suffering to our final end by threads of love. The threads are there. We just have to pick them up and follow.

Abbreviations

Introduction: The Problem of Suicide

MY STUDENTS AND THEIR peers regularly contemplate and sometimes even attempt suicide. If you are a teacher, this is true of some of your students as well. I'm only lucky that none has succeeded in completing the act. If you can't say the same, your life has been touched by an increasingly common kind of suffering, and I am deeply sorry. This tragic trend, already shocking prior to 2020, reached new heights during the COVID-19 pandemic. Between January of 2019 and May of 2021, suicide attempts among US citizens, which were already at an all-time high, rose across the board, including a breathtaking 50 percent increase among teenage girls.[1] Of course, the turn to suicide is not just a problem for the young—though I don't think that I'm alone in feeling that the despair of the young is especially painful to witness. Even pre-COVID pandemic figures from the Centers for Disease Control show a 37 percent increase in actual suicide rates in America across age groups from 2000 to 2018.[2] Though suicide rates decreased 5 percent between 2018–2020, they quickly rebounded in 2021–2022. These statistics, unthinkable just decades ago when many were already lamenting seemingly high suicide rates, have become a new normal, and not only in the United States.

Up to this point, our societal response to this epidemic of despair has been dominated by a secular, utilitarian psychotherapeutic intervention. Without disparaging in any way the hard and often thankless work done by those on the forefront of this effort, people who have

1. Centers for Disease Control, "Emergency Department Visits for Suspected Suicide Attempts."
2. Centers for Disease Control, "Suicide Data and Statistics."

1

done more for those suffering with suicidal ideation than I can fully imagine or appreciate, I would humbly submit that it has failed. We, in the modern, developed West, can boast greater access to mental health care and higher suicide rates than any civilization in recorded history. Without question, psychology must play a fundamental role in helping to reorient our civilization toward life, but its efforts must be supported by and founded on something more than an abstract desire for healthfulness and "well-being." Our problem is cultural, not purely medical. Literature, specifically Catholic literature, has a role to play in diagnosing and addressing the seemingly insoluble problem of suicide. In order to appreciate the ways in which Catholic literary modernity may signal solutions to this problem, we must first confront the dark realities of our particularly postmodern moment.

The Failure of the Therapeutic

Educators and parents in the twenty-first century are not the first to experience the phenomenon of despair among the young. Responding to a rash of student suicides in secondary schools in 1910, a now chronic state of affairs, Sigmund Freud (1856–1939) berated the school authorities for failing their charges:

> If it is the case that youthful suicide occurs not only among pupils in secondary schools but also among apprentices and others, this fact does not acquit the secondary schools. . . . A secondary school should achieve more than not driving its pupils to suicide. It should give them a desire to live and should offer them support and backing at a time of life at which the conditions of their development compel them to relax their ties with their parental home and their family. It seems to me indisputable that schools fail in this, and in many respects fall short of their duty of providing a substitute for the family and of arousing interest in life in the world outside.[3]

Freud concluded that education must play some role in inoculating young people against "melancholia" until "experience has solved this problem." This naïve belief in the power of experience is darkly comical. The general irony of Freud as a partisan for life is painful. Freud, the same thinker who in 1910 called on educators to give students reasons to live,

---

3. Freud, "Contributions to a Discussion on Suicide," 231.

became one of the major contributors to a particularly modern denial of the traditional justifications for living.

Nihilism, to speak precisely, lies at the heart of the philosophical ethos of our shared, suicidal modernity. The nineteenth-century German philosopher Friedrich Nietzsche (1844–1900) inaugurated this modernity by proclaiming the death of God. Freud theorized the nihilistic creature who emerged from the catastrophe of this divine dispossession. I use the term *nihilism* advisedly. Theologian David Bentley Hart makes the case for modernity's essential nihilism concisely:

> The word is not, I want immediately to urge, a term of abuse, and I do not employ it dismissively or contemptuously. There are today a number of quite morally earnest philosophers (especially in continental Europe) who are perfectly content to identify themselves as nihilists, because they understand nihilism to be no more than the rejection of any idea of an ultimate source of truth transcendent of the self or the world—a rejection, that is, not of the various objective *truths* that can be identified within the world but of the notion that there is some total or eternal *Truth* beyond the world, governing reality and defining the good, the true, or the beautiful for all of us here below. . . . Again, however, almost no one is entirely modern in this way, and very few of us are conscious or consistent nihilists.[4]

Freud fits this description well. He could recognize suicide as a problem, as a manifestation of a failure to give young people "a desire to live." He couldn't, in good faith, argue that students ought not to kill themselves, because he lacked recourse to any transcendent truth about who they are, what the world is, and what right action in that world signifies. At best, he could offer them his infamous "pleasure principle," the hollow promise of liberation from psychological neurosis through a loosening of moral restrictions on desire. Our culture has attempted this cure. Rising suicide rates present only the most overt of its pernicious outcomes.

Like it or not, we are all inheritors of Freud's turn away from objective notions of life's meaning and towards an ultimately, in the cosmic sense, meaningless life that must be negotiated through therapy and justified by contingent preference alone. I am intentionally avoiding the hyperbolic assertion that a life without God is necessarily devoid of all meaning. Contingent meaning may be found in a life lived in purposive relation to any value (e.g., wealth, ecological activism, Nazism, pleasure);

---

4. Hart, *Atheist Delusions*, 21.

however, such contingent values set a low bar for the human soul, which has historically and traditionally yearned for the *summum bonum*, the greatest discernible good—in a word, God. In his groundbreaking book *The Triumph of the Therapeutic: Uses of Faith after Freud* (1966), Philip Rieff credits Freud with substantially lowering the anthropological bar by developing the concept of "psychological man," an antihero whose primary measure of right action is the therapeutic maintenance of personal psychological equilibrium in an essentially meaningless world.

Freud provides no reason to live; he simply aims to manage the psychological burdens of living while it is happening in order to maximize pleasure and minimize pain. Rieff sums up the result nicely: "Freud's was a severe and chill anti-doctrine, in which the awesome dichotomy with which culture imposes itself upon men, that between an ultimately meaningful and a meaningless life, must also be abandoned."[5] Freud, building on the work of Nietzsche, took the death of God as a major premise of the psychoanalytic discipline he created. With God out of the picture, he understood all religion as an attempt to channel or repress the violent psychic impulses of humanity so that civilization, with all its material benefits, could emerge. In turn, Freud sought to dispel the delusion of religion so that humanity could escape the neurosis caused by its hypertrophied superego, its culturally constructed conscience.[6] Freud committed suicide with the assistance of his physician after a prolonged and painful bout with cancer in 1939.

Far from providing humanity with a sense of meaning that might counteract its suicidal tendencies, its willingness to reject the burden and gift of life, Freud played a part in a larger cultural evacuation of cosmic meaning and sought to mitigate the chill of the vacuum with the warmth of the psychologist's couch. I have no interest in denigrating the good work of psychologists, especially the growing number who reject Freud's premises and seek to foster better mental health within a more traditional, theistic worldview. Good psychological intervention plays a key role in suicide prevention.[7] As the numbers from the CDC indicate,

5. Rieff, *Triumph of the Therapeutic*, 24.

6. Seeking to soften the blow of Freud's brand of nihilism, Carl Jung attempted to hold on to the wisdom of the past through the accumulation of archetypal meaning-making myths. Even this ameliorative project, according to Reiff, ended in nihilism. Reiff, *Triumph of the Therapeutic*, 118.

7. The American Foundation for Suicide Prevention, "What We've Learned Through Research."

however, the mostly secularized project of mental health has failed. No culture in history has been more analyzed, psychologized, and medicated than ours. So, why are we killing ourselves in record numbers? There is no one answer to this question, a question which has broad economic, political, and cultural implications. I propose no simple solution. What seems abundantly clear to me is that our increasing inability to justify our existence to ourselves must stem at least in part from the arguments we make and the narratives we tell ourselves about that existence.

Far too often, we are content to attribute suicide wholly to the medicalized discourse of depression without thinking about the intellectual and spiritual dimensions of that mental state. There are essential problems with this approach. One, as Michael Cholbi, author of *Suicide: The Philosophical Dimensions* (2011) points out, is that blaming mental health disorders for suicide relies on disconcertingly circular reasoning. Many of the mental disorders blamed for suicide include suicidal behavior among the criteria for their diagnosis. "To the philosopher's eye," Cholbi writes, "this raises the prospect of circular explanation—of suicidal behavior being explained in terms of conditions that have suicidal behavior as one of their symptoms."[8] Acknowledging that mental disorders certainly do play a role in suicide, Cholbi insists that we must also account for other motivations. Particularly, he finds that suicidal persons are motivated by a "kind of nihilism" that springs from a "hopelessness." This hopelessness in turn can be traced back to feelings of "perceived burdensomeness" and "failed belongingness."[9] Depression and related metal disorders do not occur within a vacuum, and those sufferers who do opt for suicide tend to reflect the alienation and sense of personal nullity characteristic of our age. In short, the depressed but committed Christian faces a world far different from that of the depressed nihilist.

We can see the limitations of the suicide-as-mental-illness equation clearly in Sam Harris's *The Moral Landscape* (2010). Harris's book, while rightly interested in rejecting moral relativism, argues for a morality strictly based on the scientific method—a morality that mostly serves humanity by proving the absurdity of its own central claim.[10] Unfortunately, given Harris's star power as one of the leaders of the "New Atheism," even scathing reviews from several mainstream publications didn't stop the

8. Cholbi, *Suicide*, 165.

9. Cholbi, *Suicide,* 167–68.

10. For one of many good critiques of Harris's book, see Omelianchuk, "*Moral Landscape* (A Review)."

book from becoming a *New York Times* bestseller almost immediately. In a chapter called "The Future of Happiness," Harris relates the story of a friend who declared his intention to end his own life:

> He insisted that he was not depressed. He believed himself to be acting on a philosophical insight: everyone dies eventually; life, therefore, is ultimately pointless; thus, there is no reason to keep on living if one doesn't want to. We went back and forth on these topics, as I sought to persuade him that his "insight" was itself a symptom of depression or some other mood disorder. I argued that if he simply felt better, he wouldn't believe that his life was no longer worth living.[11]

We should note that Harris indulges in the circular reasoning debunked by Cholbi. Harris cannot conceive of ideas and beliefs as matters of importance because he assumes that all suicidal ideation is the result of mental disorders that have suicidal ideation as one of their key characteristics.

By treating his friend's suicide as the predictable symptom of a medical event, Harris shows his ignorance of some of the foundational ideas of suicidology. The founding father of modern suicidology, Edwin S. Shneidman, posits that the suicidal person is trying to resolve psychic anguish that can be caused by a host of factors but cannot be simply reduced to a clinical diagnosis. He made this point in a clear response to a 1992 study of "Rational Suicide and Psychiatric Disorders":

> The burden of their [the authors'] presentation is that the crux of suicide prevention lies in the diagnosis (and treatment) of affective disorders. I do not believe this is necessarily so. Forty years of practice and research as a suicidologist have led me to believe that the assessment and treatment of suicidal persons is best conceptualized not in terms of psychiatric nosologic categories (such as one finds in the *Diagnostic and Statistical Manual*), but rather in terms of psychological pain and thresholds for enduring that pain.
>
>   Some suicidal persons have psychiatric disorders. Many suicidal persons are depressed. Most depressed patients are not suicidal. (One can live a long, unhappy life with depression.) But it is undeniable that all persons—100 percent—who

---

11. Harris, *Moral Landscape*, 182.

commit suicide are perturbed and experiencing unbearable psychological pain.[12]

To put this another way, medical diagnosis is not sufficient to diagnose, help, or heal the suicidal person. Harris almost has a moment of clarity after his friend finally does commit suicide. At this point, he asks if it is "possible for a person to see no point in living another day, and to be motivated to kill himself, without experiencing any disorder of mood?" Unfortunately, his imagination fails him at this point, and he concludes that science simply hasn't yet progressed far enough to solve the strictly medical suicide problem.

Harris fails, as usual, in assuming that the problem of suicide is essentially or exclusively a scientific one to be solved through primarily technological means. He overlooks the essential importance of his friend's assumption that suicide is permissible, that it is an option available to anyone who has decided that life is optional. This friend makes a perfectly valid argument predicated on the very atheism espoused by Harris and like-minded "New Atheists." The argument goes like this: (1) there is no God; (2) there is no immortal soul; (3) the individual, contingently meaningful human life concludes with cosmically meaningless death; (4) life involves substantial unwanted suffering; therefore, (5) ending one's life represents a rational option for escaping life's suffering. This reasoning is, of course, flawed, but its appeal to the suffering mind is undeniable. Not surprisingly, Harris immediately abandoned any attempt to convince his friend of the inherent value of life and the wrongness of self-slaughter. For all his faults, the man is committed to his principles and no willing hypocrite. His failure is the failure of the materialist age, an inherently nihilistic age (in the precise sense defined earlier) that increasingly views suicide as not only an option but a "right."

It can be tempting to think of suicide purely as a disease of the malfunctioning mind, à la Harris, and to thereby separate it from, say, self-administered euthanasia, but no valid definition of the latter act can facilitate such a separation. Cholbi attempts to define suicide in a "value neutral" and "uncontroversial" way. He concludes that defining "suicide as intentional self-killing, regardless of its cause" is the most promising way to "satisfy these requirements."[13] Harris clearly thinks that self-killing, at least for those suffering from mood disorders, is undesirable, but

12. Shneidman, "Letter to the Editor, Rational Suicide," 889.
13. Cholbi, *Suicide*, 175.

unsurprisingly he cannot muster a meaningful moral argument against it, even in a book titled *The Moral Landscape*. There is no surprise here. After a brief survey of the many philosophical arguments against the moral permissibility of suicide, Cholbi concludes that, at best, "secular arguments" against suicide "*may* show that it is morally impermissible on certain occasions" (italics mine). [14] So long as such flaccid philosophy dominates our response to self-killing, we ought to expect it not only to increase but to find greater justification from our broader culture of death, unless we can return to and rediscover transcendent truths about the inherent value of human existence.

The Right to Die

The debate over suicide ("intentional self-killing, regardless of its cause"[15]) and euthanasia (the same action usually conducted with medical assistance of some kind) presents us with the most perniciously slippery moral slope in twenty-first-century law and ethics. Any who think this an overstatement should look to the case of Exit International, a pro-suicide group founded by Dr. Philip Nitschke, a former physician and early adopter of legalized euthanasia in Australia. Discontented with the admittedly arbitrary legal restrictions imposed by the Australian government on euthanasia practice, Nitschke left the country and founded his extralegal guerilla suicide movement in 1997. Since then, aside from hosting do-it-yourself suicide workshops and information sessions, Exit International has been regularly updating Nitschke's self-published suicide manual *The Peaceful Pill Handbook*, currently available on the group's website for ninety-five dollars.

When founded, the group used familiar arguments about the rights of those elderly people living in extreme pain and near death to exit life with a minimum of suffering. For some time, the group sought to reinforce these dubious criteria by screening the ages of their conference attendees and only providing *The Peaceful Pill Handbook* to individuals claiming to meet certain requirements. Not surprisingly, the death manual found its way into the hands of the young and distressed. Nitschke found himself in the spotlight in 2016 when twenty-seven-year-old Joshua Smith of England used the handbook to procure illegal

14. Cholbi, *Suicide*, 175.
15. Cholbi, *Suicide*, 175.

euthanasia drugs over the internet. When Joshua's body was found, his mother placed the blame squarely at the feet of Exit International.[16] Far from chastened by the story, Nitschke took it as a clear sign that his group had not been living fully into its mission. He responded by founding Exit Action, which described itself on Twitter as the "militant wing of Exit International." Since then, the militant wing has been seamlessly integrated into the main organization, whose statement of "Vision, Mission, and Values" now insists that "every adult of sound mind has the right to implement plans for the end of their life so that their death is reliable, peaceful and at a time of their choosing."[17]

This is a philosophy of death entirely in keeping with its time. Its cynical opening political gambits involve appeals to a humane concern to end extreme forms of physical suffering. Meanwhile, its internal logic moves ineluctably and relentlessly towards the assertion of suicide as a fundamental human right, the means for which ought to be made readily available to anyone with "decision-making capacity."[18] The debate about suicide in the postmodern era of radical self-determination and nearly unlimited personal license is not a medical or political debate. At heart, this is a philosophical and theological debate about the fundamental nature of the human person and its place in the cosmos.

Unfortunately, we, in the developed West, live in what is perhaps the most philosophically and certainly the most theologically illiterate age in human history. Terry Eagleton, in *Culture and the Death of God* (2014), identifies ignorance of the divine and the numinous as a hallmark of the shift to "postmodernism." This admittedly slippery and abused term gains greater clarity when we compare it with modernism in terms of its relationship with transcendent truth: "Modernism involves a readiness to encounter the dark, Dionysian forces, even the possibility of total dissolution, in its zealous pursuit of the truth. Postmodernism sees no such necessity. It is too young to recall a time when there was (so it is alleged) truth, unity, totality, objectivity, universals, absolute values, stable identities and rock-solid foundations, and thus finds nothing disquieting in their apparent absence."[19] As a consequence of this lost sense of the transcendent, I would argue, we find ourselves beset with the same suffering that has plagued human existence for all of history but are wildly unprepared to negotiate

---

16. Engelhart, *Inevitable*, 259.

17. Exit International, "Exit Vision, Mission, and Values."

18. Exit International, "Exit Vision, Mission, and Values."

19. Eagleton, *Culture and the Death of God*, 185.

that suffering with much more than the blind evasions of technological distraction, the endless hedonic pursuit of pleasure, the fervor of political activism, or the comforts of social conformity.

When these various postmodern substitutes for God, a person whose absence practically ceases to register as such, prove existentially insubstantial, the turn to suicide as a signal "right" of the postmodern era seems obvious. In a world evacuated of "absolute values," a traditional Christian insistence on the sanctity of life no longer serves as a barrier to the perfect realization of a nihilistic individual self-determination. It is worth noting that the paradigm shift from the medical model of euthanasia to the rights model of suicide in the Western world is merely symptomatic of a larger paradigm shift that predates it—i.e., the shift from a Christian to a materialist cosmology. I will not dwell on the point now, since I discuss it at length in my exploration of the novels of Michel Houellebecq in chapter 1. Suffice it to say that the expulsion of God from the common conception of the cosmos must lead inevitably to a reevaluation of the purpose of human existence as something primarily justified, if at all, by a predominance of pleasure over pain—a tenuous justification to be sure.

Most honest post-Christian thinkers can accept this characterization of the relationship between the postmodern worldview and suicide without taking umbrage. During an interview with Katie Engelhart, author of *The Inevitable: Dispatches on the Right to Die* (2021), Dr. Dirk De Wachter, a Belgian psychologist involved in his country's controversial practice of providing euthanasia for the mentally ill, waxes theological for a moment on just this subject. Their exchange is telling.

> De Wachter had started serving as a consultant psychiatrist on euthanasia cases, though he still declined to give the injection himself.
>
> "Emptiness and nihilism and no sense in life: These are, I think, the core symptoms of Western society," he said, leaning back in his chair. "What is the sense of life when there is no God? . . . We killed God and here we are."
>
> "At the same time," I [Engelhart] said, "*you* want life to stay sacred."
>
> "Yes."

"How do you do that if there's no God?"

"I don't know. I just ask questions."[20]

De Watcher, a hesitant participant in the emerging world of state-sanctioned suicide, has hit the nail on the head. The death of God is *the* prerequisite for the materialist culture of death. Belief in God remains the only thing that can make any life, no matter its sufferings, a sacred thing.

It goes without saying that mere Christianity provides no sure defense against the temptation of the suicide-as-human-right discourse. Though Catholic, Orthodox, and the majority of mainline Protestant Christians continue to reject suicide, in all its manifestations, some Protestant denominations, particularly in the Netherlands, have begun to tolerate and collaborate in euthanasia. A 2020 study in the *International Journal of Public Theology* reports that, among Protestant ministers in the Netherlands, "three-quarters of the ministers have experience with euthanasia requests from their parishioners. Almost two-thirds of them respect a parishioner's euthanasia request."[21] The twentieth century witnessed a shift among many Protestant denominations towards condoning progressive practices including contraception, divorce, gay marriage, and abortion. It is becoming increasingly clear that the twenty-first century will witness the addition of suicide to this list. Without giving in to a reactionary desire to turn back time, we may still recognize the need for and work towards a reinvigoration of the moral imagination at the heart of Christianity. This recrudescence must come in part from the great writers of the modern Catholic tradition, who, each in his or her distinct fashion, diagnose, reject, and work against the malaise of materialism.

Literature in the Age of Suicide

Given literature's perennial concern with the problem of suicide, and the radical rise in suicidal ideation and suicide attempts in the early twenty-first century, I am often surprised that academic critics and theorists show relatively little interest in the topic. Late twentieth-century concerns about climate change gave rise to an ever-expanding field of ecocriticism; recent racial unrest prompted English programs to double down on race theory. No comparable academic response to the suicide

---

20. Engelhart, *Inevitable*, 217.

21. Boer et al., "Legal Euthanasia in Pastoral Practice," 41.

crisis has emerged. Andrew Bennett's *Suicide Century* (2017) broke the predominant critical silence regarding modern literature and suicide, but it remains an outlier. Also, Bennett's book never overtly seeks out life-affirming truths in the literature he explores. It is more a project of compassion and empathy that highlights the clear need of a traumatized Western culture to make sense of its own death drive—to inhabit and understand suicide. My goal is quite different. Put simply, I believe that some works of literature manage to both castigate their age for its lies and grant us glimpses of higher, unchanging truths about life, death, and our control over them. In the modern era, such literature comes primarily from Catholics. Their warnings have gone largely unheeded, but the stories they tell offer some hope of meaningful answers to the problem of suicide. Unfortunately, many literature departments have embraced a seemingly benign nihilism that makes the appreciation and active promulgation of such wisdom difficult if not impossible.

Teachers of literature, especially at the collegiate level, have contributed to the general existential malaise that defines our suicidal era more than they have resisted it. The comparative atheism and agnosticism of the American professoriate has played its role. College and university professors are more than three times as likely to identify as atheists or agnostics compared to the general population, according to a now-famous 2009 sociological study, with only about 35 percent identifying as convinced theists.[22] At elite institutions of higher learning, the numbers are even more stark, with only 20.4 percent of professors identified as convinced theists. We can add to the growing a-religiosity of the professoriate a growing reliance on the "hermeneutic of suspicion," theorist Paul Ricoeur's notion of interpretation that rejects surface meaning as a kind of illusion concealing repressed or hidden meanings:

> According to the one pole, hermeneutics is understood as the manifestation and restoration of a meaning addressed to me in the manner of a message, a proclamation, or as is sometimes said . . . according to the other pole, it is understood as a demystification, as a reduction of illusion.[23]

22. Gross and Simmons, "Religiosity of American Professors," 113–14. National demographic trends demonstrate that the US population has become less religious since the publication of this study. This fact suggests that Gross and Simmons's numbers are, if anything, behind the curve of professorial a-religiosity.

23. Ricoeur, *Freud and Philosophy*, 30.

The three "masters of suspicion," Marx, Nietzsche, and Freud, function at the radical latter pole of interpretation and produce demystifying interrogations of economics, religion, civilization, and sexuality. A similar process of demystification and deconstruction has become the modus operandi of the postmodern study of literature to the detriment of what Ricoeur calls "the mytho-poetic core of imagination."[24] This hollowing out of the imagination is just one of the consequences of the nihilistic slide of most departments of literature. "The contrary of suspicion," Ricoeur declares, "is faith"—a virtue distinctly neglected in the modern academy.[25]

Most typically, this hermeneutic of suspicion, this anti-faith, converts the literary critic into a kind of detective who "interprets clues, establishes causal connections, and identifies a guilty party: namely, the literary work accused of whitewashing or concealing social oppression."[26] Within this assumed framework, the average literature professor initiates students, frequently victims of required freshman seminars, into an often neurotic quest to reconceptualize great literature as an inexhaustible chronicle of violations against modern sensibilities regarding race, gender, class, and sexuality. From this perspective, literature is less valuable for what it says than for what it conceals or represses, and any wisdom it may be thought to contain is invariably tainted by its unconscious reenactment of modes of oppression. God—the hegemon and patriarch *par excellence*—fares poorly in such readings.

I am, of course, painting with broad strokes in order to make a larger point. Attentive readers of this book may even note that my own readings of literary texts engage in a more modest form of suspicion and detective work, digging into texts to reveal a larger story about the emergence of our suicidal culture. Unlike too many of my colleagues, however, my goal is not deconstruction or demystification but recollection of a forgotten but perpetually valid and true order. I look to the texts examined in this book for things that postmodern literary theory tends to treat as inherently compromised: wisdom, edification, truth. Rather than debunking the authors examined herein, I go to them for the guidance and help that we desperately need.

But help with what? At times when reasoned arguments about natural and divine law, about the sacrosanct nature of human life, have

24. Ricoeur, *Freud and Philosophy*, 35.

25. Ricoeur, *Freud and Philosophy*, 28.

26. Felski, "Suspicious Minds," 215.

been rendered all but incoherent on a popular scale by the emptying of any shared sense of a higher moral order, stories, not arguments, may serve as the last bastions of sanity and truth. The stories explored in this book do not argue didactically against suicide. Instead, they call us out of the egocentric contemplation of "rights" and the desperate postmodern project of self-actualization and into an imaginative space where people (and sometimes hobbits) grapple with, overcome, and occasionally succumb to the seductions of death. In the experiential heart of that struggle, we find revelations of truth that have the potential to penetrate far deeper than any abstract arguments and may even shake some people out of acquiescence in the hegemony of death.

Chapter 1, "Beginning at the End: Michel Houellebecq's Culture of Death," turns to contemporary French author Michel Houellebecq (b. 1956) for an unflinching diagnosis of our suicidal age. Houellebecq, an often misanthropic and philosophically pessimistic agnostic, offers a trenchant critique of modern materialism and repeatedly connects the death drive of our time with the loss of Christian faith. His breakout novel *The Elementary Particles* (1998) chronicles the fictional suicide of the human race and laments the modern culture of death in a manner self-consciously reminiscent of St. Pope John Paul II's encyclical *Evangelium Vitae* (1995). Houellebecq's more recent novel *Serotonin* (2019) calls attention to our increasingly absurd attempts to use pharmaceuticals to dig ourselves out of the hole of existential despair described in his earlier novels. Together, these stories articulate the plight of our suicidal age and open the door to a Catholic alternative to our hopeless materialism.

Chapter 2, "Antinatalist Ecology and the Decadent Novel," leaps a century back in time to explore the ways in which artists of the loosely associated Decadent movement of the late-nineteenth century anticipated and rejected what philosophers today call antinatalism. This purportedly humane philosophical ethic, espoused most notably today by the philosopher David Benatar, proposes to eliminate all suffering and provide a final solution to all problems of ecology by eliminating human life through an intentional refusal to continue propagating the species. Though the antinatalist ethic does not demand individual suicide, it condones self-destruction as a rational response to the suffering of life and the harm inflected on sentient beings by sentient beings. Novelists J. K. Huysmans (1848–1907) and George Moore (1852–1933) lived and wrote a century before the advent of a formal antinatalist philosophy, but they each composed stories about young men whose philosophical pessimism anticipates antinatalism and demonstrates the disastrous consequences of this suicidal ethic.

Chapter 3, "Robert Hugh Benson's Suicide Dystopia," explores the role of suicide in the twentieth century's first and most ambitious dystopian fantasy. Little rivals *Lord of the World* (1907) for eschatological inventiveness. The novel conjures a dystopian twenty-first century in which the antichrist emerges as the leader of a humanitarian world government and wages war against the last remaining bastion of Christianity, the Catholic Church.[27] Like the many modern dystopian writers who came after him, Monsignor Robert Hugh Benson (1871–1914) sought to imaginatively follow the trend of the modern political and social experiment to its logical conclusion. Orwell shows us Victory Gin, telescreens, and brutal totalitarianism; Huxley shows us soma, Malthusian belts, and the corporate World State. Benson's visionary journey ultimately brought him to the apocalypse, but state-sponsored suicide defines his vision of modern horrors. Euthanasia serves as the defining sin of Benson's future from the novel's opening to its conclusion. Today, *Lord of the World* provides a potent warning about the consequence, temporal and eternal, of a secular materialism that worships "Life" as a substitute for God while undermining the sovereignty of individual lives.

Chapter 4, "The Stolen Gift: Suicide in Middle-Earth," moves from sci-fi to high fantasy. J. R. R. Tolkien (1892–1973) overshadows all Catholic writers of his age in terms of his influence on popular culture of the twenty-first century. Unfortunately, his profound treatment of the problem of suicide in both *The Lord of the Rings* (1954–55) and his larger legendarium has received little attention. I argue that the treatment of suicide in Tolkien's works may help to clarify their debt to a distinctly Christian view of reality. Tolkien's narratives about Middle-earth feel Christian at least in part because of their insistence on the primacy of life over death and the exclusive sovereignty of a benevolent creator over individual lives—two things distinctly lacking in both pre-Christian paganism and secular modernity. These narratives are founded on an invented mythology that treats death as the "gift" of a benevolent creator, and they repeatedly warn of the folly of attempting to steal that gift before it is freely given.

Chapter 5, "Graham Greene's Pseudo-Suicides," and chapter 6, "The Misunderstood Martyrs of Muriel Spark," delve into the

27. Benson, "Preface," in *Lord of the World.*

sometimes-heterodox fiction of two of the great novelists of the Catholic literary revival, both of whom were fascinated by the movement of soul separating the martyr and the suicide. In *The Heart of the Matter* (1948), Greene presents us with a suicide who seeks death not as an end in itself but as a means to avoid harming either of the women he loves by renouncing one in favor of the other. Similarly, Greene's novel *The Comedians* (1966) depicts suicides motivated by things as diverse as pain of lost love, the desire to escape persecution, and the wish for a heroic death. Conversely, in *The Power and the Glory* (1940), Greene orchestrates the martyrdom of a degenerate priest in a way that clearly highlights the ennobling nature of the martyr's sacrifice. Though all of these stories reveal Greene's tendency to portray most suicides as what I would call pseudo-suicides, his very investment in this process of understanding the motivation of the suicidal person comes both from his personal struggles with suicidal ideation and his abiding belief in the thoroughly unmodern notion of sin as an inescapable element of human life.

Similarly, in her novels *The Girls of Slender Means* (1963) and *The Public Image* (1968), Muriel Spark presents us with two deaths that threaten to blur the boundaries between martyrdom and suicide: one, an anarchist turned Jesuit missionary whose seeming martyrdom elicits a dubious reaction from his former associates, the other, a spiteful husband of a movie star who tries to frame his seeming suicide as a martyrdom. Ultimately, both authors remind us of the epistemological challenge of judging from the outside between a good and a bad death in a world that increasingly treats martyrdom and suicide as indistinguishable mental derangements. They also persistently recall us to the reality of sin and the mystery of God's mercy.

The seventh and final chapter, "Walker Percy: Suicide and Christian Existentialism," is dedicated to a writer who knew more about the temptations of suicide than any artist who has died of natural causes. Born into a family of suicides, Percy (1916–1990) referred to himself as an "ex-suicide," someone who has been saved from suicide by the contemplation of suicide, someone who has unflinchingly confronted the seeming absurdity of existence and found his way to the realization of transcendence. While scholars have spilled considerable ink on the subject of suicide in Percy's work and its links to existentialist philosophy, none has explored in detail his debt to the French existentialist Gabriel Marcel (1889–1973). Marcel, a convert to Catholicism like Percy, helped the great Southern author to articulate a vision of life that unflinchingly acknowledges the malaise of modern existence while still maintaining the possibility of transcending that malaise though exploration of the mystery of existence and authentic dedication of the self to others. Ultimately, Percy's seemingly dark Christian existentialism provides a vision of hope, however tenuous, in a world darkened by the cosmic meaninglessness that characterizes the nightmare of modern philosophy.

Reading about these authors and their insights will not solve the problem of suicide. This book only seeks to turn its readers' attention to those insights in the hope that they may find a broader audience. It concludes with a modest but ambitious call to arms for parents, teachers, pastors, and all those responsible for the formation of the young. Only by intentionally forming the moral imaginations of this and the next generation can we hope to fight for the seemingly lost cause of life in a suicidal culture. In fighting for that cause, we may wish to keep the words of T. S. Eliot in mind:

> If we take the widest and wisest view of a Cause, there is no such thing as a Lost Cause because there is no such thing as a Gained Cause. We fight for lost causes because we know that our defeat and dismay may be the preface to our successors' victory, though that victory itself will be temporary; we fight rather to keep something alive than in the expectation that anything will triumph.[28]

Suicide, like all evils and misfortunes, will always be with us. In an increasingly materialist culture that treats sovereignty of the individual and self-determination as nearly absolute, we are unlikely to turn the tide in any final way. But the cause of life is intimate. If the literature explored in this book and the few insights contained herein can help inspire those supporting this cause, then my humble project will have been worth the effort. If this book leads just one suffering soul to see the inherent, transcendent, eternal meaningfulness of life and seek to realize that meaning by continuing the seemingly unendurable struggle of living, which I pray it will, then it will have achieved something greater than I dare hope for.

---

28. Eliot, "Francis Herbert Bradley," 199–200.

1

Beginning at the End: Michel Houellebecq's Culture of Death

> I had no more reason to kill myself than most people did. . . .
> And yet I knew I was close to suicide, not out of despair or even
> any special sadness, simply from the degradation of "the set
> of functions that resist death," in Bichat's famous formulation.
> The mere will to live was clearly no match for the pains and ag-
> gravations that punctuate the life of the average Western man.
> —Houellebecq, *Submission*

> The modern philosopher had told me again and again that
> I was in the right place, and I had still felt depressed even in
> acquiescence.—G. K. Chesterton, *Orthodoxy*

> Can the restoration of Catholicism to its former splendor repair
> our damaged civilization? Here we are in agreement—it's much
> simpler, almost self-evident. The answer is "Yes."—Houellebecq,
> "Restoration"

THE NOVELS OF MICHEL Houellebecq, a misanthropic, postmodern,
decadent agnostic, may seem an odd starting point for a book primarily devoted to the problem of suicide in modern Catholic literature.
Nevertheless, I choose to "begin at the end" with Houellebecq because
his work provides the clearest and most brutally unflinching vision of
our current predicament. For the average Christian partisan of life, the
horror of the growing suicide rights movement is akin to the horror of
the abortion rights movement. Both legal and cultural agendas highlight

the fundamental discontinuity between the Christian cosmic imagination and that of a secular materialist culture. No writer captures the existential whiplash of this shift from the sacramental to the materialist worldview better than Houellebecq, even if he experiences the loss of that sacramental worldview only as a nostalgic longing for a good never fully possessed in the past and virtually unattainable in the future.

The consensus *enfant terrible* of contemporary French literature, Houellebecq made considerable waves in 2015 with his novel *Submission (Soumission)*. Released in the immediate wake of the Charlie Hebdo massacre, the novel follows the ascent of Islamic political power in France and the parallel movement of a dissolute intellectual antihero, François, from hedonistic materialism, to flirtation with a culturally decrepit but spiritually vital Catholicism, to opportunistic conversion to Islam. The book received both praise as a sophisticated satire and condemnation as an Islamophobic rag.[1] I was drawn to *Submission* not by the brouhaha regarding its depiction of Islam, but by my scholarly interest in the work of the decadent Catholic novelist J. K. Huysmans, François's intellectual obsession. In *Submission*, Huysmans serves as a reminder of a world in which a secular intellectual might actually experience meaningful conversion from soulless materialism to traditional Christianity, something François never achieves, though he does enact a more mercenary submission to Islam at the novel's conclusion.

Submission combines the existential bleakness and gratuitous depictions of sex that serve as hallmarks of Houellebecq's aesthetic in all of his novels. Largely because of a misanthropy bordering on sadism, Houellebecq's extremely graphic depictions of perverse sex are far less titillating than horrifying, though they seem to revel in walking a tightrope between the two. I remember as a college student cringing while reading the nightmarish sex scenes in Walker Percy's *Lancelot*. Houellebecq typically brings me closer to nausea than discomfort. I can teach Percy with a straight face; I wouldn't subject my students to his twenty-first century inheritor, even though the two share the project of diagnosing and denouncing modernity's failures. Most notably, both authors identify the modern age as one in which suicidal ideation is not only rife but seemingly reasonable. Percy's pseudo-self-help book *Lost in the Cosmos* (1983) poses a question that runs implicitly through Houellebecq's work: given our unprecedented opportunities for "self-growth" in the liberated post-1960s era, why are

---

1. For examples of each, see Preston, "Submission by Michel Houellebecq Review," and Zia-Ebrahimi, "There is No Islamophobic Elephant in This Room."

we so depressed and even suicidal?[2] One likely answer is that we ought to
be. According to Percy's self-help persona, "Any person, man, woman, or
child, who is not depressed by the nuclear arms race, by the modern city,
by family life in the exurb, suburb, apartment, villa, and later in a retirement home, is himself deranged" (*LC*, 75).

Both Percy and Houellebecq agree on the basically rotten nature
of modern existence; however, Percy was able to attain to a solution that
Houellebecq can only set up as an all-but-unattainable alternative, Catholic faith. Not everyone would agree with my assessment of Houellebecq's
essentially anti-modern and implicitly pro-Catholic project. Though a
New York Times review characterized his breakout novel *The Elementary
Particles* (*Les Particules élémentaires*, 1998) as "a frontal attack on the generation of '68," a writer for *The New Criterion* insisted that the book "does
not challenge but rather epitomizes the nihilism we have inherited from
the 1960s."[3] Likewise, while there are critics ready to declare Houellebecq
a Catholic sympathizer, however unlikely, there are others convinced that
the author's interest in Catholicism is nostalgic at best.[4]

Houellebecq's Christian champions have found in the French author
a popular voice that echoes their own concerns about the ascendence of
secular materialism in the developed West. Rod Dreher, author of the
controversial *Benedict Option* (2017)—which espouses the formation of
intentional Christian communities at some remove from mainstream
secular life—has carried on a "bittersweet" love affair with Houellebecq's
novels for years because of their "prophetic" nature.[5] Dreher's investment
in Houellebecq as anti-modern prophet finds detailed and impressive
support in Louis Betty's *Without God: Michel Houellebecq and Materialist
Horror* (2016). According to Betty, "Houellebecq's novels represent a kind
of fictional experiment in the death of God" that examines the existential
fallout of the triumph of post-Enlightenment scientific materialism over
religion."[6] The outcome of these literary experiments is invariably bleak:
"Life whittled down to the play of atoms thus represents a kind of

2. We should note that Percy asked this question well before the sharp rise in suicide rates in the first two decades of the twenty-first century.

3. *The New Criterion*, "False Advertising."

4. See, for example, McQueen's "Zombie Catholicism Meets Zombie Islam," which
wholly rejects the idea that Houellebecq is interested in Catholicism as a potentially
vital force in the modern world.

5. Dreher, "France's Master Of 'Materialist Horror.'"

6. Betty, *Without God*, 5.

materialist horror, and characters unable to see the world in anything but physicalist terms are inevitably prey to depression and suicide."[7]

The development of Betty's thesis—Houellebecq's novels are essentially religious in their exposition of the failure of philosophical materialism to address humanity's metaphysical needs—leaves little room for detailed consideration of suicide. In this chapter, I intend to confirm and expound upon Betty's thesis by exploring Houellebecq's fascination with suicide in novels separated by two decades, *The Elementary Particles* (1998) and *Serotonin* (*Sérotonine*, 2019). Together, these books demonstrate Houellebecq's abiding belief that madness and suicide (of both individual and species) are the only fitting *telos* of a truly materialist philosophy. Together they diagnose the problem of suicide in the postmodern world in a manner that highlights the need for the very wisdom offered by the great thinkers of a specifically Catholic literary modernity.

As a novel about the decline of Christendom and the consequences of secular materialism, *The Elementary Particles* is ultimately more visionary and intellectually daring than the even more controversial *Submission*. Published just three years after Pope John Paul II's landmark encyclical *Evangelium Vitae* (*The Gospel of Life*, 1995), Houellebecq's novel provides unexpected support for John Paul II's central thesis regarding an emergent "culture of death" and follows that thesis to its logical conclusion: the suicide of the human race. Though it may seem shocking at first, there are unmistakable and essential parallels between the visions of these two very different men, the beatified pontiff and the iconoclastic novelist. After establishing the essential continuity between *Evangelium Vitae* and *The Elementary Particles* as works that diagnose the culture of death that has given birth to the current crisis of suicide in the West, I turn to a consideration of Houellebecq's more recent novel, *Serotonin*. Twenty years after elaborating the logic of suicide at the heart of our age, Houellebecq shifts his attention to our increasingly absurd attempts to dig ourselves out of the hole of existential despair with pharmaceuticals. Together, these two important novels continue the literary tradition of their Catholic predecessors by pointing to faith as the only consistent and conceivable solution to the problem of suicide.

7. Betty, *Without God*, 4.

Houellebecq's Culture of Death

The central action of *The Elementary Particles* concerns two half-brothers, Bruno and Michel. By-blows of a neglectful mother of the sixties generation who was more interested in her own sexual liberation and self-realization than the two unfortunate products thereof, the boys are nearly allegorical opposites. Bruno is a perpetually failed hedonist whose attempts to compensate for the pain of life through excessive indulgence in first food and then increasingly perverse sexual experimentation lead to the destruction of his life and the lives of anyone who attempts to love him. Michel, by contrast, is the consummate scientist whose alienation from his own body reflects his immersion in quantum theories that deny the very existence of a reality underlying the observable world. Together, Bruno and Michel serve as complementary avatars of what the narrator dubs "the age of materialism (defined as the centuries between the decline of medieval Christianity and the publication of Djerzinski's [Michel's] work)" (*EP*, 258). In their separate ways, the brothers are defined and destroyed by their age.

As the narrator's definition of the age of materialism implies, *The Elementary Particles* divides modern history into three main eras separated by "metaphysical mutations—that is to say radical, global transformations in the values to which the majority subscribe" (*EP*, 3). Just as Rome gave way at the height of its power to the Christian mutation, Christendom gave way to the rationalism, scientism, and individualism of the materialist mutation. Houellebecq's novel chronicles the life of the man, Michel, who ushered in the third and most radical paradigm shift in world history by engineering the voluntary suicide of the human species.

The book's framing narrative becomes clear only at its conclusion. In homage to a humanity that has willingly ceased to reproduce itself, the post-human "gods" manufactured by Michel's scientific breakthroughs have composed a semi-fictitious biography of their creator. Our post-human narrator is immortal and asexual. Its genetic code has been stripped of the markers of "egotism, cruelty, and anger" and the entire surface of its skin embedded with the pleasure-producing corpuscles formerly restricted in such a miserly fashion to the genitals (*EP*, 263). We will discuss these creatures and their role in the abolition of humanity shortly. For now, suffice it to say that Houellebecq's pseudo-god narrator has great sympathy for his human subject but no nostalgia for the age of materialism, which he (better to say "it") describes in the book's opening paragraph: "[Michel] lived through an age that was miserable and troubled. . . . [O]ften haunted by misery, the men of his generation lived out their lonely, bitter lives. Feelings such as love, tenderness and human fellowship had, for the most part, disappeared" (*EP,* 3). Throughout the story of Michel's life, the narrator breaks in to comment retrospectively on the reasons for the failures of the age of materialism and the extinction of the human species.

Houellebecq's narrator presents a bleak cultural history of the late twentieth century. In it, the sexual liberation of the 1960s, made possible by widely available contraception, led in the 1970s to "the cult of the body beautiful" and the "substantial increase in the consumption of the erotic" (58, 41). In 1974 this hyper-sexualization of youth culture was accompanied by the institutionalization of divorce and legalization of abortion—followed "some decades later" by euthanasia. These changes flew in the face of "Christian doctrine, which long had been the dominant moral force in Western civilization" (59). Unlike this earlier Christian metaphysic, which "accorded unconditional importance to every human life" because of the "belief in the existence within the body of a soul," the ascendent "materialist anthropology" was "more moderate in its ethical councils" (59). As a result, the fetus was "no longer acknowledged as a viable individual" and "the new concept of *human dignity* meant that the elderly person . . . had the right to life only as long as it continued to function well enough" (59). Suicide proved the final, logical *telos* of this materialist anthropology.

Lest we think that Houellebecq's narrator may be providing a disinterested account of the last stage of human evolution before its heroic creation of a better and glorious replacement, our post-human historian follows its retrospective with a damning assessment:

> The agnosticism at the heart of the French republic would facilitate the progressive, hypocritical and slightly sinister triumph of the materialist worldview. Though never overtly discussed, the question of the *value* of human life would nevertheless continue to preoccupy people's minds. It would be true to say that in the last years of Western civilization it contributed to a general mood of depression bordering on masochism. (59)

Humanity did not continue to evolve as part of a steady march of species progress. Instead, it created a replacement species because it stopped believing its existence was justified. Michel used his mastery of science to give his fellow humans, now known to themselves as suffering bodies devoid of souls, a, shall we say, humane justification for satisfying their communal desire for nonexistence.

As if to give existential substance to the narrator's abstract condemnation of modernity, the lives of Michel and Bruno provide a horrifying glimpse of the collapse of Western civilization in microcosm. Both lives (the hedonist's and the scientist's) are scarred by the absence of a maternal figure and defined by suicide. Michel, more fortunate at first, lands with a grandparent who raises him with some experience of love. His older half-brother Bruno is less fortunate. Relegated to a boarding school, the weak and timid Bruno becomes the focus of brutality at the hands of his sadistic schoolmates. His subsequent pubescent attempts to find love crash and burn because, among other things, of an inability to express love as anything other than sexual appetite. When Bruno finds a woman willing to marry him and has a son, he briefly attempts to repair himself by becoming a Catholic. He reads Charles Péguy's mystical poetry and joins a "Living the Faith" group. The poetry is depressing for someone who has lost all sense of sin and salvation and the only interesting thing about the group is a pretty young Korean girl, whom Bruno slobbers over shamelessly. Incapable of love, he slides deeper into the pit of his own bathetic carnality, spending ridiculous sums on pornography and generally ignoring his wife and son.

Though seemingly incapable of living a Christian life, Bruno finds an explanation for his predicament in the writings of John Paul II, who "was the only person—the only person—who really understood what was happening in the West" (150). Inspired by John Paul II's insights, Bruno writes both an article and a poem detailing the obliteration of the family, the blight of his own existence:

> There are families still, more or less
> (Sparks of faith among atheists,
> Sparks of love in the pit of nausea),
> And we do not know how
> These sparks glow. (151)

The poem goes on to describe humanity's failed attempt to replace the traditional family with the atomized pleasures of self-indulgence. Trapped in bodies that are "ever more exhausted" by the marketplace of pleasure, our species disappears into "the shadow of sorrow / Into true despair." This exhaustion culminates in suicide:

> We go down the long, solitary road to the place where all is dark,
> Without children, without wives,
> We enter the lake
> In the middle of night
> (and the water on our ancient bodies is so cold). (152)

Set adrift from each other, like the elementary particles of the novel's title, humans sink into despair and realize their proper end in self-destruction.

This is more or less what happens to Bruno. His marriage crumbles. He becomes estranged from his son. The closest thing to solace he discovers is a hedonistic partnership with Christiane, with whom he explores France's nudist resorts and swingers' clubs. They share a sad parody of love until Christiane's degenerative medical condition lands her in a wheelchair. Unable to even pretend to care for someone who can no longer provide him with sexual satisfaction, Bruno finds that he "had no more been capable of love than his parents before him" (205). Christiane likewise concludes that, given her crippled condition, life has ceased to be worth living. At this point, the post-human narrator steps in again to sum up the suicidal logic of the materialist era:

> Contemporary consciousness is no longer equipped to deal with our mortality. Never in any other time, or any other civilization, have people thought so much or so constantly about aging. Each individual has a simple view of the future: a time will come when the sum of pleasures that life has to offer is outweighed by the sum of pain. . . . This weighing up of pleasure and pain, which everyone is forced to make sooner or later, leads logically, at a certain age, to suicide. (204)

Compelled by this logic, Christiane throws herself down a flight of stairs. Bruno admits final defeat and checks himself into the psychiatric clinic where he will spend the rest of his life.

Michel fares no better. He is, in Bruno's estimation, worse off than his older brother (57). Incapable of even physical pleasure and affection, he fails to return the love of his beautiful childhood sweetheart, Annabelle. Michel pursues the only thing he knows, scientific knowledge. Annabelle, in turn, undergoes a string of unsatisfying romances and their attendant abortions. When the two reunite in their disillusioned forties for one last attempt at happiness, it's far too late. After conceiving a child in a desperate attempt at intimacy, they find that Annabelle's reproductive system is wracked by cancer. An abortion and a hysterectomy leave her feeling gutted and depressed. Like Christiane, she opts for suicide. Michel, convinced of the failure of the human experiment, dedicates the rest of his life to perfecting the science of cloning a genetically perfected and undying replacement species. That task accomplished, he, like the speaker in Bruno's poem, walks into the sea. His suicide anticipates the rational suicide of the whole species. Slowly, humans cease procreating in order to allow their post-human inheritors to replace them. The only holdouts are "some humans of the old species, particularly in areas long dominated by religious doctrine," whose gradual extinction seems, nevertheless, "inevitable" (263).

Houellebecq is neither the only nor the most eminent French thinker to trace the suicide drive in Western civilization directly back to the rise of materialist philosophy. In the second volume of *Democracy in America* (1840), Alexis de Tocqueville, one of Houellebecq's heroes,[8] writes about the shocking restlessness and melancholia found in prosperous countries. He distinguishes America from France in that the anxieties of the former lead to high rates of madness and those of the latter lead to high rates of suicide. Though these cases of madness and suicide are both symptoms of the same illness, Americans "do not put an end to their lives, however disquieted they may be, because their religion forbids it; and among them materialism may be said hardly to exist."[9] At the time, Tocqueville wrote about France and America as essentially distinct cultures: one increasingly materialist and the other doggedly religious. That philosophical gap has closed significantly. The secular materialism underlying Houellebecq's denunciation of Western civilization in *The Elementary Particles* is now explicitly transatlantic, and since 2016 the US suicide rate has outstripped that of France, according to the World Health Organization.[10]

Setting aside the science fiction framing the narrative of *The Elementary Particles*, the major contours of the cultural history of the materialist age provided by Houellebecq's post-human narrator and informed by Tocqueville are inescapably familiar to anyone conversant with John

8. In *The Map and the Territory*, Houellebecq the character calls *Democracy in America* "a masterpiece, a book of unheard-of visionary power" (161). Also, in a revelatory 2011 interview, Houellebecq credits Tocqueville with foretelling the breakdown of larger communities into isolated nuclear families, but notes that even Tocqueville did not anticipate the breakdown of the family unit and the mass atomization of individuals common in late modernity. See Houellebecq, "Houellebecq, Tocqueville, Democracy."

9. Tocqueville, *Democracy in America*, 139.

10. World Health Organization, "Suicide Mortality Rate."

Paul II's *Evangelium Vitae*. In the encyclical, he famously denounces the rise of a "culture of death" characterized most notably by abortion and euthanasia. These practices, according to John Paul II, emerge from the failure of the family, a threatened institution that he repeatedly refers to as the "sanctuary of life." Our culture of death finds its biblical origins in Cain's murder of his brother Abel, an act that violates the "kinship uniting mankind in one great family, in which all share the same fundamental good: equal personal dignity."[11] At the heart of all of these violations of the "gospel of life," John Paul II identifies the same degraded anthropology that characterizes Houellebecq's age of materialism, which, to use John Paul's words, "reduces human life to the level of simple 'biological material' to be freely disposed of."[12] In a "cultural climate that fails to perceive any meaning or value in suffering" because of an "absence of religious outlook," modern man has assumed a "Promethean attitude" that leads people to think that they can master life and death through, most notably, abortion and euthanasia.[13] Coupled with this Promethean attitude is a perverse "notion of freedom which exalts the isolated individual in an absolute way."[14] Readers of *The Elementary Particles* will recognize the predicted result: "Thus," John Paul II writes, "society becomes a mass of individuals placed side by side, but without any mutual bond."[15] In this familial and relational wasteland, the human person, reduced to an animal that exercises its freedom in blind pursuit of hedonic fulfillment, becomes both the agent and the subject of an emergent culture of death that finds its logical conclusion in suicide.

John Paul II insists that the culture of death can be summed up in Cain's rhetorical question: Am I my brother's keeper? Houellebecq confirms this assertion by focusing his novel about the collapse of the materialist age on the lives of two brothers who cannot save each other or anyone else from ruin. Even Bruno, who reads John Paul II and grasps the truth of his message about the centrality of the family, cannot be bothered to care for his brother, his wife, his son, or his crippled lover because to do so would encroach upon his isolated world of atomized freedom. Michel seeks to remedy the problem by replacing mankind with creatures more suited to a world without God, creatures who are genetically programed

11. John Paul II, *Evangelium Vitae*, 21.
12. John Paul II, *Evangelium Vitae*, 29.
13. John Paul II, *Evangelium Vitae*, 30–31.
14. John Paul II, *Evangelium Vitae*, 36.
15. John Paul II, *Evangelium Vitae*, 37–38.

to find contentment in "immortality" and sensual pleasure. The remedy is, of course, illusory. Houellebecq's post-human narrator admits that its supposed happiness and immortality are a sham. "Men," it writes at the conclusion of the novel, "consider us happy," and "the rule of history is inexorable" (263). Happiness, like suffering, has ceased to mean anything for a species as incapable of salvation as it is incapable of damnation; furthermore, time and death remain unconquered adversaries. Michel's "gods" will pass away eventually, and their homage to the human race "itself will one day disappear, buried beneath the sands of time" (263). In its state of pseudo-happiness and pseudo-immortality, humanity's successor species waits for the eventual end of the material world with patient disinterestedness. Meant to serve as science's riposte to death, they are, in fact, the rear guard of the militant culture of death.

As much as the teachings of John Paul II inform Houellebecq's diagnosis of the failure of materialism to justify, let alone sanctify, life, the saint was perhaps too hopeful to anticipate the novelist's vision of a post-human apocalypse. Another influential Christian author of his century did. In the conclusion of *The Abolition of Man* (1943), C. S. Lewis argues that the radical subjectivism of the modern age is leading to a materialist anthropology that rejects any notion of the law of human nature. Lewis calls this endangered "doctrine of objective value," this "belief that certain attitudes are really true, and others really false, to the kind of thing the universe is and the kind of things we are," the Tao.[16] The end of a technologically advanced science that denies the Tao, according to Lewis, will be the recreation of humanity in its own arbitrary image. Those who have mastered nature to the point that they have conquered human nature (the "Conditioners") can have no coherent sense of a natural moral law. They will, therefore, have to either give up on life completely or fall back on the treacherous standard of "their own pleasure" because "If you will not obey the *Tao*, or else commit suicide, obedience to impulse . . . is the only course left open."[17] These Conditioners, empowered by future scientific techniques only intuited by Lewis in the 1940s but familiarly called gene editing today, will end by creating a post-humanity.

Houellebecq's Michel does just this. To use Lewis's famous phrase, Michel creates "men without chests." His gods, his sterile, immortal hermaphrodites, are no longer susceptible to the threat of decay and physical

16. Lewis, *Abolition of Man*, 18.
17. Lewis, *Abolition of Man*, 65, 67.

degeneration. They are no longer even bothered by questions of meaning and purpose. As befits gods, they simply are, but what they are no longer exists in any relation to the Tao. Living as they do beyond the boundaries of good and evil, joy and pain, they patiently await the heat death of the planet and the end of their pseudo existence. Lewis scholar Michael Ward chose *After Humanity* (2021) as the title of his book-length companion to *The Abolition of Man* because that text envisions a world in which humanity has engineered its own replacement with something non-human. Ward notes that *Abolition* ends on an uncharacteristically dark and "hollow note" in a manner that indicates that Lewis's "main purpose is less to change our destination than to predict our destiny."[18] Given his unfeigned misanthropy, it is hard to say whether Houellebecq views humanity's abolition as altogether undesirable. But his prophecy, like that of Lewis, ultimately conveys a greater sense of horror than hope. Of course, Lewis, a convinced Christian, spent his life attempting to cultivate such hope. *That Hideous Strength* (1945), his sci-fi exploration of the abstract ideas contained in *The Abolition of Man*, ends with the overthrow of the Conditioners and a scene of ideal sexual consummation between the married protagonists. Lacking Lewis's access to the theological virtues of faith, hope, and love, Houellebecq provides the materialist alternative to this scene of triumph in the conclusion to *The Elementary Particles* by opting for death—a very different consummation, but one too often "devoutly to be wish'd" in a world deaf to the gospel of life.

Serotonin and the Failure of the Therapeutic

The Elementary Particles makes the logic of suicide in the age of material-ism radically clear and simultaneously validates both *Evangelium Vitae*'s diagnosis of "the culture of death" and Lewis's fears about the abolition of man. Houellebecq's subsequent novels return to the subject of suicide like vultures to a carcass. For example, *The Map and the Territory* (*La carte et le territoire*, 2010) follows the career of photographer turned painter, Jed Martin. Jed's mother commits suicide while he is still a child, and he spends the rest of his life under the shadow of a primal loss that reasserts itself when his father opts for euthanasia late in the novel. But these events are peripheral. They are, the novel implies, common parts of the modern human experience. Most of the first part of the story deals with Jed's artistic

18. Ward, *After Humanity*, 188.

development and his relationship with the novelist Michel Houellebecq. Jed commissions this fictionalized Houellebecq to write the catalogue for an upcoming exhibition. The Houellebecq we meet in *The Map and the Territory* is at first secluded in a house in Ireland, deranged and utterly depressed. This depiction echoes those found in the popular press leading up to the publication of *The Map and the Territory*. Commenting on the real-life author's isolated existence in Ireland, Emily Eakin had this to say in *The New York Times* in 2001: "Houellebecq's friends don't wonder at his self-imposed exile abroad. They wonder at his being alive at all. 'He has suffered a lot,' Beigbeder [Houellebecq's friend and fellow novelist] said. 'I think he has come back from a place where a normal person would have committed suicide. And that explains everything.'"[19]

Rather than imagining his own suicide in *The Map and the Territory*, Houellebecq offers his fictional counterpart something like the redemption that continues to elude him in real life. While Jed mounts the heights of artistic success and plumbs the depths of his own loveless life, Houellebecq leaves Ireland to take up residence in his childhood home in France. There, Jed discovers, Houellebecq adopts a dog, reads Tocqueville, and seems almost content: "There was in the voice of the author of *The Elementary Particles* something that Jed had never noticed before, that he'd never expected to find, and that he took some time to identify, because basically he hadn't found it in anyone, for many years: he seemed happy."[20] This less depressing state of affairs proves short lived. Midway through the novel, Houellebecq is found brutally murdered. In the aftermath, his friends and fans are surprised to find that "the author of *The Elementary Particles*, who throughout his life had displayed an intransigent atheism, had very discreetly been baptized, in a church in Courtenay, six months before [his murder]."[21] Suicide has been a consistent theme throughout Houellebecq's work. Catholicism recurs with comparable consistency as a cultural force at odds with and mostly outmatched by the Western death drive. Here, however, the Church gains an unexpected victory over both the author's suicidal ideation and his murderer.

Houellebecq's recent novel, *Serotonin* (*Sérotonine*, 2019), drops the science fiction of *The Elementary Particles* and the self-portraiture of *The Map and the Territory*, but retains a fascination with the seemingly unavoidable logic of suicide. For Houellebecq, self-destruction serves as

19. Eakin, "Michel Houellebecq."
20. Houellebecq, *Map and the Territory*, 147.
21. Houellebecq, *Map and the Territory*, 202.

the ultimate realization of the materialist failure to cope with spiritual despair. The failure in *Serotonin* is specifically medical. The novel begins and ends with a brief description of its subject: "It's a small, white, scored, oval tablet." Having given up on any ultimate justification for human existence other than the pursuit of a Freudian pleasure principle, Western civilization has turned in large part to pharmacology as a means of mitigating the depression experienced by those inhabitants of the materialist era who are sensitive or thoughtful enough to do the obvious thing: be depressed. Like Walker Percy before him, Houellebecq relentlessly savages the industry of post-Freudian psychological therapy. The traditional soul doctors, the priests, have devolved into therapists, who offer in place of the bread of life and the promise of eternity the latest anti-depressant and the possibility of side effects.

Let me be clear. From my perspective, both Percy and Houellebecq exaggerate the failure of psychology. Their work is, after all, satirical in nature and prone to artistic hyperbole. Psychological and pharmaceutical interventions have saved and enriched many lives. Both authors are most insightful not in rejecting the practice of psychology in toto, which they never do, but in highlighting the failures of a purely materialist psychology to adequately tend to the complete psyche, the soul. David H. Rosmarin, associate professor at Harvard Medical School, made a similar point more recently in a 2021 op-ed for *Scientific American* titled "Psychiatry Needs to Get Right with God." Rosmarin calls for a more "spiritually integrated form of cognitive-behavioral therapy,"[22] something that neither Percy nor Houellebecq would be likely to oppose in the same way they respectively oppose Freudian analysis and metaphysically unmoored pharmacology. It would be a mistake on our part to read Houellebecq's satire of the triumph of the therapeutic as a repudiation of all psychological practice. He does not denigrate medical science, but he does acknowledge its inability to solve the problem of the suicidal logic of modern materialism.

In *Serotonin*, anti-depressants are Band-Aids on severed limbs. They offer no salvation, only extended suffering. Such is undeniably the case with Houellebecq's protagonist, Florent-Claude Labrouste, whose attempts to cope with existential despair by means of a pill produce only the added indignities of emotional numbness and erectile dysfunction. Unlike many of Houellebecq's characters, Florent (as he prefers to be

22. Rosmarin, "Psychiatry Needs to Get Right with God."

called) had an essentially happy childhood. His parents loved each other
ardently and included him somewhat in the penumbra of that love.
Things take a turn for the worse when his father receives a brain cancer
diagnosis. Unable to live without each other, Florent's parents commit
suicide together on their fortieth wedding anniversary. The realities of
death mar their grand romantic gesture somewhat: "It was easy to tell by
their positions on the bed that they had wanted to hold hands until the
end, but they had suffered from convulsions in their death throes, and
their hands had parted" (*Ser*, 68).

As usual, Houellebecq immediately contrasts suicide with Catholicism in a manner that highlights the metaphysical chasm between his
characters and the historical faith of their culture. A priest presides over
the funeral. Clearly knowing nothing about two nonpracticing Catholics who asked to be buried in the same coffin, the good-natured cleric
takes this gesture of love as the basis for a generic sermon about the
triumph of love in the afterlife. The Church is somewhat divided on the
question of funeral rites in the case of suicide. Suicides, who for parts of
Church history were denied Christian burial, are today typically granted
funerals because individual pastors cannot clearly judge when the act is
a "free and deliberative act of the will" as opposed to the involuntary result of a mental collapse.[23] However, Canadian bishops, who have been
living with legalized euthanasia since 2014, have been divided on the
question of funeral rites in cases of euthanasia. In his 2017 guidelines
regarding this question, Archbishop Michael J. Miller of the Diocese of
Vancouver made a strong distinction between cases of suicide and more
obviously deliberate and "rational" cases of suicide by euthanasia, insisting that priests should consider the possibility of denying funeral rites
in such cases.[24] In spite of their deliberate rejection of Church teaching,
Florent's parents receive a ceremonial burial. It leaves their son more
resentful than comforted. He recalls that the "priest annoyed me a little
during his sermon, glibly talking about the magnificence of human love
as a prelude to the ever greater magnificence of divine love; I found it
a bit indecent for the Catholic Church to try to *recover* them" (*Ser*, 69).
Always somewhat removed from his parents' shared world of affection
in life, Florent cannot stand the idea that the Church would attempt to
gather that love, however misguidedly expressed, within the bounds of

23. McNamara, "Funeral Masses for a Suicide."
24. Miller, "Guidelines Regarding Funeral Rites."

a higher, divine love. Like his parents, and like so many of Houellebecq's characters, Florent's failure to understand or adequately express love plays a major role in his journey toward suicide.

Under the shadow of the loss of his parents, Florent carries on a life marked by a successful career as an agricultural consultant. From this vantage point, he witnesses the slow collapse of traditional French agriculture under the weight of globalization (one of the novel's primary concerns). Simultaneously, Florent experiences the failure of his own life as a string of love affairs degenerate into transactional sexual relationships because of his inability to practice fidelity even to those he loves the most. Florent regularly interrupts his narrative, which turns out to be an extended suicide letter, with recollections of the women he has loved and the ways in which he has betrayed that love. He sees no hope for redemption or improvement. By the time we meet him at the beginning of the novel, the forty-six-year-old man (the same age, he mentions offhandedly, at which Nerval hung himself and Baudelaire died) is languishing. Lately, he can only look back on memories of the good women he has done wrong as he deals with the fallout of discovering the perverse infidelities of his much younger girlfriend, Yuzu. When life with Yuzu proves unendurable, the middle-aged Florent flees his apartment in search of freedom. What follows reads like an insider's narrative of the slide into clinical depression.

From page to page, Florent contemplates self-destruction, his own and that of other people. In a last-ditch effort to stay alive, he turns to a doctor, who prescribes the new antidepressant Captorix. The series of evasions that follows necessitates increasingly larger doses of Captorix, which manages to artificially raise his serotonin but can do little for his ennui. Florent's physician, the hard-bitten but well-intentioned Dr. Azote, can offer more pills but has no illusions about his work: "My job is basically to stop people from killing themselves; well, for a while" (*Ser*, 134). Rendered impotent and listless by the drugs that keep him from killing himself, Florent retreats to the country and occupies a seaside cabin owned by his college friend Aymeric d'Harcourt-Olonde, the recently divorced son of an ancient and noble family whose idealistic attempts to revive traditional cattle farming have been undercut by the economic policies of the European Union. The two men, stupefied by the failures of their lives, drink, play with guns, and generally wallow until Aymeric leads a group of farmers in an armed demonstration that culminates in a fatal exchange of gunfire with the police, sparked by Aymeric's decision to shoot himself in the head.

By the time Aymeric kills himself in a gesture of defiance against globalism and life in general, the book's fascination with suicide has become almost monotonous. The topic appears seemingly on every other page and elicits less and less of a reaction. This, I believe, is part of Houellebecq's point. The tragic suicide of an individual, which has served as the grand dénouement of so many works of literature and to which this novel is clearly building, lacks pathos in a postmodern world that has lost its sense of the tragic along with its sense of the transcendent. Terry Eagleton makes the necessary link between tragedy and God explicit in *Culture and the Death of God*:

> Whereas modernism experienced the death of God as a trauma . . . as well as a cause for celebration, postmodernism does not experience it at all. There is no God-shaped hole in the center of its universe, as there is in the center of Kafka, Beckett or even Philip Larkin. . . . This is one of the several reasons why postmodernism is post-tragic. Tragedy involves the possibility of irretrievable loss, whereas for postmodernism there is nothing momentous missing.[25]

In a world as utterly divorced from the divine as the one depicted by Houellebecq, suicide risks losing all contact with tragedy. The novel concludes with a fumbling attempt to reestablish that contact.

Following Aymeric's death, Florent attempts to reconnect with the only other person on earth with whom he might still hope to form something like a human bond capable of tethering him to life, the love of his youth, Camille. When this too fails in utterly horrific fashion, Florent decides to give up on the possibility of love and life: "I understood that it was over . . . that the mechanism of unhappiness was the strongest of all, that I would never regain Camille, and that we would both die alone, unhappy and alone, each in our own way" (*Ser*, 268). Florent sinks deeper into despair only to find there an intimation of something like God.

> I had entered an *endless night*, and yet there remained, deep within me . . . something less than a hope, let's say an uncertainty. One might also say that even when one has personally lost the game . . . for some people . . . the idea remains that *something in heaven* will pick up the hand, will arbitrarily decide to

---

25. Eagleton, *Culture and the Death of God*, 186.

> deal again . . . even when one has never at any moment in one's
> life sensed the intervention or even the presence of any kind of
> deity, even when one is aware of not especially deserving the
> intervention of a favorable deity. (*Ser*, 270–71)

As spiritual epiphanies go, this could be worse. Florent senses something like the hope abandoned by so many people in the postmodern
inferno; however, this intuition can only do so much for someone for
whom the final cause of all hope, God, remains a remnant of a past culture rather than a vital part of the present one. Like the protagonist of
Submission, who explains away a seemingly mystical vision by blaming
it on hunger, Florent lacks any point of meaningful reference outside of
the psychosomatic.

Rather than intentionally chasing his intimation of a "hope beyond
hope" (*Ser*, 270) to some kind of spiritual awakening, to some sense of
inherent meaning in life, Florent decides that he should ask his doctor
for a yet higher dose of antidepressants. Dr. Aotze demurs after review-
ing his patient's bloodwork. Florent's hormones are now so out of balance that he can neither increase nor decrease his dosage without dire
consequences. The pills that promised to keep despair at bay have, pre-
dictably, failed. Houellebecq seemingly deserves some credit for artistic
prescience on this point. Not long after the publication of *Serotonin*, a
group of researchers made waves with their 2022 umbrella review of the
medical literature regarding the relationship between serotonin and depression, which found no meaningful link between the two. The study's
authors note that many practitioners and most laypeople continue to
think of depression as the result of a "chemical imbalance"; however,
their synthesis of all available research found no meaningful connection between lowered serotonin levels and clinical depression.[26] Were
the researchers behind this study interested in an imaginative account of
the worst case scenario of treating depression as a purely chemical imbalance susceptible to purely pharmacological intervention, they could
have asked for no better text than Houellebecq's novel.

Confronted with but not entirely surprised by the failure of his own
pharmacological intervention in Florent's life, Dr. Azote recommends pay-
ing for sex as a short-term solution to his hormonal catastrophe, but the
formerly libidinous protagonist has been robbed of the desire for this most
basic of vices by the pill that had been keeping him stupefied enough to

26 Moncrieff et al., "Serotonin Theory of Depression," 3243, 3253.

stay alive. Strangely enough Dr. Azote advises against euthanasia because of a sentimental attachment to the last vestiges of the Hippocratic Oath. He is professedly "not on the side of death" even though his profession lacks the vocabulary to affirm life once life has stopped producing enough pleasure to outweigh its many pains (*Ser,* 282). Aside from recommending the palliative benefits of illicit sex, he can offer nothing to his patient except a half-formed notion that life ought to be preserved. In this way, Dr. Azote becomes a stand-in for the entire secular medical profession, which doggedly, and often heroically, fights to keep people alive without being able to argue coherently for the inherent value of life.

At the novel's conclusion, Houellebecq once again contrasts the vision of life provided by the age of materialism with that provided by Christianity in a manner that highlights the bankrupt quality of the former. Having exhausted the resources of clinical medicine and intent on "abandoning all hope of a possible life" (*Ser,* 293), Florent retreats to a studio apartment in an ugly high rise on the outskirts of Paris. There he intends to waste the last of his savings on expensive food, sex being off the table, while he prepares himself to make use of his apartment window. His enigmatic final reflections touch on three main things: (1) the failure of his medication to tether him to life; (2) the failure of post-1960s individualism to provide happiness; and (3) the sacrifice of Christ. The first two are predictable. By this point in the narrative, the reader has been told often enough that antidepressants do no more than help "people to live, or at least not die—for a certain period of time" (308). Without question, "death imposes itself in the end" (308). Florent also returns to the recurrent idea that he could have been happy and made someone else happy if he had been able to love faithfully, if he had rejected "the illusion of individual freedom, of an open life, of infinite possibilities" that "were part of the spirit of the age," an age of suffering (309). His final thoughts come as more of a surprise.

Faced with his immanent suicide, Florent finds himself giving a definite name to the "hope beyond hope" (270) he sensed but could not name earlier in his depressive free fall. He identifies "God" as the source of all love and claims that those "surges of love" we experience in life are "inexplicable if we consider our biological nature . . . as simple primates" (309). In essence, Houellebecq refutes the idea that the core demand of the human soul to love and be loved can be explained away biologically. Synthetic hormonal adjustment could not save Florent. The experience of love cannot be reduced to a material phenomenon because it is "an extremely clear sign" of God's love. However simplistic in his articulation, Florent uses love as a proof for the existence of a benevolent God, an explicitly Christian God. The concluding paragraph demands quotation in full:

> And today I understand Christ's point of view and his repeated horror at the hardening of people's hearts: all of these things are signs, and they don't realize it. Must I really, on top of everything, give my life for these wretches? Do I really have to be explicit on that point?
>
> Apparently so. (309)

My first reading of this concluding paragraph left me with a sense of whiplash. In subsequent readings, I began to see the subtle ways in which Houellebecq prepares the way for this epiphany.

References to God appear early in the novel as something like traces of a bygone psychological and cultural order. Relieved that a beautiful girl's skirt has not been lifted by a gust of wind and annihilated him with a vision of the thing he has treated as a god most of his life, the middle-aged Florent comments offhandedly that "God is merciful and compassionate" (6). Fantasizing about driving his car off the freeway, he concludes, "I would give the Lord my uncertain soul" (19). In these instances, references to God are covered in a film of irony. By the middle of the novel, Florent graduates to directly denigrating God: "God is a mediocre scriptwriter, that's the conviction that almost fifty years of life have led me to form, and more generally God is mediocre" (157). Later still, he slips into speaking of God as an intelligent creator: "unlike Gogol, I couldn't have said that God had given me a complex nature. God had given me a simple nature, infinitely simple in my opinion—it was more the world around me that had become complex, and now I could no longer deal with complexity of the world" (255). By the novel's conclusion, at his absolute nadir, Florent has found his way circuitously but believably to a positive affirmation of a benevolent, Christian God.

This conversion does not make Florent a good theologian. The conclusion depicts a man ready to end his life in a perverse parody of Christ's sacrifice on the cross. The Christ of the Bible agonizes over what he must suffer for the sake of humanity in the garden of Gethsemane, but he never refers to his people as wretches. Of course, Florent's lifelong alienation from religion constitutes a major part of his existential predicament. So, he was never likely to become an orthodox Catholic overnight. Neither does he seem likely to abandon his planned suicide. If anything, the novel's abrupt conclusion implies its narrator's abrupt conclusion. But his epiphany represents perhaps the most meaningful event in a broken life. Stripped of the pseudo-freedom offered by unfettered individualism, stripped of the atomized self that postmodernity holds up as a god, he receives a fleeting but concrete and unironic glimpse of a God who gives the lie to that world. Houellebecq may never find his way to that God, as he does in *The Map and the Territory*, but the fact that his art wanders so regularly in the direction of that end suggests one potential reason why the artist has not yet imitated his art and forsaken the life he so bitterly laments.

We would be hard-pressed to find any contemporary author as steeped in the problem of suicide as Michel Houellebecq. *The Elementary Particles* tells a grand historical narrative about the genesis of our suicidal age by tracing it back to the rise of materialism and the decline of religion, specifically Catholicism. *Serotonin* tells a far more intimate and psychologically driven story about one man's experience of our culture's failure to palliate its cosmic meaninglessness with therapeutic drugs. Houellebecq paints an almost irremediably bleak picture of modern existence, but his vision does suggest an alternative. Christianity—with its divine anthropology, promise of an eternal *telos*, belief in the possibility of self-sacrificial love, and ennoblement of suffering—still exists in Houellebecq's world. There is, as Eagleton puts it, a "God-shaped hole" in Houellebecq's cosmos that allows us to see the rejection of life for the tragedy that it truly is. This is a starting point. The Catholic writers explored in the remainder if this book will help lead us from this dismal beginning to a more complete vision of reality by offering diverse, and sometimes even hopeful, responses to the problem of suicide.

2

Antinatalist Ecology and
the Decadent Novel

IT SHOULD COME AS no surprise that Houellebecq, the subject of chapter 1, was fascinated by the literature of the late-nineteenth-century Decadent movement. Decadence, if I may permit myself to paint with overly broad strokes, celebrated artifice over nature, reveled in sensual experimentation, and blended ancient classicism and modern philosophical pessimism with a nostalgia for a particularly medieval Christianity. Oscar Wilde stands out as one of the most recognizable Decadents in the English tradition, with his novel *The Picture of Dorian Gray* (1890) capturing much of the essence of the movement. Houellebecq draws repeatedly on the work of Wilde's most profound influences among the French Decadents, such as the poet Charles Baudelaire, infamous for his collection of poetry *Les Fleurs du mal* (*The Flowers of Evil*, 1857), and especially J. K. Huysmans, the Decadent novelist turned Catholic convert and oblate. Houellebecq shares Huysmans's immersion in the pessimism of figures such as the German philosopher Arthur Schopenhauer (1788–1860) as well as his obsession with the nature and the narrative consequences of sin and moral degeneration. He also shares the general Decadent horror of children. When they do appear in his fiction, their one role seems to be that of heightening our awareness of the degradation of the world adults have created for them. Children appear in Houellebecq's novels, if at all, to suffer.

In general, Decadent literature is no place for a child, and its aversion to children goes hand in hand with its investment in philosophical pessimism and its thematic fixation on individual and even species suicide. Long before twenty-first-century philosophical antinatalists such as David Benatar and Sarah Perry sought to convince humanity to stop having babies in order to avoid the suffering inherent in human existence and save the planet from human despoilment, the protagonists of decadent novels routinely affirmed both the undesirability of human life and the vulgarity of procreation. In doing so, decadent literature anticipated the essential arguments of the most radical ecological ethic of our day.

This chapter will first outline the essential arguments of modern antinatalism, a philosophical movement that becomes less obscure with each passing year. Second, it will theorize the manifestation of proto-antinatalist sentiment in Huysmans's Decadent novel, *À Rebours* (1884). Third, it will explore in detail the particular brand of Decadent antinatalism at play in Irish artist George Moore's inheritor novel, *Mike Fletcher* (1889). Moore's book plays with the idea of voluntary extinction as a heroic and ethical response to the catastrophe of human existence and demonstrates that decadence has a role to play in current discussions of antinatalism, suicide, and ecology. *Mike Fletcher*, I will argue, plays the role of devil's advocate to its own protagonist's fantasies of human species extinction. Far from affirming Fletcher's misanthropy and antinatalism, Moore negates his antihero's grand act of renunciation by affirming human life through a narrative that reveals the horrific consequences of philosophical pessimism. Mike Fletcher the character is undone by *Mike Fletcher* the novel, which advocates for human life and affirms the importance of the human species in the ecology of existence. Like Huysmans before him and Houellebecq after him, Moore demonstrates that those works of literature that most fully embody pernicious ideologies in an individual life may be our best argumentative resource against some of the emergent nightmares of nihilistic modern philosophy.

Antinatalism, Ethics, and Ecology

Procreation has lost its attraction for an increasing number of people in the modern, developed world. In the United States, which is faring better than many countries, the birth rate reached a new low of 1.62 in 2023, down 2 percent from 2022 and down 57 percent from the historic high of almost 3.8 in 1957.[1] Though many are quick to point to economic factors, an increasing number of potential parents have indicated a simple unwillingness to bring children into a world they see as essentially broken and unfit for new human life. Among this set, many cite specifically ecological concerns.[2] This turn against procreation for utilitarian and ethical reasons finds its philosophical counterpart in antinatalism.

If we were honest with ourselves, antinatalist thinkers insist, we would accept the unavoidable logical conclusion that existence isn't all it's cracked up to be. David Benatar—philosopher at the University of Cape Town and author of *Better Never to Have Been: The Harm of Coming into Existence* (2006), *Debating Procreation: Is it Wrong to Reproduce?* (2015), and *The Human Predicament: A Candid Guide* (2017)—serves as a modern John the Baptist for the gospel of antinatalism. In 2017, Benatar achieved a level of recognition usually denied to philosophy professors, when *The New Yorker* requested an interview. An excerpt from that interview puts the case against existence succinctly:

> "For an existing person, the presence of bad things is bad and the presence of good things is good," Benatar explained. "But compare that with a scenario in which that person never existed—then, the absence of the bad would be good, but the absence of the good wouldn't be bad, because there'd be nobody to be deprived of those good things." This asymmetry "completely stacks the deck against existence," he continued, because it suggests that "all the unpleasantness and all the misery and all the suffering could be over, without any real cost."[3]

Benatar pulls up short of recommending immediate and violent species suicide (he considers himself a compassionate antinatalist). "Life is bad, but so," he concedes, "is death. Of course, life is not bad in *every* way. Neither is death bad in every way. However, both life and death are, in a crucial respect, awful. Together, they constitute an existential vise—the wretched grip that enforces our predicament."[4] Two obvious ways out of this predicament present themselves: suicide and refusal to procreate.

Concluding that nonexistence is objectively superior to existence does not necessitate suicide, Benatar insists: "The view that coming into existence is always a harm does *not imply* that death is better than

1. Calfas and DeBarros, "U.S. Fertility Rate Falls to Record Low."
2. Gayle, "More People Not Having Children."
3 Rothman, "Case for Not Being Born."
4. Benatar, *Human Predicament*, 1–2.

continuing to exist, and a fortiori that suicide is (always) desirable."[5] Antinatalists do not demand heroic suicide. Camus may have been able to conceive of something like heroic effort in the face of life's meaninglessness, but Benatar prefers to stick to a neo-epicurean quality-of-life calculus. Once someone concludes that the awful experience of death is preferable to an unbearable life, "rational suicide," understood as neither cowardice nor a mental aberration,[6] ought to be readily available. While arguing that suicide provides one acceptable means of achieving the goal of nonexistence, Benatar insists that we can act most rationally, justly, and compassionately by simply ceasing to procreate. Those who are never born need never suffer, harm others, or face death. Any pleasure or transitory happiness denied to the unborn cannot be considered an actual loss because something that has never existed cannot experience loss. Were we all to embrace this final solution, we would end the suffering of a human race that has too often deluded itself, primarily with the aid of religion, into pretending that suffering might be anything other than categorically bad. Benatar identifies this as the "philanthropic" core of his message. He laments that it is "unlikely that many people will take to heart the conclusion that coming into existence is always a harm" and "even less likely that many people will stop having children"; nevertheless, he holds out hope that some people might be persuaded to make the ethical decision against procreation.[7]

Aside from its direct benefits for those humans spared the pain of existence, Benatar's philanthropic ethic comports with many of what he calls "misanthropic" secondary benefits, particularly in the realm of ecology.[8] Mass rejection of procreation would, without a doubt, save countless other species from extinction and provide almost immediate amelioration of pollution, deforestation, ocean acidification, and global warming. At the very least, we would prevent ourselves from committing the ultimate sin of creating, through artificial intelligence, new forms of consciousness capable of experiencing the pain of existence.[9]

This argument speaks to a central crisis of materialist postmodernity, which attempts to simultaneously and paradoxically reject objective notions of ultimate meaning and to rationalize continued existence.

5. Benatar, *Better Never to Have Been*, 212.

6. Benatar, *Better Never to Have Been*, 129.

7. Benatar, *Better Never to Have Been*, 225.

8. Benatar, *Better Never to Have Been*, 224.

9. Benatar, *Better Never to Have Been*, 136.

Its ecological implications are profound. Serious environmentalists often recommend that humans reduce their carbon footprint or their detrimental effect on other species by reducing global population or controlling birth rates. The argument for this position is simple: we are part of nature; we are destroying other parts of nature; we should find ways to mitigate our detrimental effects on nature. What this argument generally assumes is that nature itself is somehow inherently good. This assumption even holds true for our most radical philosophers of ecology. Object-oriented ontologists, such as Graham Harman, Timothy Morton, and Ian Bogost, reject human exceptionalism and insist upon the ontological parity not only of all species of animal life but of all elements of the material world. Bogost presents the argument for OOO (pronounced "Triple O") concisely:

> Ontology is the philosophical study of existence. Object-orient-ed ontology ("OOO" for short) puts *things* at the center of this study. Its proponents contend that nothing has special status, but that everything exists equally—plumbers, cotton, bonobos, DVD players, and sandstone, for example. In contemporary thought, things are usually taken either as the aggregation of ever smaller bits (scientific naturalism) or as constructions of human behavior and society (social relativism). OOO steers a path between the two, drawing attention to things at all scales (from atoms to alpacas, bits to blini), and pondering their nature and relations with one another as much as with ourselves.[10]

Even those who claim to view all elements of the universe (sentient and otherwise) as equal in ontological status surprisingly assume that the sentient bits of that universe are somehow good and worth preserving. Morton's 2018 monograph is called simply *Being Ecological,* and it makes no bones about its interest in getting humans to act differently in order to prevent the extinction of animal species and preserve an ecological world in which humans and toasters exist on a footing of ontological parity.

Traditional essentialists, including most Christians, would call this ontological parity distorted and illogical. Antinatalist thinkers like Benatar call this perverse essentialism—this insistence that nothing is essentially superior to anything else but that all sentient things are essentially worth preserving—into question by insisting on the undesirability of all sentient existence. "My argument," writes Benatar in the Introduction to *Better Never to Have Been,* "applies not only to humans

10. Bogost, "What is Object-Oriented Ontology?"

but also to all other sentient beings. . . . Although sentience is a later evolutionary development and is a more complex state of being than insentience, it is far from clear that it is a better state of being."[11] If we question the notion that sentient life is *essentially* good; if we resist the unexamined assumption that sentient beings ought to be because they currently are, we open the door to antinatalism.

Though animal and human sentience are separated by an evolutionary gap, in this reading, antinatalists assume that this same basic insight regarding the undesirability of existence holds as true for other species as it does for homo sapiens. Sarah Perry, author of *Every Cradle Is a Grave: Rethinking the Ethics of Birth and Suicide* (2014), devotes a chapter to "The World of Nature of Which We Are a Part." Like Morton, Bogost, and other object-oriented ontologists, she rejects an anthropocentric view of suffering. Life for most animals, she reminds us, is nasty, brutish, and short. Even without humans in the equation to destroy and pollute habitats, animals would continue to face lives more characterized by suffering than anything else. Perry goes so far as to insist that we could "simply prevent their [animal] reproduction, or even merely cease our 'conservation efforts' that involve breeding animals. Breeding wild animals and releasing them into the wild is doing the ugly work of Genesis all over again—and cruelly claiming that it's 'good.'"[12] For Perry, we are just the sentient part of a material nature, and our sentience only gifts us with suffering. Our treatment of nature as something separate from us, and even something good, is a delusion that keeps us wedded to the life that harms us. We humans, as Morton reminds us in nearly all of his commentary on literature and ecology, developed a Romantic notion of nature as separate from ourselves, as something to be contemplated and enjoyed as an ontologically distinct other. This is an illusion. We are part of nature. We are not special, simply more capable of affecting our ecological surroundings than other animals. Wed that capability to an antinatalist ethic, and there is only one justifiable response to other sentient life: "Responsible people spay or neuter their pets," Perry reminds us. "Why not spay Nature Herself?"[13]

It would be both accurate and misleading to call antinatalism a fringe movement. You cannot find thoroughgoing antinatalist arguments in *The Norton Anthology of Theory and Criticism* alongside selections from

11. Benatar, *Better Never to Have Been*, 2.

12. Perry, *Every Cradle Is a Grave*, 200.

13. Perry, *Every Cradle Is a Grave*, 200.

Morton's *The Ecological Thought*, at least not yet. Its proponents don't give TED Talks. Neither *The Journal of Ecocriticism* nor *ISLE* (*Interdisciplinary Studies in Literature and Environment*) regularly publishes articles on antinatalism in literature. There is no academic conference for antinatalist thought in Europe or the United States. That said, antinatalist blogs, Reddit pages, podcasts, and books boast a substantial audience. Compared to most academic subfields, including literary ecocriticism, the antinatalist branch of philosophy has touched a popular nerve and spoken to a growing suspicion regarding both the inherent value of life and the desirability of the human species in the post-secular Western world. Its reasoning strikes many as inescapable. I claim that seemingly pessimistic and misanthropic Decadent novels provide powerful counter-arguments to the brutal logic of postmodern materialism by showing us what lives truly informed by such nihilistic philosophy amount to. The degraded and tragic narratives of Decadent protagonists provide an unexpected apologia for humanity's continued existence and an implicit argument for life and meaning over death and existential absurdity.

Decadence and Antinatalism

On its face, suicide seems a perfectly fitting end for a truly Decadent text or character. Wilde's Dorian Gray could not remain physically young and beautiful forever while his soul became more desiccated with each passing year. He had to die, and his own hand was the only tool for the job. And no Decadent antihero would dream of polluting an already vile world with more life. Children play a minor role in Decadent literature. Rather than think of them as better seen and not heard, most Decadent texts treat them as better not seen at all. The world of "Wine and woman and song" depicted in Decadent poet Ernest Dowson's "Villanelle of the Poet's Road" or the East End opium dens of *Dorian Gray* (or, for that matter, the fashionable dinner parties of *Dorian Gray*) or the salacious pictures of the artist Aubrey Beardsley leave little room for innocent Victorian children. When boys and girls do appear in Decadent literature, they do so primarily as objects of direct or sublimated erotic attention.[14] Overwhelmingly, opposition to the cruel banality of life weds itself to nausea at the vulgarity of procreation in the imagination of the Decadent antihero.

---

14. For more on pedophiliac tensions in Decadent literature, especially *Dorian Gray*, see Ohi, *Innocence and Rapture*.

One such antihero, the eponymous aristocrat of Villiers de l'Isle-Adam's *Axël* (1890), after meeting the love of his life, proposes that they commit suicide together, since their future lives could never match the intensity of their present passion: "Living? Our servants will do that for us." Add to this general antipathy between the Decadent novel, children, and life in general the fact that almost none of the artists associated with the Decadent movement, with the obvious exception of Oscar Wilde, bothered to marry or procreate or, in many cases, have sex at all.

I would be remiss not to mention the distinctly queer element to the implicit antinatalism of Decadence, though it is not a major feature of my current argument. Lee Edelman's groundbreaking book *No Future: Queer Theory and the Death Drive* (2004) posits an essential link between modern queer identity and a rejection of future-oriented procreative existence. Edelman insists that the queer figure implicitly disrupts the stability of political systems and that "*queerness* names the side of those *not* 'fighting for the children,' the side outside the consensus by which all politics confirms the absolute value of reproductive futurism."[15] I would not be the first to see an attempt at queer antinatalism in Edelman's theorization of the "sinthomosexual"—that figure who stands outside the future-oriented fetish of the child, a figure of the Decadent antihero if ever there was one. Stanimir Panayotov makes the connection explicitly in a manner that Edelman himself does not:

> What can be called "antinatalism" in Edelman is "where the future stops," the "desire to die" now where "now" does not pass as the "future." The lesson to be learned from Edelman is not a Foucaultian [sic.] notion of writing the ontology of the present; it is to live the now as an unsignified future coming in the figure of the NO, and not NOW. Just as being antinatalist does not morally involve the committal of suicide, just as non-procreation does not necessarily mean human extinction, so the desire to die, or the stopping of future [sic.], does not mean to stop living: it only means to start dying without signifying death as life—to stop the world.[16]

At first blush, it seems like Edelman's brand of queer antinatalism captures much of the *fin-du-globe* essence of Decadent antiheroes such as Huysmans's Des Esseintes, Wilde's Dorian Gray, and Moore's Mike Fletcher. This likeness even extends to the postmodern inheritors of

15. Edelman, *No Future*, 3.
16. Panayotov, "Heart's Unreason," 131.

this tradition, such as Houellebecq's Florent and Gabriel Brockwell—the suicidal misanthrope at the heart of DBC Pierre's *Lights Out in Wonderland* (2010), who embraces the death drive with open arms as a means of escape from his own failures at masculinity and radical political reform. But, as we well know, these characters are not their creators, and they are not the sum of their stories. I hold that the seeming or implicit antinatalism of Decadent characters is repeatedly undermined or subverted by a more explicit affirmation of life, and human life in particular. But more on that later. For now, I would like to investigate that seeming Decadent antinatalism in order to give it proper shape and to show it for what, at base, it is: a pose.

The clearest and most explicit expression of Decadent antinatalism, other than Moore's *Mike Fletcher*, is without a doubt Huysmans' *À Rebours*. His "breviary of decadence," as Arthur Symons would later christen it, anticipates the central tenet of the antinatalist movement. In the novel, a Parisian hedonist, Jean des Esseintes, leaves the city to create an aesthetic retreat in the suburbs, where he enacts increasingly elaborate experiments in pursuit of intellectual and sensual pleasure. It doesn't end well. Late in the novel, in the depths of his misery, unable to sleep or eat and suffering from oppressive summer heat, Des Esseintes finds that his perverse suburban monastery has become a place of torture. Seeking some relief, he does the unthinkable and leaves his aesthete's cell in order to sit in his garden for the first time. There, he turns his attention to humanity and the tragedy of existence.

In the shade of his garden tree, Des Esseintes watches a group of local urchins at play. Some are eating a peasant's snack of bread smothered with cheese and garlic, which momentarily stirs the starving appetite of a man whose history of sensual excesses has led to an ironic inability to desire or keep down food.[17] Des Esseintes immediately rushes to the kitchen and orders his servants to secure such a snack. Upon returning to the garden, he finds the boys fighting over their meager food. Quickly, the larger boys gang up on and abuse their smaller companions. Musing on the lives of these filthy peasant children leads Huysmans' protagonist into an extended antinatalist reverie: "Faced with the savage fury of these vicious brats, he reflected on the cruel and abominable law of the struggle of life; and, contemptible though these children were, he could not help feeling sorry for them and thinking it would have been better

17. Huysmans, *Against Nature*, 154.

for them if their mothers had never borne them."[18] He then devotes a paragraph to considering the miserable lot of such children, from colic in infancy, to betrayal in manhood, to ignoble and painful death in old age. This, he realizes, is the condition not just of the poor but of all people: "And the future, when you came to think of it, was the same for all, and nobody with any sense would dream of envying anyone else."[19] True enough in this case. None of those poor but healthy boys would wish to trade places with their wealthy but physically decaying voyeur. Having established the undesirability of life, Des Esseintes spins a web of antinatalist theories and policies.

Characteristically, his mind turns to its most fondly hated obsession, that behemoth champion of life and fecundity, the Catholic Church: "What madness it was to beget children. . . . And to think the priestery, who had taken a vow of sterility, had carried inconsistency to the point of canonizing St. Vincent de Paul because he saved innocent babes for useless torments!"[20] Priestly celibacy might seem consistent with antinatalist thinking, but it conceals far more sinister practices, most notably St. Vincent de Paul's sadistic insistence on saving the lives of orphaned infants because of "an absurd theological code."[21] What's worse, the practice caught on and "won universal acceptance; for instance, children abandoned by their mothers were given homes instead of being left to die quietly without knowing what was happening." Lamentably, to the deranged mind of Des Esseintes, even the rise of secular governments and laws offers no hope of an escape from the Catholic delusion that each human life is inherently dignified and worth preserving. The pseudo-philanthropic army of Homais produced by the Enlightenment had swallowed a version of this absurd belief, made more absurd by its lack of theological grounding, and inscribed it in the laws of the state. These same laws, Des Esseintes complains, make it both legal to practice contraception and illegal to perform an abortion should such measures fail. This hypocrisy stings even more than that of the celibate priests. If only Des Esseintes had had the comfort of knowing that this oversight would be corrected by most of the Western world in less than a century, he might have slept better. Of course, it had to be corrected for the very reasons he cites.

18. Huysmans, *Against Nature*, 155.
19. Huysmans, *Against Nature*, 155.
20. Huysmans, *Against Nature*, 155.
21. Huysmans, *Against Nature*, 156.

A modern secular democracy cannot possibly argue with any consistency for the inherent value of human life. In his encyclical *Evangelium Vitae* (1995), St. Pope John Paul II, a thorn in the side of death if ever there was one, insisted that Western policies of contraception went hand in hand with the logic of a broader "culture of death" that was itself a realization of secular modernity's tendency toward voluntaristic and nihilistic notions of freedom:

> In seeking the deepest roots of the struggle between the "culture of life" and the "culture of death," we cannot restrict ourselves to the perverse idea of freedom. . . . We have to go to the heart of the tragedy being experienced by modern man: the eclipse of the sense of God and of man, typical of a social and cultural climate dominated by secularism, which, with its ubiquitous tentacles, succeeds at times in putting Christian communities themselves to the test. Those who allow themselves to be influenced by this climate easily fall into a sad vicious circle: when the sense of God is lost, there is also a tendency to lose the sense of man, of his dignity and his life.[22]

A decade after John Paul II's forceful proclamation, French anthropological philosopher René Girard cited the importance of this argument in modern ethical discourse, noting that "John Paul II's idea of recovering 'a culture of life' from the 'culture of death' has framed a whole set of issues, from abortion to stem cell research, capital punishment and war."[23] For evidence of the veracity of this claim, we need look no further than the late pope's role as analyst of the culture of death in Houellebecq's *Elementary Particles*. As much as it continues to help frame such debates, however, even John Paul II's apocalyptic vision of secular modernity's death drive failed to anticipate the rise of explicitly antinatalist philosophy. Even he could not conceive of mainstream philosophers calling for the cessation of sentient life itself in the name of ethics. Had he read more Decadent literature, he might have seen it coming.

Huysmans does not share Des Esseintes's "charitable reflections" on legalized and universally practiced abortion and suicide. Instead, he implicitly insists upon the misanthropic roots of all such philanthropic plans for the eradication of life. After relating the unfolding of Des Esseintes's thought process for three pages, the narrator shows us the actions that such thoughts produce. When the peasant's snack requested prior to

22. John Paul II, *Evangelium Vitae*, 39–40.
23. Girard, "Gospel and Globalization," 59.

his antinatalist reflections arrives on a silver platter, Des Esseintes greets this manifestation of incarnate life, this humble sustenance, with nausea: "His gorge rose at the sight; he had not the courage to take even a bite at the bread, for his morbid appetite had deserted him."[24] His appetite gone, Des Esseintes shows his detestation for the boys whose welfare he momentarily pretended to care about. As if to highlight the importance of the ensuing exchange between master and servant, Huysmans allows his protagonist to speak to another human being, an extremely rare occurrence in a novel whose narrator does nearly all the talking:

> "You see those children fighting in the road?" he said to the man. "Well, throw the thing to them. And let's hope that the weaklings are badly mauled about, that they don't get so much as a crumb of bread, and that on top of it all they're soundly thrashed when they get home with their breeches torn and a couple of black eyes to boot. That'll give them a fore-taste of the sort of life they can expect!"[25]

For all their pretense to philanthropic concern about the suffering of humanity, those who disdain life and fantasize about species extinction, Huysmans suggests, primarily wish to see their own misery amplified. These wretched apostles of death cannot be content with their own annihilation; they long to see it realized on a global scale. Huysmans clearly demonstrates that Decadent antinatalists should not be equated with their creators.

Huysmans made the distance between his views and those of his creature, Des Esseintes, clear in a 1903 preface to À Rebours. In it, he argues that his turn to Catholicism some years after the publication of À Rebours was less a rejection of the Schopenhauerian pessimism of his early work than it was a realization that Catholicism both contains and transcends such philosophy. The point is complex and worth quoting at length:

> I did not imagine that it was only a short step from Schopen-hauer, whom I admired beyond reason, to *Ecclesiastes* and the *Book of Job*. The premises about Pessimism are the same, only when the time comes to reach a conclusion, the philosopher disappears. I liked his ideas about the horror of life, the stupid-ity of the world, the mercilessness of destiny; I like them also

24. Huysmans, *Against Nature*, 157.
25. Huysmans, *Against Nature*, 157.

in the Holy Scriptures; but Schopenhauer's observations lead
nowhere; he leaves you, so to speak, in the lurch; in the end,
his aphorisms are only an herbarium of dry plaints; whereas
the Church explains the origins and the causes, indicates the
conclusions, offers remedies. She does not limit herself to giving
you a spiritual consolation, but treats and cures you, whereas
the German quack, once he has proven the incurability of your
condition, simply sneers and turns his back on you. . . . After
all these years, when I reread these pages where such resolutely
false theories are presented as true, I smile.[26]

Huysmans does not deny the suffering entailed in life. Schopenhauer was
exceedingly right about one thing: life involves a great deal of suffering.
He was also exceedingly wrong about the implications of this assertion.
Suffering makes human life qua human life an intolerable burden if, and
only if, that suffering is not bounded by divine providence, the turning of
all things to the good in the fullness of time. If God is truly dead, Huysmans would tell us, the antinatalists are right; if God is not dead, then
their philosophy mistakes the part for the whole. Huysmans concludes
his retrospective on À Rebours by returning to the notion of suicide. He
cites a famous review of the novel by Barbey d'Aurevilly, in which the
reviewer asserts that "After such a book, the only choice left open to the
author is between the muzzle of a pistol and the foot of the cross."[27] The
Decadents consistently chose the foot of the cross, but their art consistently obsessed over the barrel of the pistol.

The earliest critics of literary decadence associated the movement
with a suicidal death drive. In his 1936 introduction to the *Oxford Book
of Modern Verse*, W. B. Yeats directly links Decadent poetry with the desire for self-annihilation. When Walter Pater instructed the readers of his
"Conclusion" to *The Renaissance* to live life like a "hard, gem-like flame,"
he cast a sinister shadow, Yeats tells us. The aesthetic dictum provided
momentary inspiration but insufficient motive for life. Pater's Decadent
followers found in that shadow a call to suicide that their pragmatic
Victorian fathers never would have heeded. The Decadents were "the
sons of men who had admired Garibaldi or applauded the speeches of
John Bright," men, in short, who "knew exactly what they wanted and
had no intention of committing suicide."[28] Unlike their vital fathers, men

26. Huysmans, "Preface," 208–9.
27. Huysmans, "Preface," 217.
28. Yeats, "Introduction," ix.

like Lionel Johnson, Ernest Dowson, and Count Eric Stenbock—author
of both *Shadows of Death: A Collection of Poems* (1893) and *Studies of
Death: Romantic Tales* (1894)—found no justification for life. Yeats tells
us that his father christened these men the "Hamlets of our age."[29] I would
contend that John Yeats hit the nail on the head with that one, but not
quite in the way his son thought. W. B. Yeats saw in his father's pronounce-
ment a simple acknowledgment of the brooding, self-destructive desire at
the heart of what he dubbed "The Tragic Generation." True, like Hamlet,
the Decadents often spoke of death as "a consummation devoutly to be
wished." Like Hamlet, they were largely driven to this conclusion by a disdain for a corrupt and corrupting world and entertained dreams of human
extinction. Also like Hamlet, they never chose to make their quietus with
a bare bodkin. For all their fascination with suicide, the canonical British
Decadents disdained the act itself. Incidentally, they also preferred nun-
neries, at least as aesthetic objects, to marriage beds.

My point, and my point overall, is that this obsession with species
suicide in decadent texts, like that in *Hamlet*, is not an endorsement. Ultimately, Decadent authors, as opposed to individual Decadent characters, prove surprisingly life affirming. So, how do we explain the seeming
ubiquity and earnestness of the Decadent obsession with death? Suicide
in Decadent literature acts as one prop for the Decadents' larger pose of
rebellion. In *The Rebel* (1951), Camus rightly points out that the Decadents, especially Baudelaire, never truly rebel. "Baudelaire," Camus tells
us, "despite his satanic arsenal, his taste for Sade, his blasphemies, remains too much a theologian to be a proper rebel."[30] Camus only brings
up the Arch-Dandy because Baudelaire "was the most profound theo-
retician of dandyism and gave definite form to one of the conclusions
of romantic revolt."[31] The romantic artist is a dandy who must not only
exalt "beauty for its own sake," but must also "define an attitude" and,
eventually, assert that "art is his ethic." From this point on, the artist
has three options: madness, self-destruction, or careerism: "When the
dandies fail to commit suicide or do not go mad, they make a career and
pursue prosperity."[32] The key reason dandyism fails to live up to Camus's
admittedly dubious criteria for meaningful existential revolt is that the

29. Yeats, "Introduction," x.
30. Camus, *Rebel*, 53.
31. Camus, *Rebel*, 53.
32. Camus, *Rebel*, 53.

ANTINATALIST ECOLOGY AND THE DECADENT NOVEL

romantic rebel cannot help reaffirming the metaphysical order of God, even in the act of blasphemy:

> Dandyism, of whatever kind, is always dandyism in relation to God. The individual, in so far as he is a created being, can oppose himself only to the Creator. He has need of God, with whom he carries on a kind of a gloomy flirtation. . . . Despite its Nietzschean atmosphere, God is not yet dead even in romantic literature. Damnation, so clamorously demanded, is only a clever trick played on God. . . . The romantic rebel's ambition was to talk to God as one equal to another. Evil was the answer to evil, pride the answer to cruelty. . . . Obviously, the point is to raise oneself to the level of God, which already is blasphemy. But there is no thought of disputing the power or position of the deity. The blasphemy is reverent, since every blasphemy is, ultimately, a participation in holiness.[33]

The greatest form of rebellion available to the decadents fell short not because they lacked boldness but because they still conceived of a God against whom they must struggle.

Here, Camus reads more like T. S. Eliot than anyone else on the subject of late romanticism, blasphemy, and belief. Twenty years before publication of *The Rebel*, in his essay "Baudelaire" (1930), Eliot identified his subject as a blasphemer and argued that the French poet's blasphemy is a forceful affirmation of the existing metaphysical order. Unlike Camus, Eliot saw in this blasphemous decadence not a rebellion that failed because the dandy neglected to kill himself and insisted on wrestling with a fictional God, but a partially realized pursuit of the truth of existence that gave meaning to degraded modern existence:

> Baudelaire perceived that what really matters is Sin and Redemption. . . . The recognition of the reality of Sin is a New Life; and the possibility of damnation is so immense a relief in a world of electoral reform, plebiscites, sex reform and dress reform, that damnation itself is an immediate form of salvation—of salvation from the ennui of modern life, because it at last gives some significance to living.[34]

Affirming sin as a metaphysical reality, Baudelaire found salvation from the ennui of a banal modern world and an escape from the death drive at the heart of decadence. He was not the only Decadent artist to turn to

33. Camus, *Rebel*, 55.
34. Eliot, "Baudelaire," 236.

God, however grotesque the flourish of that turn. Though much criticism of Decadent literature downplays or avoids the subject, Decadent literature is nearly all identifiably Christian literature, albeit a strange species of that particular genus. However strange it might seem, the often misanthropic and pessimistic Decadents were secret agents—and sometimes explicit champions—of a religion that not only affirms the importance of human existence in the ecology of the cosmos but treats suicide as utterly anathema. We have seen this phenomenon in Huysmans. George Moore's Schopenhauerian fantasy, *Mike Fletcher*, puts the thesis to a harsher test.

George Moore's Antinatalist Fantasy

Though far less popular today, George Moore (1852–1933) was easily the most prominent Irish novelist of his time before being overshadowed by his younger compatriot James Joyce. Moore may be counted among the Decadents, at least in his early work; however, unlike his Decadent contemporaries, his interest in Catholicism, like that of Joyce after him, was largely agonistic. A Catholic by birth, Moore spent much of his life in rebellion against his native faith. His response to the stultifying effects of an often Jansenistic Irish Catholicism was not what Joyce would successfully manage in forging "the uncreated conscience of my race"—if success can be measure by one's ability to catalogue and subtly precipitate the degeneration of an entire country into a-religiosity. Moore gave forging the Irish conscience a pass, preferring to renounce those bits of himself that he associated with his homeland and direct his energies toward a more continental audience. His early short story collection *The Untilled Field* (1903), which served as a model for Joyce's *Dubliners* (1914), provided mostly non-Irish readers with a portrait of a priest-ridden island antipathetic to freedom, sexual fulfilment, and artistic expression.[35] In the same year as the publication of *The Untilled Field*, the already atheistic Moore attempted to score political points against the Catholic Church by publicly converting to the Anglican Church of Ireland. He made the move somewhat awkward for the Rev. Gilbert Mahaffy, the minister who received him, by repeatedly insisting that his conversion did not indicate a belief in any of the central theological doctrines of trinitarian

---

35. For more on the influence of Moore's short stories on Joyce, see Beckson, "Moore's *The Untilled Field* and Joyce's *Dubliners*."

Christianity—a position he made abundantly clear in his late novel *The Brook Kerith* (1916), which retells the story of the passion in a manner that explicitly denies Christ's divinity. As his biographer Adrian Frazier puts it, Moore's "notion of a Protestant had been an English atheist in favor of morality and independent judgement."[36] Suffice it to say, Moore never enjoyed an orthodox relationship with his native faith.

An early apostate from Catholicism, Moore also apostatsized from both his nationality and the long tradition of Western philosophy presumably debunked by an emergent radical pessimism. Such momentous self-transformation, however, never achieved its goal completely. To put it more directly, Moore couldn't shake his Catholicity or its distinctively natalist commitments—the theologically sponsored fecundity of its laity being one of its most distinctive hallmarks. This natalist Catholicism reemerged in his early writing as a foil to the nihilistic pessimism of Schopenhauer, with which he had so earnestly attempted to indoctrinate himself. At least in part, his failure can be attributed to an ill-advised decision to apprentice himself to Huysmans, whose pessimism came to be just one part of a larger, providential Catholicism. Moore's failed rebellion against his Catholic roots can be seen in his largely neglected decadent novel *Mike Fletcher*, a book that ultimately rejects pessimistic proto-antinatalism in favor of a distinctly more Catholic appreciation for the propagation of life.[37]

The antinatalist trope we have already seen at work in *À Rebours* found its fullest expression just five years later with the publication of *Mike Fletcher*. Early in his career, Moore wrote his "Don Juan" trilogy about a group of young men who capture the essence of their age. *Mike Fletcher* is the final novel in the trilogy. Published a year before *The Picture of Dorian Gray*, *Fletcher* was also directly inspired by Huysmans's "breviary of the decadence."[38] In spite of its provocative nature and captivating prose style, Moore's novel has received less serious

36. Fraizer, *George Moore*, 332.

37. In 2006, Kirsten MacLeod dedicated two pages of her book *Fictions of British Decadence* to *Mike Fletcher*. She correctly identified *Mike Fletcher* as one of the "ur-texts of Decadence" and credited Moore with "bringing Decadence to England" (66). Since then, the most significant critical studies of Decadent literature—Sherry's *Modernism and the Reinvention of Decadence* (2015), Hext and Murray's *Decadence in the Age of Modernism* (2019), Desmarais and Weir's *Decadence and Literature* (2019), and Murray's *Decadence: A Literary History* (2020)—have been content to mention Moore in passing and have entirely overlooked *Mike Fletcher*.

38. See Steward, "J. K. Huysmans and George Moore," 200.

attention than it merits, given the undeniably important role it plays in the history of Decadent literature in English. The final section of this chapter will focus on the novel as an extension and elaboration of the antinatalist pessimism found in *À Rebours*. Like Huysmans before him, Moore indulges in proto-antinatalist fantasy through his protagonist only to disavow the fantasy with a final affirmation of life over death. This extension of Huysmans's rejection of the premises of antinatalism is especially important because it suggests that even the apostate Moore was able to grasp some of the lessons about the meaning of life that Huysmans learned from his conversion to Catholicism. The antinatalism of *Fletcher* also feels much closer to the spirit of our time in part because it mirrors some of the ecological concerns that play a role in twenty-first-century opposition to procreation.

Mike Fletcher follows the fortunes of three young men: John Norton, Frank Escott, and Mike Fletcher. According to Mark Llewellyn, through these three characters "Moore analyses what he sees as the three main subject-positions available to the modern man—the celibate and melancholic aesthete; the husband and father; and the artist and debauchee."[39] Fletcher, a young Irish dandy, is the last in Llewellyn's list. Over the course of the novel, he obsesses over a beautiful novice nun, contributes Decadent poetry to a literary periodical, gains a fortune by seducing a rich old dowager, and eventually renounces everything by committing suicide in what he believes to be a philosophically consistent and heroic rejection of life. Though Fletcher is the primary focus of the novel, its opening chapter largely concerns itself with "the celibate and melancholic aesthete," Norton. Fletcher's friend and confidant, Norton shares his poetic vocation, his attraction to the pessimism of Schopenhauer, and his disdain for human procreation. This interest in Schopenhauer marks both characters as Decadents. In his preface to *The Case of Wagner* (1888), Nietzsche identifies Schopenhauer as the philosopher of decadence.[40] Schopenhauer's rejection of life made his philosophy a natural complement to the terminal myths and Decadent sense of entropic time best captured in the companion phrases *fin de siècle* and *fin du globe*—it has also made him the go-to philosopher for the modern antinatalist movement and one more prop in the Decadent pose of rebellion. Even in his blasphemous prime, the anti-Catholic

39. Llewellyn, "Masculinity in *Mike Fletcher*," 131.
40. Nietzsche, *Complete Works of Friedrich Nietzsche*, xxx.

Moore, like the Catholic convert Huysmans before him, creates a story that sides with God and life over nihilism and death.

Moore establishes an opposition between Catholicism and Schopenhauer's pessimism at the outset of the novel in the figure of Norton. At the beginning both he and Fletcher are hard at work on long "pessimistic" poems. This artistic sympathy shocks their friends because Fletcher's pagan hedonism and Norton's ascetic Catholicism appear so antipathetic, and so they prove. Norton knows from the start that his philosophy and his religion cannot be reconciled; he reels at the realization that he must choose between his religion and publishing his magnum opus—a collection of pessimist poetry culminating in the long poem *The Last Struggle*:

> But his poems were all he deemed best in the world. For a moment John stood face to face with, and he looked into the eyes of, the Church. The dome of St. Peter's, a solitary pope, cardinals, bishops, and priests. Oh! Wonderful symbolization of man's lust of eternal life!
>
> Must he renounce all his beliefs? The wish so dear to him that the unspeakable spectacle of life might cease for ever; must he give thanks for existence because it gave him a small chance of gaining heaven?[41]

The obvious answer for a Catholic is, yes. Life is a gift; death is the enemy; eternal life begins in the next world; and you'd best be ready for it. Like a good antinatalist, Norton rejects the first two assertions, but he clings to the last.

Trapped by this moral conundrum, Norton seeks the counsel of a priest. In the somewhat comic scene that ensues, Norton attempts to outline Schopenhauer's philosophy to a priest whose only reference point for modern philosophy is Cardinal Newman and who warns against "inclining too willing an ear to the specious sophistries of German philosophers" (10). Norton's insistence that Christ "is the perfect symbol of the denial of the will to live" meets with justifiable skepticism. Overcome by the priest's pious ignorance of the desirability of nonexistence, Norton can only bend his head "before the sublime stupidity of the priest" and crush his "rebellious spirit" (10; 11). Rather than submitting his poems for review and approval by the clergy, he decides to burn them. Here is Camus's dandy. His rebellion against God, which ought rightly to end in suicide—in this case the figurative

---

41. Moore, *Mike Fletcher*, 7. All subsequent citations from this text will appear parenthetically.

suicide of a literary holocaust—only affirms the authority of the thing it struggles against. Norton's blasphemous pessimism is yet another pose. As if not to be outdone, the novel's Decadent protagonist, Fletcher, will make Norton's figurative suicide literal.

The son of an Irish peasant and a French maid, Mike Fletcher lacks the pedigree and Jesuit upbringing of Des Esseintes, yet he has a great deal in common with Huysmans's protagonist. Whereas *À Rebours* begins with the exhausted hedonist's retreat from the world into a sort of Decadent retirement home, however, *Mike Fletcher* presents us with a young, British version of the Decadent antihero seen in his prime. A notorious Casanova, Fletcher is Dorian Gray with no need of a Lord Henry. First among the rabble-rousers and aesthetes of 1880s London, he has ruined hundreds of young women and made pleasure his god. He clearly agrees with Des Esseintes that life is an enemy best exploited and then rejected.

After Norton relates the destruction of his poems to Fletcher, he confesses surprise that his frivolous, hedonistic friend should also be writing a long poem about Schopenhauer's philosophy. Fletcher responds that his lifestyle is a perfect realization of pessimism:

> If you want a young and laughing world, preach Schopenhauer at every street corner. . . . The optimist believes in regeneration of the race, in its ultimate perfectibility, the synthesis of humanity, the providential idea, and the path of the future; he therefore puts on a shovel hat, cries out against lust, and deprecates prostitution. . . . The optimist counsels manual labor for all. The pessimist believes that forgetfulness and nothingness is the whole of man. He says "I defy the wisest of you to tell me why I am here, and being here, what good is gained by my assisting to bring others here." (46)

If Norton represents a pessimism of cold spirituality, Fletcher embodies a pessimism of burning carnality. Rather than asserting that humanity's goal ought to be an escape from the fleshly to the spiritual via death, he asserts that humanity has no telos and, therefore, ought to maximize pleasure and leave suffering and procreation to the beasts. Delighted by this radically different realization of their shared beliefs, Norton asks Fletcher to describe his own great pessimistic poem. What follows is the most fully realized antinatalist fantasy in literature.

In the poem, Fletcher envisions a human race that has rejected the will to live by embracing self-destruction. "Man," he tells Norton, "has at last recognized that life is in equal parts misery and abomination, and has resolved that it shall cease" (46). What has brought about this change? "There have been Messiahs, there have been persecutions, but the Word has been preached unintermittently. Crowds have gathered to listen to the wild-eyed prophets. . . . The world, grown tired of vain misery, accepts oblivion" (46). Realizing the pointlessness and horror of endless procreation, humanity has accepted oblivion. The prophets of a new religion of nonexistence have replaced the biblical "Word" of creation with the new gospel of merciful oblivion and successfully converted the masses—a consummation only dreamed of by modern antinatalists such as Benatar. In Fletcher's millenarian vision, only one young, beautiful man remains. He is, of course, French, and he "stands like a saint of old, who, on the last verge of the desert, turns and smiles upon the world he has conquered" (48). Here the story shifts its focus momentarily to the ecological.

Wandering the postapocalyptic world, Fletcher's last man watches the Anthropocene landscape, the landscape of the human epoch, crumble and give way to nature. Trees and other vegetation have reduced the bridges of Paris to rubble; the sea destroys the paintings of Veronese in Venice; the wolf cubs of Florence rip to pieces the last remaining copy of Dante's *Commedia*. Fletcher's hero cannot be distressed for long by these sights because the glory of humanity's accomplishment reveals itself in the flourishing of nature. Standing in Rome "amid the orange and almond trees, amid a profusion of bloom that the world seems to have brought for thank-offering, amid an apparent and glorious victory of inanimate nature, he falls down in worship of his race that had freely surrendered all, knowing it to be nothing, and in surrender had gained all" (49). Like the thoroughgoing antinatalists of our day, Fletcher envisions the ecological windfall of humanity's self-erasure not as an ultimate good—there can be no such thing in an ultimately meaningless universe—but as a testament to the great achievement of auto-extinction.

There's only one problem. The cries of a beautiful dying woman disrupt the hero's moment of "intense consciousness" and introduce a reverse existential threat. Upon being nursed back to health, the woman blasphemously proposes that they continue the human race. Unable to escape the wiles of this *femme vitale*, the protagonist of Fletcher's poem does the only ethical thing, at least from an antinatalist perspective. He commits one final act of salvific murder. Following the path of Des Esseintes, Fletcher finds in Schopenhauer's pessimism a corollary of what he perceives as the Christian disdain for the physical world without the false promise of mysterious providence and a just afterlife. Unlike

Huysmans's protagonist, Fletcher does not end by begging God for pity. Instead, he follows his philosophical convictions to their logical conclusion by committing suicide.

Surprisingly enough, Schopenhauer, who asserted every person's right to end his or her own life, also disdained suicide as an affirmation of the will to live and a capitulation to circumstance. "The suicide," he laments, "wills life and is only dissatisfied with the conditions under which it has presented itself to him."[42] The pessimists of *Mike Fletcher* deny this conclusion and embrace suicide not as an escape from life but the consummation of a philosophical system. Moore notes Schopenhauer's disapproval of suicide midway through the novel during a conversation between Fletcher and one of his would-be conquests, Lady Helen Seymour. Not content simply to add Lady Helen to his list, Fletcher seeks to seduce her intellect by introducing her to Schopenhauer. She surprises him by both cultivating a real understanding of the philosopher and carrying his ideas to their logical conclusion. The night of her suicide, she points out and forcefully rejects Schopenhauer's opposition to self-destruction by espousing suicide as a solution to the will to live. "Schopenhauer is wrong when he asserts that suicide is no solution of the evil; so far as the individual is concerned suicide is a perfect solution, and were the race to cease tomorrow, nature would instantly choose another type and force it into consciousness" (87). She opines that the only real relief will come when the earth is "ice or cinder" (88). Melodramatic as this sounds, Lady Helen's comments anticipate the more extreme fantasies of modern antinatalists who, in their most ambitious online flights of fancy, muse on whether, after humanity has chosen voluntary extinction, we ought not stack the deck against an unfortunate reemergence of consciousness on Earth by simply obliterating the planet.[43] Lady Helen's suicide is not an affirmation of the will to live; it is the realization of a philosophy that denies any meaning in existence. Following the act, Fletcher's friend Frank Escott, a former hedonist turned responsible family man, accuses Fletcher of corrupting Lady Helen by introducing her to Schopenhauer. Not surprisingly, Fletcher takes no responsibility for Lady Helen's death. After all, for him suicide is perfectly reasonable and pessimism means debauching while Rome burns.

42. Schopenhauer, *World as Will and Idea*, 48.
43. r/antinatalism, "How Do You Feel About Blowing up the World?"

Over the next seven years, Fletcher remains resolute in his philosophical convictions as his status rises and he moves from one conquest to the next, but Moore continues to offer alternatives to his hero's dark philosophy. As Mark Llewellyn correctly points out, Fletcher's friends Norton and Escott present explicit alternatives that both attract and repel the protagonist. During his time with Norton, who, like Huysmans, has rejected Schopenhauer for Catholicism, Fletcher momentarily imagines himself starting a religious order. During his time with Escott, Fletcher fluctuates "between outright contempt and unrecognized enviousness" of his friend's simple domestic life. Rejecting both Norton's faith and Escott's family, Fletcher maintains his allegiance to Schopenhauer and reaffirms opposition to life as his "highest" ideal: "Not to create life is the only good; the creation of life is the only evil; all else which man in his bestial stupidity calls good and evil is ephemeral and illusionary" (128).

Ultimately, Fletcher's antinatalism provides him with the inspiration and justification for an increasingly destructive life. Seeking to anticipate the essentialist objection that a life without cosmic meaning may easily degenerate into one of moral turpitude, modern antinatalists often employ altruistic and humanitarian principles to defend their philosophy and serve them as the spoonful of sugar necessary to make their nihilistic medicine go down. In the conclusion to his latest book, *The Human Predicament*, Benatar argues that, given the inherent meaninglessness of life and the competing unpleasantness of suicide, a good antinatalist might embrace a "pragmatic pessimism" and "busy oneself with projects that create terrestrial meaning, enhance the quality of life (for oneself, other humans, and other animals), and 'save' lives (but not create them!)."[44] It strikes me as patently unfair to convince people of the ultimate meaninglessness of life and then turn around and insist that they might pass the remainder of their pointless and painful existence in philanthropy. Moore sees past such ruses. His antinatalist antihero embraces the fact that he cannot both deny ultimate meaning to human existence and affirm consistent categories of ethical behavior.

Fletcher's brand of pessimism affirms the conclusion of Camus's favorite romantic rebel, Ivan Karamazov, who accepts that in the absence of "God and immortal life" all human actions indeed become "lawful."[45] His disdain for life provides ultimate license. Fletcher has not yet

44. Benatar, *Human Predicament*, 211.
45. Dostoyevsky, *Brothers Karamazov*, 717.

discovered the more complex existentialist sophistries of the twentieth century, which assert that the construction of meaning, the act of authentic revolt in the face of an absurd existence, justifies life. The life of existential revolt, Camus tells us, "is remote from suicide" because suicide rejects one of the premises of absurd existence (i.e., human life).[46] Because he has never learned to endure torture with a smile—to my mind a dubious alternative to suicide—Fletcher also has no answer to the famous introductory conundrum of Camus's *Myth of Sisyphus* (1955): "Judging whether life is or is not worth living amounts to answering the fundamental question of philosophy."[47] In the prime of life and wealthy beyond his dreams, Fletcher begins to intuit this dilemma looming on the horizon of his pessimist's bacchanal. He ought to be reveling in life. He ought at least, like Camus's Don Juan, to embrace all the pleasure of life while young and then ratify its absurdity by spinning out old age in a Spanish monastery, not praying to a nonexistent God but contemplating "through a narrow slit in the sun-baked wall, some silent Spanish plain, a noble, soulless land in which he recognizes himself."[48] But Don Juan never read Schopenhauer. Fletcher finds, as Lady Helen did before him, that ideas have consequences.

By the time we reach the final chapter, Fletcher's "moods of passive happiness" are "interrupted more frequently than they had been in earlier years by the old whispering voice, now grown strangely distinct, which asked, but no longer through laughing lips, if it were possible to discern any purpose in life. . . . The dark fruit that hangs so alluringly over the wall of the garden of life now met his eyes frequently" (270). Seeking escape in distraction, he throws himself with new abandon into drunkenness and debauchery, courtesans and champagne, gambling and prizefights. None of these can distract him for long from his one "besetting sin" (271). It is worth noting at this point that Moore's narrator adopts a distinctly Catholic disdain for Fletcher's idolization of death. He routinely disparages Fletcher's fleshly excesses, but these pale in comparison to the impending transgression of the antihero's suicide. In fact, the narrator makes clear that Fletcher's whoring and drinking emanate directly from the morbid contemplation of suicide. His rejection of the will to live and refusal to see a purpose in life lead to a diabolical desire to destroy the lives of others. No longer a simple hedonist

46. Camus, *Myth of Sisyphus*, 54.

47. Camus, *Myth of Sisyphus*, 3.

48. Camus, *Myth of Sisyphus*, 76.

or a gullible Faust, Fletcher anticipates Dorian Gray by embracing his role as a destroyer of souls: "'Before I kill myself,' he said, 'I will kill others; I'm weary of playing at Faust, now I'll play at Mephistopheles'" (271). Part of his corruption of the youth involves the development of a heroic philosophy of species suicide.

Fletcher and an old friend develop this philosophy of death in front of several young men at a party one evening. The human psyche, they agree, combines instinct and reason. Animal instinct rejects the idea of suicide out of hand. Reason sees the ultimate sense of suicide and concludes that "being of all acts the least instinctive, it is of necessity the most reasonable" (274). Because of irrational instinct, most men would rather wait for the benefit of an inheritance from a suffering and aged relative than realize the unlimited benefit of nonexistence, which they could reap at any time. When Fletcher proposes that his friend publish these conclusions, a young man nearby entreats him not to, fearing that "We should have every one committing suicide all around us—the world would come to an end" (276). Fletcher responds with a wry laugh and bemoans the fact that no "bit of mere scribbling will terminate life. . . . Very seldom, if ever, has a man committed suicide for purely intellectual reasons" (276). We soon learn that Fletcher intends to realize such an achievement.

Following a few half-hearted attempts at moral reform, which bore more than they edify, Fletcher realizes that he has been too long adrift on the sea of pessimism to find, like his friends Norton and Escott, either a Catholic or a domestic haven. Even the seduction of innocent girls ceases to stave off ennui. The only logical conclusion is suicide, but Fletcher abhors the idea that anyone might mistake his decision for a momentary impulse of depression: "He would go to death in the midst of the most perfect worldly prosperity the mind could conceive, desiring nothing but rest, profoundly convinced of the futility of all else, and the perfect folly of human effort" (289). He wants the world to know that he is obliterating instinct with reason with no ulterior motives, that he rejects life qua life. Leading up to the act, Fletcher asks and answers a central question of antinatalism: "Why were we born? Why are we taught to love our parents? It is they whom we should hate" (296). He takes time before shooting himself to dress as neatly as he would for a fashionable party so that the police and the press might see his act as one of "philosophic deliberation and judicious reflection" (298). In a fit of last-minute philanthropic fervor, Fletcher delays death long enough to leave money to the impecunious family man Frank Escott and an illegitimate son he has never met. Then, he turns to the pistol.

The dark joke in any narrative about suicide as a grand gesture of despair, love, or philosophical conviction is that while life may cease, narrative refuses to. As Andrew Bennett repeatedly notes in his book *Suicide Century: Literature and Suicide from James Joyce to David Foster Wallace*, one of the central paradoxes at the heart of suicide is that the act promises ultimate individual sovereignty over life while simultaneously annihilating "sovereignty, identity, and autonomy."[49] This holds especially true for characters in stories, whose actions are necessarily framed and made sense of by a larger narrative apparatus. Judas, Werther, Madame Bovary, Mike Fletcher, none can stop the movement of narrative when they stop the beating of their heart. They cannot ultimately escape life and meaning because they are subsumed in the narrative flow of story.

Moore's narrative concludes with a conversation between Frank's wife, Lizzie Escott, and Lottie, the mother of Fletcher's illegitimate son. As the women discuss Fletcher's irresponsibility and disregard for his child, the abandoned boy listens in silence, and a paperboy cries "Suicide of a poet in the Temple!" in the background (303). Upon learning of Fletcher's death, Lizzie and Lottie, ignorant of his will, predict that the callous man surely left nothing for them; nevertheless, Lottie confesses that she could never stop loving Mike. At this point, Moore signals the futility of Fletcher's gesture by giving his son the last word. "Now," the boy pipes in, "I'm sure you're talking about father" (304). For all his philosophical conviction of the futility and meaninglessness of life, for all his investment in his suicide as a grand heroic act of intellect over instinct, Mike fails utterly; he is not a martyr for reason, just another suicidal poet who, despite his best efforts, has even done his part to continue the existence of the species he deplores. Moore never had children, but even he chose to give life, in the form of Mike's son, the last word over death. Moore's rejection of the antinatalism embodied in his protagonist mirrors that of Huysmans and provides a razor-sharp riposte to the sterile logic of a philosophical movement that would not find a voice or name for well over a hundred years after the publication of his Decadent novel.

In or own time, these Decadent novels may provide an important reminder that there is nothing terribly new or radical about twenty-first-century pessimist philosophies. Even their specious ecological claims have

49. Bennett, *Suicide Century*, 16.

been made before. As the novels explored in this chapter demonstrate, the result of adhering to these philosophies is generally disastrous. For those who even suspect that the purpose of human life might be something like happiness, these ideologies of despair must be rejected. They may have new names and new proponents, but our philosophies of death remain both predictable and pernicious. Unfortunately, as I noted at the beginning of this chapter, cratering birthrates in the developed world strongly suggests that the pessimist philosophies once limited to Decadent antiheroes have become an implicit part of our popular paradigm. There can be no simple solution when a civilization, and even a species, demonstrates that it no longer intuits the goodness of its existence; however, great Catholic literature can at least help to expose the diabolical roots of this despair. Our next author, Monsignor Robert Hugh Benson, does just that in the twentieth century's first dystopian novel.

3

Robert Hugh Benson's Suicide Dystopia

ICONIC EARLY TWENTIETH-CENTURY DYSTOPIAN fiction proved surprisingly unimaginative and myopic on the topic of suicide. The two most conspicuous examples of the genre, *Brave New World* (1932) and *1984* (1949), treat the act as a desperate, last-ditch means of resistance to state control and coercion. In the dramatic conclusion of the former, John Savage hangs himself in despair when he realizes that he and his self-flagellatory attempts at atonement and spiritual purgation have been coopted into the soulless orgies of The World State. This despairing and transgressive act is left open to him only because he grew up outside of the soma-benumbed and sex-stupefied social and genetic engineering that keeps the citizens of Huxley's imaginary state in check. Self-destruction supposedly occurs more frequently in Orwell's brutal Oceania, but, there too, totalitarian control largely circumscribes the act. Certain of an imminent arrest to be followed by torture and execution, Winston Smith wishes to commit suicide but lacks the easy means and the will to carry it out because Big Brother has removed both: "The proper thing was to kill yourself before they got you. Undoubtedly some people did so. Many of the disappearances were actually suicides. But it needed desperate courage to kill yourself in a world where firearms, or any quick and certain poison, were completely unprocurable."[1] In

---

1. Orwell, *1984*, 106.

this case, the protagonist's failure to commit suicide anticipates his total capitulation to the state and to Big Brother.

Huxley and Orwell, who were prescient about many of the potential scientific and political modes of control that might be exerted by totalitarian governments, failed to anticipate the ways in which an emerging world government might embrace suicide as a human right implicit in secular humanitarianism. Their predecessor, Msgr. Robert Hugh Benson (1871–1914), saw this vision with clear eyes. Benson, youngest son of the Archbishop of Canterbury, first joined the Anglican clergy before becoming one of the most famous Catholic converts of his age in 1903. Ordained soon after his conversion, Benson lived the life of both a priest and a major literary figure, writing prolifically and achieving substantial fame in his own lifetime. He has, unfortunately, received little critical attention in the last fifty years. The only sustained study of Benson, Janet Grayson's *Robert Hugh Benson: Life and Works* (1998), opens with this telling question: "Does anyone read Robert Hugh Benson anymore?" Since the publication of Grayson's book, Benson famously received endorsements from Pope Benedict XVI and Pope Francis, both of whom admonished the faithful to read Benson's Catholic dystopian fantasy *Lord of the World* (1907).

Following this call, Catholic critics have invested some time in exploring the novel's often prescient vision of the near future. A 2016 edition of the novel, published by Ave Maria Press, includes a brief "Theological Reflection" by Michael P. Murphy that correctly identifies *Lord of the World* as a novel about the "transvaluations" that follow upon the death of God proclaimed by Nietzsche at the end of the nineteenth century and the subsequent attempt to replace metaphysics with spiritualized materialism. What results is a "theodrama," a term borrowed from Hans Urs von Balthasar, in which the stage is set for a "play of ideas where the stakes are, quite literally, life and death."[2] Murphy goes on to argue that the religion of man that emerges as a replacement for Christianity in the novel ultimately reveals the violent heart of a humanity unredeemed by Christ. While Murphy is exactly right in identifying the link between cycles of violence and a godless materialism—the post-Nietzschean world can boast more bloodshed than all human history prior—he and other Benson scholars have yet to appreciate the penetrating insight of the treatment of suicide in *Lord of the World*. Within the context of the

2. Murphy, *"Tantum Ergo,"* 11.

larger thesis of my book, that Catholic literature has something meaningful to say about our crisis of self-destruction, Benson's dystopian novel
demonstrates the, to me, inescapable truth that only a fiction cognizant
of humanity as both material and spiritual, as made in the image of God,
can account for and suggest meaningful responses to the problem of suicide. To put it another way, Benson was able to predict our predicament
more astutely than his fellow early twentieth-century dystopian novelists because he knew his subject, humanity, more completely. Because he
knew the resurrection, he could imagine the horror of a life lived with
knowledge of nothing but the guarantee of the crucifixion.

Before diving into *Lord of the World*, it is worth noting that Benson
wrestled with suicide in his work on more than just this one occasion.
The Conventionalists (1908) tells the story of a decadent young man
named Christopher Dell, who, after falling from grace, must undergo
a radical spiritual treatment at the hands of the mystic Mr. John Rolls.
Chris is driven to the point of attempting suicide only to be saved by
Rolls at the last minute. This experience represents the first step in
Chris's spiritual regeneration. Likewise, Val Medd, the protagonist of
The Coward (1912), is forced to confront his own shortcomings when
he, fortunately, fails to prove his strength of will by committing suicide.
In both cases, the possibility of suicide becomes a kind of precondi-
tion for a desperate pursuit of personal recrudescence. Benson seems to
anticipate the existentialists of the mid-twentieth century by identifying
suicide as a critically modern philosophical problem with implications
about the nature of human existence and the burdens of cosmic meaning, or a lack thereof. Far more than any of Benson's other work, however, *Lord of the World* tackles the problem of suicide head-on and signals
the inherently modern nature of that problem. In the novel, Benson
highlights the paradoxical but essential role of suicide and euthanasia
in any secular society that substitutes abstract humanity for individual
souls and "Life" for God. In so doing, he implicitly anticipates the ethically compromised hylozoism—the belief that all matter is alive—that
defines much postmodern academic and popular discourse about everything from ontology to ecology to politics to suicide.

Little in twentieth-century Catholic literature rivals *Lord of the
World* for eschatological inventiveness. The novel conjures a dystopian
twenty-first century in which the antichrist emerges as the leader of a
humanitarian world government and wages war against the last remaining bastion of Christianity, the Catholic Church. Benson acknowledged

the extraordinary, especially from a secular perspective, nature of this premise in his very brief preface to the book: "I am perfectly aware that this is a terribly sensational book, and open to innumerable criticisms on that account, as well as on many others. But I did not know how else to express the principles I desired (and which I passionately believe to be true) except by producing their lines to a sensational point."[3] Like the many modern dystopian writers who came after him, Benson sought to imaginatively follow the trend of the modern political and social experiment to its logical conclusion. Orwell shows us Victory Gin, telescreens, and brutal totalitarianism; Huxley shows us soma, Malthusian belts, and the corporate World State. Benson's visionary journey ultimately brought him to the apocalypse, but state-sponsored suicide defines his vision of modern horrors.

The twenty-first century, as depicted in *Lord of the World*, is divided politically between three superpowers: Europe; the American Republic; and the Eastern Empire. The novel's action takes place in Europe, where Communist "Humanitarianism" has nearly eradicated all religion through bloodless social and political change and mostly relegated the remaining Catholic "Individualists" to ideological quarantine zones: Rome and an Irish Free State. The rest of Europe is comfortably godless and enjoys the conveniences afforded by rapid transit, mass production, terminal marriage contracts, and, most notably, ready access to death.

Euthanasia serves as the defining sin of Benson's future from the novel's opening. In chapter 1, Mabel Brand, wife of the virulently anti-Catholic MP Oliver Brand, steps off a train just before the calamitous crash of a volor, a sort of sophisticated ornithopter. Amid the wreckage, she encounters two radically different approaches to death and dying. The first is that of the novel's protagonist, Fr. Percy Franklin:

> There was a sort of articulate language coming from [the dying man at her feet]; she caught distinctly the names of Jesus and Mary. . . . She stood . . . dazed by the suddenness of the whole affair, and watched almost unintelligently the grey-haired young priest on his knees, with his coat torn open, and a crucifix out; she saw him bend close, wave his hand in a swift sign, and heard a murmur of a language she did not know. Then he was up again, holding the crucifix before him, and she saw him begin to move forward into the midst of the red-flooded pavement, looking this way and that as if for a signal. (*LW,* 34)

3. Benson, "Preface."

The second approach, that of the state, follows immediately: "Down the steps of the great hospital on her right came figures running now, hatless, each carrying what looked like an old-fashioned camera. She knew what those men were, and her heart leapt in relief. They were the ministers of euthanasia" (34). The priest administers the sacrament of Extreme Unction; the state administers painless death.

After the event, Mable returns to her husband and mother-in-law at the family home, where Benson puts on display all the dysfunctions of the society in miniature. Aristotle identifies the household, or *oikos*, as the foundation of the larger political order. Its political regime does not match that of the larger city-state necessarily, but the health of the domestic order says much about the health of the larger political order. The Brand household is sick. Oliver, apprised of the volar crash by the news and certain his wife must have died, finds his panic augmented by rage at the suspicion that his aged mother has been praying. Lacking any meaningful framework for death, he can only rage at the woman who gave him life for resisting the ideology of his dead materialism. Ironically, when Mable walks through the door, Oliver greets her with an exclamatory, "Christ!" The word has lost all meaning for Oliver, but it is beginning to mean something to his wife, whose direct encounter with death has begun in her a reexamination of her assumptions about life.

Due to the utterly hygienic nature of modern existence, neither Mabel nor Oliver has witnessed death before. Mable relates the priest's action at the scene of the crash to her husband and reveals her own sense of incompleteness and speechlessness in the face of mortality: "You know, if I had had anything to say I could have said it too. They were all just in front of me: I wondered; then I knew I hadn't. I couldn't possibly have talked about Humanity" (36). Her husband's response— "you know it doesn't really matter" (36)—offers no solace but does demonstrate ideological consistency. Faced with the dying of a creature that only has value in relation to the state and only has existence so long as it is breathing, humanitarianism can offer no words of solace or acts of grace. The best it has to offer is a speedy death. Oliver confirms as much. After denouncing Fr. Franklin's beliefs as antiquated mumbo jumbo, he tells Mabel "you know in your heart that the euthanatisers are the real priests" (37). Not only are the Catholic clerics charlatans who prey on people's superstitions; they are servants of the Church that "had so long restrained the euthanasia movement with all its splendid mercy" (39). Benson's future is one in which humanity has accepted the supreme dominion of death to the point of acting as its priests. Paradoxically, this culture of death finds its ideological basis in a humanitarianism that treats an abstract notion of "Life" as divine.

Hylozoic Heresies

Benson's antichrist, Julian Felsenburgh, emerges from political obscurity in the American Republic to prevent impending war and broker a miraculous peace between the Eastern Empire and the Western super nations. Soon after, jubilant world leaders rush to hand him the reins of power and beg him to assume political control over the whole world. After his acceptance, Felsenburgh also becomes the head of a secular religion of Life. Unlike the French revolutionaries of the eighteenth century, who attempted the worship of the human faculty of reason, Felsenburgh's followers embrace a pantheistic worship of Life itself.

This religion of Life already bolstered Europe's "Communist-Humanitarianism" before the emergence of the antichrist. It was, as it were, a religion waiting for a god. At the book's outset, we are told that "Humanitarianism, contrary to all persons' expectations, is becoming an actual religion itself, though anti-supernatural. It is Pantheism . . . it has a creed, 'God is Man'" (*LOTW*, 10). The first liturgy of this new religion of Life takes place in Westminster Abbey. Our protagonist, Fr. Franklin, finds himself astonished "at the skill with which the new cult had been framed. It moved round no disputed points; there was no possibility of divergent political tendencies to mar its success, no over-insistence on citizenship, labour and the rest, for those who were secretly individualistic and idle. Life was the one font and center of it all, clad in the gorgeous robes of ancient worship" (210). Benson's imagined culture of death finds justification for euthanasia and suicide as corporal works of mercy in the worship of Life in the abstract. Building on this logic, Felsenburgh, as the self-appointed guardian of Life, will go on later to dictate forced euthanasia for the Catholic enemies of Life and eventually oversee the carpet-bombing of Rome itself.

Such formal Life-worship has not emerged in our own twenty-first century, a century in which participation in any form of ritual religious worship continues its sharp decline, but we can recognize a substantial parallel in various contemporary academic discourses that fall under the umbrella of hylozoism—the belief that all matter is alive.

In "Life's Return: Hylozoism, Again" (2020) Matthew Taylor argues that the various brands of new materialism and neoanimism found in modern academic discussions of anthropology and ecology are recapitulations of an earlier fad for hylozoism: "The specific political and ethical stakes of these hylozoisms ('all matter is alive') and panpsychisms ('all things have mind or a mind-like quality') vary, but universal life often is posited as the necessary restorative for anthropocentrism's deadening effects."[4] In other words, those theorists who lament the ecological effects of human beings on the planet regularly invoke a quasi-spiritual notion of universal Life. Not surprisingly, this hylozoic perspective results in rather flimsy ethics.

As Taylor demonstrates, the theory that all matter is vital led many nineteenth-century thinkers to social Darwinism and eugenics. The line of thinking is disturbing but easy to follow: All of existence participates in Life. Very well, let the most highly developed forms of that Life prosper and the rest diminish. Taylor sees in such thinking "a secular providence, a mundane predestination, in which a profane-yet-ideal eternal life either dethrones or approximates God."[5] When Life supplants God, death quickly reveals itself as the only rational *telos* for all living things. If all matter lives, then all matter must die; that death is its final cause, to use the Aristotelian formulation. Acknowledging the inescapable brutality of this logic, Taylor notes that even the German pessimist Schopenhauer "regarded hylozoism with horror."[6]

Taylor demonstrates the essential connection between Life-worshiping hylozoism and its logical conclusion, universal death, in Mark Twain's short story "Three Thousand Years Among the Microbes" (1905). The story, written just two years before *Lord of the World*, follows a man who has become a cholera germ within a human body and, in the process, discovered that humans and bacteria are essentially the same. Most notably, they both engage in wars of colonization. Twain's satire had colonial expansion and exploitation in its crosshairs but inadvertently fired upon human existence itself. By positing that there is "no moral difference between a germicide and a homicide,"[7] Twain inadvertently creates a "flat ontology" that "casts us all as bare life."[8] His hylozoism, which was

4. Taylor, "Life's Return," 474.
5. Taylor, "Life's Return," 480.
6. Taylor, "Life's Return," 480.
7. Quoted in Taylor, "Life's Return," 482.
8. Taylor, "Life's Return," 483.

meant to address injustice, implicitly embraces a "universal nihilism" that denies the possibility of justice and "democratizes death."[9]

The dangers of Life-worship degenerating into nihilistic death-worship are inherent in materialist hylozoism and will come as no surprise to readers of twentieth-century political philosopher Hannah Arendt. In the penultimate chapter of her book *The Human Condition* (1958), titled "Life as the Highest Good," Arendt argues that there is both a continuity and a fundamental disconnect between the Christian and the modern, secular insistence on the fundamental importance of human life. The latter inherited its prioritization of life from Christianity but without maintaining the metaphysical justifications for such a position. She contrasts this tenuously shared prioritization of life with the earlier pagan, and especially Roman, assertion of the importance of the cosmos and the relative insignificance of the individual. Disturbingly, this ancient position has reemerged among twenty-first-century self-help gurus under the umbrella of "Cosmic Insignificance Therapy," a kind of therapeutic neo-stoicism that promises to help people overcome emotional turmoil by reminding them that their lives have no ultimate significance.[10] Christianity stands in stark opposition to such denigration of the individual, both in its ancient and modern manifestations. Arendt tells us that by proclaiming "the immortality of the individual life," Christianity "reversed the ancient relationship between man and the world and promoted the most mortal thing, human life, to the position of immortality, which up to then the cosmos had held."[11]

This Christian endorsement of the essential sanctity of life presented an affront to antiquity, whose emphasis on the relative insignificance of the individual, except as a potential aid to the state, expressed itself in both the exposure of unwanted or malformed children and the general approbation of suicide as a reasonable means of evading suffering or protecting honor: "One could no longer with Plato despise the slave for not having committed suicide rather than submit to a master, for to stay alive under all circumstances had become a holy duty, and suicide was regarded as worse than murder."[12] From the Roman perspective suicide was an acceptable and often laudable means of ending a life that, ultimately, only has value in relation to the potential immortality

9. Taylor, "Life's Return," 483.
10. Schaffner, "On 'Cosmic Insignificance Therapy.'"
11. Arendt, *Human Condition*, 314.
12. Arendt, *Human Condition*, 316.

of the body politic. Individual life only becomes radically important once Christianity reverses the paradigm and ascribes immortality to the individual, not the cosmos or the state. Thus, Benson had to reject the kind of communal Life worship that he saw emerging from the collectivist ideologies of his time.

According to Arendt, herself a vocal opponent of such ideologies, this reverence for Life remains central to Western thought even as it rejects God in terms of naturalism and materialism—exactly the state of affairs described by Benson. The emergent conception of man as material organism allowed philosophers to "bridge the ever-widening chasm between philosophy and science" by making contemplation just another material phenomenon. This suited many radical modern philosophers, who take the vital importance of Life for granted even while rejecting the tenets of Christianity that justify such reverence. Nietzsche, Marx, and Bergson are the "greatest representatives of modern life philosophy . . . inasmuch as all three equate Life and Being." To the extent that these philosophers of Life "emphasize action as against contemplation," they represent a "last stage of modern philosophy," which is "perhaps best described as the rebellion of the philosophers against philosophy."[13] Because these thinkers take Life as their fundamental principle of being in the absence of transcendent truth, they end up producing a materialist anti-philosophy.

Unfortunately for the inheritors of these anti-philosophers, the modern attempt to enshrine Life as the greatest good, while simultaneously rejecting the immutable metaphysical foundations of the Christian reverence for life, left the individual in a fix: "The only thing that could now be potentially immortal, as immortal as . . . individual life during the Middle Ages, was life itself, that is, the possibly everlasting life process of the species mankind."[14] Left in a state of existential drift, Arendt claims, modern humanity can blindly cling to the remnants of a coherent Christian reverence for life, but it cannot ultimately justify the defense of individual lives on its own terms. Life itself becomes the animating force of an existence whose only *telos* is "Life" in the abstract and species continuation in the aggregate. For the Christian, individual life has inherent dignity because it is granted by a creator and serves as the prelude to immortality. Modern vitalist materialism submerges the individual life into

13. Arendt, *Human Condition*, 313n76.
14. Arendt, *Human Condition*, 321.

"the over-all life process of the species," thereby stripping individual life of anything like inherent dignity. You are not a unique and distinct self, granted dignity by a creator, but one part of the overall aggregate of Life granted the privilege or burden of a brief existence prior to a complete reintegration back into the whole of an indifferent nature.

Benson's suicide dystopia depicts the horrific consequences of any hylozoic heresy that replaces reverence of the individual life with abstract Life-worship. As the followers of Benson's antichrist, Julian Felsenburgh, declare, "We do not explain nature or escape from it by sentimental regrets: the hare cries like a child, the wounded stag weeps great tears, the robin kills his parents; life exists only on condition of death; and these things happen however we may weave theories that explain nothing. Life must be accepted on those terms; we cannot be wrong if we follow nature" (*LOTW,* 284). Devoid of a creator or ordering intelligence to give an ought to the is, Life as material nature becomes a viciously self-contained system, an unintelligible prelude to death. In such a world, as Benson demonstrates, painless death and painless suicide must be not only tolerated as rights but exalted as goods.

Benson's Dystopia

Benson clearly intuited the hylozoic tendency to reduce all existence to material "Life" and anticipated Arendt's critique of any philosophy or culture that takes a vague notion of deified Life in general or species life as its highest good. Projecting that tendency forward in time, he shows us a future in which belief in a quasi-divine and impersonal Life can quickly pervert the human relationship with death.

When contemplating the impending death of her beloved mother-in-law, the only Christian in her life, Mabel's perverse Life worship leads her to see death as concomitantly beautiful: "It seemed curiously pathetic to the girl to watch that quiet old spirit approach its extinction, or rather, as Mabel believed, its loss of personality in the reabsorption into the Spirit of Life which informed the world.... What a strange and beautiful thing death was, she told herself—this resolution of a chord that had hung suspended for fifty, thirty, or seventy years—back again into the huge stillness of the huge Instrument that was all in all to itself" (77, 79). Rather than tell her mother-in-law of the doctor's prognosis, that the old woman could live for ten years or die any minute, Mabel keeps her in the dark.

The narrator explains that it was not "part of Mabel's idea of duty to tell her that she was in danger, for there was no past to set straight, no Judge to be confronted. Death . . . was a peaceful Gospel; at least, it became peaceful as soon as the end had come" (78). We see one consequence of devotion to the secular-materialist "Spirit of Life," which is also a Gospel of Death, in Mable's decision to hide the truth and deny an old woman the rites of absolution. We see another consequence not long after this reverie, when she has her mother-in-law forcibly euthanized while the woman cries out for a priest to hear her confession (130). When Oliver comes home to his dead mother, Mabel, in one of the novel's most truly unsettling moments, says simply "She resisted, but I knew you would wish it" (131). Such is the mercy granted by Life.

We see another example of Life-worship's inevitable reversion to death in Mable's decision, near the book's climax, to end her own life at a suicide clinic. To her great credit, Mabel, who has never known any other worldview than that of secular Life-worship, loses faith in its god, in the Lord of the World. Felsenburgh announces that, for the sake of sustained peace, all citizens must take a loyalty oath that will force the few remaining theists to renounce their belief in God or face forced euthanasia. Oliver, Mable's husband and a prominent government official, explains that "there is going to be no violence; it will all be quite quiet and merciful" (324). Again, Benson drives home the point that painless death represents the closest approximation to mercy in a world without God, a world in which the dominion of pitiless Life has made mercy anathema. Over the course of the novel, Mabel has become increasingly interested in Christianity. Unsettled by this painless persecution of Christians but unable to contemplate an alternative to her faith in Felsenburgh as the highest incarnation of Life, Mabel makes the rational and consistent decision to end her own life. "It was her belief, as of the whole Humanitarian world," we are told, "that just as bodily pain occasionally justified the termination of life, so also did mental pain. . . . It was the most charitable act that could be performed" (337). *Caritas* in the realm of Life cannot mean self-sacrificial love because such love involves pain, and the highest realization of Humanitarian charity is the cessation of pain.

Mabel repairs to the Manchester Home of Rest, which provides a peaceful retreat in which those wishing to end physical or mental pain can spend the eight days of probation required before legal, state-provided suicide—though she might have gone abroad, "where laxer conditions prevailed" (362). The nurse practitioners, commonly referred to as

"Sisters" in Benson's time, recall to mind a time long ago when the sick were treated primarily by the religious seeking to give comfort to God's children. In Benson's future, the secular sisters provide the modern cult of death with its own attendant nuns. Mabel's sanitized and sanctioned journey to death fills an entire chapter and runs parallel, in the timeline of the story, to the novel's apocalyptic denouement. It represents one of the most lengthy and detailed examinations of an individual suicide in all of literature. It also stands apart in its willingness to follow the suicide beyond physical death into the borderlands between this life and the next. Mabel's eight days of preparation are characterized by clearheaded resolve and unshakable certainty in her decision; however, as the day of death draws closer, her "whole sentient life" begins to protest and must be repeatedly subdued by her will (334).

Gripped by this atavistic abhorrence of self-destruction, Mabel catches glimpses of a truth outside of her orthodox materialism. In the depths of this agony, her mind finds temporary solace in the intimation or "half-hinted promise of some deeper voice suggesting that death was not the end" (335). She forces down this heretical "hope of continued existence" and reminds herself that "men [are] but animals—the conclusion was inevitable" (335). As just another animal momentarily participating in the movement of life, Mabel sees death as truly inevitable and must, therefore, be the desirable fulfillment of her *telos*. When Sister Anne brings in the euthanasia box and finishes instructing Mabel in its use, her charge asks "And what then?" Like a cheerfully reassuring Hamlet, Sister Anne affirms the ultimate nullity of human existence and the ultimate dominion of death: "There is nothing more" (344). Benson demurs.

Rather than simply killing Mabel and implicitly consigning another suicide to perdition, Benson provides a sympathetic and moving vision of her passage from this life to the next in a manner that at least hints at her salvation and invites his readers to contemplate the difference between secular and divine mercy. On the cusp of the act, Mabel suddenly feels the boundaries of the material world, the only world she has ever known, begin to blur, and she becomes momentarily aware of "some other mode of existence" (347). Inspired by "neither intellect nor emotion" but by something beyond both, she erupts in spontaneous prayer:

> O God, I know that You are not there—of course You are not.
> But if You were there, I know what I would say to You. I would
> tell You how puzzled and tired I am. No—No—I need not tell
> You: You would know it. But I would say that I was very sorry

for all this. Oh! You would know that too. I need not say anything at all. O God! I don't know what I want to say. I would like
you to look after Oliver, of course, and all Your poor Christians.
Oh! they will have such a hard time. . . . God. God—You would
understand, wouldn't You? (347)

This prayer, faltering and heterodox, expresses both Mabel's depression and her deep desire to be forgiven. In spite of the fact that she has
grown up without any notion of sin, some part of her soul realizes that
what she is about to do demands repentance and forgiveness. She also
understands, perhaps better than many a devout Christian, that God's
understanding, his mercy, are all encompassing. Throughout *Lord of the
World*, Benson decries suicide. Near the novel's conclusion, he softens
this condemnation without softening his convictions by reminding us
that even the godless inhabitants of a dystopia might intuit God and
seek him with fumbling steps.

Mabel's attempted prayer is not enough to turn her away from
self-destruction. A life defined by materialism cannot be easily or immediately attuned to a higher reality; however, the description of her
suicide leaves open the door of hope. As the world around her crumbles
away and her physical senses give way, another reality asserts itself: "it
seemed as if she had penetrated at last into some recess of her being into
which hitherto she had only looked as through a clouded glass" (349).
No Christian reader could miss the allusion to Paul's famous statement
about the difficulty of apprehending God: "For now we see through a
glass, darkly; but then face to face: now I know in part; but then shall
I know even as also I am known." Within this hitherto unknown part
of her soul, Mabel perceives a "limitless space . . . alive, as a breathing,
panting body is alive . . . immaterial, yet absolutely real—real in a sense
in which she never dreamed of reality" (350). This vision ends with a
revelation: "Then she saw, and understood. . . ." (350). The concluding
ellipses leave Mabel's ultimate fate uncertain, but her soul's vision of
God, "a center, round the circumference of which she had been circling
all her life," invites us to hope that her final, imperfect prayer of contrition made her receptive to salvation (349).

Mabel's prayer and her mystical vision gain greater clarity within
the context of the novel's abiding preoccupation with prayer. In particular, Benson dedicates a great deal of time to exploring Fr. Franklin's
prayer life. During one four-page narrative description of the priest's
internal state at Vespers, Fr. Franklin passes beyond sense and self into

a "Presence" and the "veil of things" (49). There, he finds "that strange region where realities are evident . . . where all things meet, where truth is known and handled and tasted, where God Immanent is one with God Transcendent" (49). In the presence of this reality, he experiences a revelatory mystical vision before returning to the world of the senses. Following Mabel's groping, earnest attempt at prayer, she puts on the gas mask that will end her life, but, rather than experiencing a cessation of all experience as her body dies, she undergoes a transformation of perception akin in description to Fr. Franklin's experience of prayer. Benson himself, in response to a reader who was dismayed by Mabel's suicide, made clear that he believed in his character's ultimate salvation because of both her invincible ignorance and her final prayer: "I think Mabel was all right, really. Honestly, she had no idea that suicide was a sin; and she did pray as well as she knew how at the end."[15] Clearly Benson meant to highlight the pathos of her death as an act worthy more of pity than condemnation.

By recounting Mabel's suicide from her perspective, rather than the sanitized perspective of the Life-worshiping state, Benson engages in a Christian version of what Michel Foucault, Giorgio Agamben, and others have termed thanatopolitics. This thanatopolitics provides an alternative perspective to a life-oriented biopolitics, the "productive power that necessitates or silently calls for death as the consequence of 'making live.'"[16] In giving voice to those that biopolitical power "lets die" to preserve other life, thanatopolitics describes death's ability to function politically and rhetorically. The Catholic Church, the mother to countless martyrs, has understood for centuries the power of the dying witness, even without the aid of Foucauldian neologisms. Benson demonstrates this understanding by giving voice to Mabel's experience. The suggestion of potential salvation at the conclusion of her horrific and truncated "Dream of Gerontius" both denies the ultimate authority of the world state that coerced her into self-destruction and affirms the higher authority of a Divinity that truly opposes death by throwing open the gates of eternal life to those willing to humble themselves enough to walk through. Benson's dystopia is of this world. His novel calls its readers to reject the deified "Life" of that world in favor of the promise of immortality.

15. Quoted in Martindale, *Life of Monsignor Robert Hugh Benson*, 75.
16. Murray, "Thanatopolitics," 718–19.

Canticle for Leibowitz and the Legacy of the Suicide Dystopia

Benson's diagnosis of state-sponsored suicide as the signal sin of a secular postmodernity finds confirmation in another Catholic science fiction novel, Walter Miller's *A Canticle for Leibowitz* (1959). I won't attempt to do Miller or *Canticle* full justice in this brief aside. Because I simply aim to point out that Benson's suicide dystopia has at least one major inheritor in the Catholic literary tradition, I will limit myself to a brief overview before concluding this chapter.

Miller (1923–1996), a veteran of World War II, converted to Catholicism after the war and published *Canticle* in 1959. He subsequently left both the Church and his writing career behind. Ralph Wood opines that Miller's "leaving the church may have . . . prompted the desiccation of his literary imagination."[17] I think it reasonable to suggest that it also may have weakened his commitment to the uncompromising anti-euthanasia stance found in *Canticle*. Following the loss of his faith and the death of his wife, Miller committed suicide in 1996. I point this out not to suggest that faith always prevents suicide—it does not—or that loss of faith always leads to despair, but rather to suggest that Miller's one great literary achievement owed a large part of its insight and force to the same Catholic moral imagination that animated Benson's *Lord of the World* and many of the works explored in this book.

A Canticle for Leibowitz takes place in a postapocalyptic America devastated by nuclear war. The novel revolves around an order of monks whose scientific discoveries inadvertently help to begin the next cycle of nuclear weapons development. Like *Lord of the World*, *Leibowitz* is apocalyptic in the biblical sense, a point made succinctly and convincingly by Wood:

> The strange power of *Leibowitz* is hard to define. It is not a conventional work of science fiction, despite its obsession with technology, since most of its action and characters are quite realistically depicted. Neither is it another dystopian novel in the fashion of George Orwell's *1984* or Aldous Huxley's *Brave New World*, though it certainly depicts a nightmarish future. I believe that it should be read, instead, as an apocalyptic work. Even here qualifications are necessary. It is not apocalyptic merely because it concerns the final culmination of things in an atomic holocaust. Rather it is an apocalypse in the literal sense:

17. Wood, "Lest the World's Amnesia Be Complete," 25.

an "unveiling," a revelation of the deeply destructive urges at work in late modern life.[18]

Though Wood does not pay special attention to this detail, I would contend that the most significant modern destructive urge "unveiled" in *Leibowitz* has less to do with the mass destruction of nuclear war than the distinctly individual destruction of euthanasia.

Late in the novel, the order's abbot, Zerchi, must face off against the well-intentioned Doctor Cors as he and the forces of the secular state establish a Mercy Camp, where the wounded survivors of the second nuclear holocaust can seek relief from their irreversible radiation poisoning through euthanasia. Abbot Zerchi is carrying on a long tradition. For millennia, the Catholic Church has been the one bulwark against mercy killing. In the centuries following the first nuclear fallout, only the Church's injunction against taking innocent life prevented some parents from killing those babies born mutated and deformed by the effects of radiation:

> Even within the Church, some had dared espouse the view that such creatures truly had been deprived of the *Dei imago* from conception, that their souls were but animal souls, that they might with impunity under the Natural Law be destroyed as animal and not Man . . . but for men to take it upon themselves to judge any creature born of woman to be lacking in the divine image was to usurp the privilege of Heaven. Even the idiot which seems less gifted than a dog, or a pig, or a goat, shall, if born of woman, be called an immortal soul, thundered the *magisterium*, and thundered it again and again.[19]

Insisting that even natural law, unaided by divine revelation, could not countenance a parent killing a child because of mental or physical deformity, the Church released repeated condemnations of infanticide.

Though written over a decade before the legalization of abortion in America and multiple generations before the emergence of today's euthanasia debates, *Leibowitz* anticipates the clash between natural law and divine mandate, on the one hand, and individual license on the other. Miller, less preachy and more prone to irony than Benson, conceives of a world in which the unwanted mutants of the human race are dubbed the "Pope's children." In doing so, he highlights both the seeming absurdity

18. Wood, "Lest the World's Amnesia Be Complete," 27.
19. Miller, *Canticle for Leibowitz*, 80.

and fundamental beauty of the Church's position. Relatively few people, unaided by an outside moral authority, would opt to preserve the life of a child with a genetic mutation, even with a mutation that causes no particular pain to the child. This harsh reality is borne out by both the widespread historical practice of infanticide, especially in the ancient world, and by the modern practice of aborting children with genetic abnormalities. In the past few decades, children with Down syndrome have virtually disappeared from the first world, as the vast majority of parents elect for abortion once genetic screenings reveal the mutation.[20] Miller understood this dynamic well and, like Benson, he grasped that a world without the guidance of a religion that affirms the inherent dignity of all human life would quickly become a world of state-sanctioned suicide.

The inheritor of the Church's centuries-long war against infanticide and mercy-killing, Abbot Zerchi struggles to convince a government official deputized with administering euthanasia that his apparent compassion in ending individual suffering is not only misguided, but evil. Like most Catholics resisting the modern tendency towards self-destruction, Zerchi fails. He can neither convince a mother to allow her baby to suffer from radiation poisoning, nor persuade Doctor Cors that what he believes to be mercy is a fundamental rejection of God's order, a kind of cheap replacement for God's mercy. He fails because, in purely material terms, suffering becomes the ultimate evil; it becomes the one thing worthy of sacrifice. Near death and experiencing a good deal of suffering at the novel's conclusion, Zerchi contemplates what he should have said to Cors:

> Really, Doctor Cors, the evil to which even you should have referred was not suffering, but the unreasoning fear of suffering. *Metus doloris.* Take it together with its positive equivalent, the craving for worldly security, for Eden, and you might have your "root of evil," Doctor Cors. To minimize suffering and to maximize security were natural and proper ends of society and Caesar. But then they became the only ends, somehow, and the only basis of law—a perversion. Inevitably, then, in seeking only them, we found only their opposites: maximum suffering and minimum security.[21]

Linking both the global destruction of nuclear war and the individual destruction of euthanasia to our attempts to insulate ourselves from

20. Zhang, "Last Children of Down Syndrome."
21. Miller, *Canticle for Leibowitz*, 271.

that suffering through technology, Zerchi reaches a horrifying conclusion. In extremis, and unguided by God's injunction against playing God, humanity will willingly sacrifice itself on its own savage altar in a misguided attempt to evade suffering.

Both Benson and Miller clearly understood that euthanasia can only take root in a civilization as a legitimate response to suffering if that civilization has embraced a false cosmology and anthropology. If the cosmos is mere matter, then man is mere matter. Human life becomes indistinguishable from the abstract "Life" of the cosmos. Within this flattened hylozoic existence, the only spiritual comfort offered by the world spirit is the comfort of oblivion. By calling us into dystopian and apocalyptic worlds in which this anti-Christian paradigm has achieved ascendency, these authors warn against a future that we already partially inhabit and remind us that, though we may never hope to prevent the apocalypse or build a heaven on earth, we may yet hope for the salvation offered by a truly merciful God if we refuse to bow to Life or preach the gospel of death.

J. R. R. Tolkien, the father of the modern fantasy genre and focus of my next chapter, understood the all-too-human desire to master life by mastering death. Rather than exploring this desire in an imagined future, he created a secondary world that provides one of the most compelling literary responses to the problem of suicide by calling its readers to a heroic ideal largely missing from the modern world.

4

The Stolen Gift: Suicide in Middle-Earth

> Fairy tales, then, are not responsible for producing in children
> fear, or any of the shapes of fear; fairy tales do not give the
> child the idea of the evil or the ugly; that is in the child already,
> because it is in the world already. Fairy tales do not give the
> child his first idea of bogey. What fairy tales give the child is
> his first clear idea of the possible defeat of bogey. The baby has
> known the dragon intimately ever since he had an imagination.
> What the fairy tale provides for him is a St. George to kill the
> dragon.—G. K. Chesterton, "The Red Angel"

IN HIS ESSAY "ON Fairy-Stories," first given as a lecture at the University
of St. Andrews in 1939, J. R. R. Tolkien distinguishes between the "primary world" we inhabit and the "secondary world" of fantasy—a world
produced by an act of what he calls "sub-creation." This sub-creative
act, he claims, springs from our status as creatures with a divine creator:
"Fantasy remains a human right: we make in our measure and in our
derivative mode, because we are made: and not only made, but made
in the image and likeness of a Maker."[1] The majority of the literature
discussed in this book concerns itself with imaginatively exploring what
Tolkien would call "primary creation." In these works, the phenomenon
of suicide presents itself as one possible human action within a universe
made and animated by the God of Christianity, however seemingly absent that God may be in the lives of those characters who feel compelled
to end their own lives.

1. Tolkien "On Fairy-Stories," 145.

Tolkien set himself the monumental task of creating a world quite different from the one we know, a universe with its own myths, languages, races, and beliefs. In spite of Tolkien's fervent personal adherence to Catholicism and occasional comments confirming the Christian dimensions of his work, scholars have struggled to reach consensus on the nature of the relationship between Tolkien's secondary world and his primary religious beliefs. Critics have spilled considerable ink attempting to define the degree of correspondence between Middle-earth and Tolkien's Christian understanding of our primary world. Some see an explicitly Christian and even apologetic text. Others see a story that contains Christian themes only if readers choose to see them. Synthesizing the clearest point of critical near-consensus, Paul Kerry identifies what he calls "Tolkien's critical move—to expel allegory and yet absorb in his work applicable religious elements."[2] I believe that the treatment of suicide in Tolkien's works may help to clarify their debt to a distinctly Christian view of reality. Tolkien's narratives about Middle-earth feel Christian at least in part because of their insistence on the primacy of life over death and the exclusive sovereignty of a benevolent creator over individual lives—two things distinctly lacking in both pre-Christian paganism and secular modernity.

As we discussed at length in an earlier chapter, Hannah Arendt notes a certain continuity between the Christian and the modern, secular insistence on the fundamental importance of human life over and against paganism's insistence on the importance of the cosmos and the relative insignificance of the individual. This reverence for life remains so central to Western thought, according to Arendt, that even the troika of modern anti-philosophers—Nietzsche, Marx, and Bergson—take life as their fundamental principle of being in the absence of truth. Unfortunately, and here I repeat myself, this evacuation of the immutable metaphysical foundations of the Christian reverence for life left the modern human in a fix: "Far from believing that the world might be potentially immortal, he was not even sure that it was real."[3] Tolkien's work signals its particularly Christian perspective on life by highlighting both the pagan neglect of the fundamental dignity of individual human life and the modern neglect of any metaphysical foundation for that life's meaning.

2. Kerry, "Historiography of Christian Approaches to Tolkien's *The Lord of the Rings*," 25.

3. Arendt, *Human Condition*, 320.

It would be too tidy to claim that Tolkien simply reiterated Catholic moral teaching about suicide with elves and dwarves thrown in. In the process of creating a new world, or at least a mythical precursor to our own, that could express the eternal verities of primary creation, Tolkien effectively needed to rediscover the substance of the truths underlying Christianity by a different path. In this process of rediscovery, he approached suicide as something new and gave us characters who both accept and reject its attractions. His writings capture the tragic pathos of self-destruction while developing and unfolding a larger, competing ethos of self-sacrifice and service to life. In order to explain the development of this life-affirming ethic, I will begin by considering the paradoxical nature of death in Tolkien's mythology as the "gift" of a benevolent creator. Next, I will analyze prominent examples of suicide in *The Silmarillion* and the early legendarium more broadly. Finally, I will consider the development of Tolkien's philosophy of suicide in *The Lord of the Rings*, which discovers anew a distinctly Christian view of the act as both an evasion of duty as right action, and a usurpation of divine sovereignty.

The Gift of Ilúvatar

Death is not simply a reality in Tolkien's work; it is a matter of central importance. In a 1958 response to an enthusiast, one Miss Beare, who had written requesting clarification about everything from the bridle on Glorfindel's horse to the fashion of the winged crown of Gondor, Tolkien concludes with a surprisingly sweeping assertion about his created world. He claims that his work is founded on religious ideas and identifies its central theme as death. Rejecting the common notion that his book is "about 'power,'" he insists that it is instead "mainly concerned with Death, and Immortality; and the 'escapes': serial longevity, and hoarding memory."[4] Tolkien had said much the same thing two years earlier in a letter written, but never sent, in response to the theory that his story was an allegory for atomic power.[5] In it he similarly dismisses

4. Tolkien, *Letters*, 284.

5. Power does, of course, play a substantial role in Tolkien's secondary world. Jane Chance's *The Lord of the Rings: The Mythology of Power* (1992) goes so far as to compare Tolkien's notion of power to that of his contemporary Michel Foucault. Though there are legitimate connections to be made between the two thinkers, this line of reasoning breaks down in large part because Foucault makes all human action part of a dialectic of power. Tolkien implicitly rejects this position by placing greater emphasis on death and immortality in a world suffused with the presence of the supernatural—a category

power struggle as the book's essential theme. War and struggle merely provide "'a setting' for characters to show themselves."[6] In a move typical of his competing need to clarify his own thinking and protect the integrity of his sub-creation from definitive authorial statements, Tolkien opines that the "real theme for me is about something much more permanent and difficult: Death and Immortality: the mystery of the love of the world in the hearts of a race 'doomed' to leave and seemingly lose it; the anguish in the hearts of a race 'doomed' not to leave it, until its whole evil-aroused story is complete."[7]

Tolkien's creation myth, the "Ainulindalë" (The Music of the Ainur), provides the foundation for this assertion that the ultimate stakes in Middle-earth are eternal, not ephemeral. As in Christianity, individual life and death are of ultimate importance because life as we know it is both the result of an intelligent and benevolent creator and the first stage in an existence that stretches beyond mortality and into eternity. Tolkien's secondary universe is neither the absurd universe of the atheist existentialists, nor a materialist soup in which human consciousness arises arbitrarily and, ultimately, pointlessly. It is the product of immortal, divine powers under the guidance of a supreme and benevolent creator, singing existence into being. The universe that proceeds from the ordering intelligence of the Ainur is marred by the discordant will of the evil Melkor (later renamed Morgoth), but even this taint of evil finds itself enfolded in the providential direction of Eru Ilúvatar, whom, in his letters, Tolkien routinely refers to simply as "God." Life is the animating theme at the heart of this universe. As in Christianity, the creation of life is a totally gratuitous gift from a benevolent creator. In a surprising twist, however, Tolkien also identifies death as a gift. It is here we must begin if we are to follow Tolkien's rediscovery of suicide as a stolen gift.

The Christian creation myth clearly marks death as something alien to human nature, an aberration and punishment resultant from the disobedience and hubris of Adam and Eve. In order to better understand Tolkien's philosophy of death, we must first accept that his sub-created world is not ours. Most notably, it contains persons both mortal (e.g., Men and Hobbits) and immortal (e.g., Valar and Elves). Understanding the distinctions between these groups is essential for understanding the

---

that Foucault categorically denies.

6. Tolkien, *Letters*, 246.

7. Tolkien, *Letters*, 246.

nature of death in Tolkien's world. Men, the Atani (the second people), are distinct from Elves in several ways. Mortality is the most essential difference. According to the "Quenta Silmarillion," Ilúvatar himself described human mortality as a gift: "'But the Quendi [Elves] shall be the fairest of all earthly creatures . . . and they shall have the greater bliss in this world. But to the Atani I will give a new gift'" (S, 41). We are told that this discrepancy in mortal lifespan, and good looks, coincides with greater freedom of choice and a restlessness of spirit. Ilúvatar "willed the hearts of men should seek beyond the world and should find no rest therein; but they should have a virtue to shape their life . . . beyond the Music of the Ainur, which is as fate to all things else" (41). In Tolkien's world, the reality of death somehow enables humans to transcend the fate ordained by the Powers that created Eä (the whole material universe): "It is one with this gift of freedom that the children of Men dwell only a short space in the world alive, and are not bound to it, and depart soon whither the Elves know not" (42). Death estranges humans from the created, time-bound world and signals that they are in some sense alien to it. It is a "gift," which "as time wears even the Powers shall envy" (42). Grant Sterling sums the matter up succinctly in "'The Gift of Death': Tolkien's Philosophy of Mortality" (1997), noting that "although God intends that we love the world . . . He also intends that we see death, in its appropriate time, as a blessing, for through it we may escape the world and serve Him in other ways, and receive from Him a greater reward."[8]

The reason mortals perceive this gift as a curse is yet another consequence of the influence of Melkor, who "has cast his shadow upon it, and confounded it with darkness, and brought forth evil out of good, and fear out of hope" (S, 42). In the primary world, which is for Tolkien an objectively Christian world whether people acknowledge that fact or not, this perspective on death might come uncomfortably close to heresy because it turns the punishment of death from Genesis into a kind of reward. Well aware of the theologically dicey nature of his reframing of death as the "Gift of Ilúvatar,"[9] Tolkien insisted on the orthodoxy of his understanding of death-as-gift in a follow-up letter to Miss Beare, which he drafted but never sent. First, he reiterates that his legends are written by the Elves, and do not "necessarily have anything to say for or against such beliefs as the Christian that 'death' is not part of human nature, but a punishment

---

8. Sterling, "'Gift of Death,'" 18.
9. Tolkien, *Letters*, 285.

for sin."[10] The Elves have no direct access to death, so they speak of it as they believe it "should now become for Men, however it arose." "A divine 'punishment,'" from this Elvish perspective, "is also a divine 'gift,' if accepted, since its object is ultimate blessing, and the supreme inventiveness of the Creator will make 'punishments' (that is changes of design) produce a good not otherwise to be attained."[11] From this premise, we can easily see the development of Tolkien's mythical exploration of humanity's rightly and wrongly oriented relationships with death.

Nowhere does this philosophy of mortality find fuller expression than in the stories surrounding the kings of Númenor, the noblest representatives of humanity in the long history of Middle-earth. The Númenóreans are the focal point of the second of Tolkien's three ages. Descendants of the Edain, those men of the first age who strove alongside Elves against Morgoth, the Númenóreans were given both "life more enduring than any others of mortal race" and their island home of Andor, which, tellingly, means "Land of Gift." The story of the rise and fall of the Númenóreans is the story of their corruption by Sauron, their rejection of the "Gift of Ilúvatar," and their consequent loss of the "Land of Gift."

At first, the long lives of the Númenóreans lead to wisdom, power, and majesty. These lives were bounded by a mortality that was accepted rather than shunned or feared. Fittingly, the first ruler of Andor was Elros, brother of Elrond half-Elven, who guides the formation of the fellowship in *The Lord of the Rings*. As descendants of Lúthien, to whom Ilúvatar gave the choice of mortality because of her love for the human Beren, Elros and Elrond were likewise allowed to choose between Elven and human life. Elros chose the latter and thereby signaled his willingness to receive the "Gift of Ilúvatar." The kings of Númenor lived hundreds of years. Rather than dying of old age, they would accept death at a time that seemed, in their wisdom, fitting. This act of accepting death at its proper time and in the proper way tells us much about Tolkien's philosophy of life. Aragorn continues the tradition of the early, good kings of Númenor after the conclusion of *The Lord of the Rings*. Tolkien relates Aragorn's conversation with his wife Arwen about his decision to die in an appendix to the book. The conversation highlights both the appropriateness and difficulty of the Númenórean approach to death:

10. Tolkien, *Letters*, 285.
11. Tolkien, *Letters*, 286.

Arwen knew well what he intended, and long had foreseen it; nonetheless she was overborn by her grief. "Would you then, lord, before your time leave your people that live by your word?" she said.

"Not before my time," he answered. "For if I will not go now, then I must soon go perforce. . . . Take council with yourself, beloved, and ask whether you would indeed have me wait until I wither and fall from my high seat unmanned and witless. . . . I am the last of the Númenóreans . . . and to me has been given not only a span thrice that of Men of Middle-earth, but also the grace to go at my will and give back the gift."[12]

In order to grasp the distinction between Aragorn's acceptance of death and the suicides that arise elsewhere in Tolkien's work, we must remember that in writing about the good Númenórean kings Tolkien is writing about people granted a special "grace." If we overlook this fact, we risk reading Aragorn's words about dying "unmanned and witless" as a justification for euthanasia. Aragorn clarifies that the option of this choice is reserved for the kings of Númenor. Similarly, Arwen's line of half-Elves were given the grace to choose mortality, though, in the face of her husband's passing, she confesses that "the gift of the One to Men . . . is bitter to receive."[13] Just as ordinary humans cannot choose to be immortal, they cannot choose to approach death in the exact manner of the Númenórean kings. This, Tolkien implies, is almost certainly for the best. As the fall of Númenor reveals, along with the special grace of choosing to "give back the gift" comes the disastrous option of attempting to evade it.

If Aragorn's acceptance of death at the fitting time portrays an idealized version of a Númenórean response to mortality, because it accepts its own ordained limitations, the fall of Númenor shows the horrific consequences of what happens when we reject our mortality. Far from being content with their long lives, power, and dominion over their island kingdom, the Númenóreans began to envy the immortality of the Valar in the far west. Slowly, they "began to murmur, at first in their hearts, and then in open words, against the doom of Men, and most of all against the Ban which forbade them to sail into the West" (S, 264). This discontent with mortality grew. The gift of Ilúvatar "became a grief to them only because coming under the shadow of Morgoth it seemed to them that they were surrounded by a great darkness, of which they were afraid" (S, 265).

12. Tolkien, "Appendix A," *Lord of the Rings*, 1062–1063.
13. Tolkien, "Appendix A," *Lord of the Rings*, 1063.

Filled with fear of death, they refused to accept it at its appropriate time, devised elaborate means to delay it, and even sought to find some way to recall the dead to life. When these measures failed, the Númenóreans resorted to the false immortality of monuments and "filled all the land with silent tombs in which the thought of death was enshrined in the darkness" (S, 266). In spite of, or perhaps because of this obsessive and corrupting fear of death, the Númenóreans became more temporally powerful. At the height of this power, their king Ar-Pharazôn brought an army to the mainland of Middle-earth in order to face the massing hoards lead by Morgoth's lieutenant, Sauron. Perceiving their superior strength, Sauron abased himself and became a prisoner. With lies and flattery, he convinced Ar-Pharazôn to reject Ilúvatar and the Valar in favor of the lord of the dark, Melkor, for whom he built a mighty temple on the spot where they once worshiped Ilúvatar. Atrocities ensued: "Thereafter the fire and smoke went up without ceasing; for the power of Sauron daily increased, and in the temple, with spilling of blood and torment and great wickedness, men made sacrifice to Melkor that he should release them from death" (S, 273). Disaster follows close on the heels of disobedience. In an attempt to overthrow the Valar and claim the undying lands of the West for themselves, the corrupt Númenóreans sail a fleet westward. Ilúvatar, in an uncharacteristic example of direct intervention, destroys the fleet and sinks Númenor itself. Tolkien's message is clear. Fear of death begins with evasion and ends with obsession, sacrilege, and self-destruction. Tolkien was, by his own admission, concerned primarily with what becomes of mortals when we reject the "Gift of Ilúvatar." But, as we will see, Tolkien's texts are also profoundly concerned with the tragic consequences of attempts to take that gift before it is offered.

Stealing the Gift in *The Silmarillion*

Tolkien recounts two especially prominent suicides in the legends of the First Age of Middle-earth. The first involves a tragic story first told among the earliest sketches of his mythology, elaborated upon in *The Silmarillion* (1977), and more recently published in its complete form as *The Children of Húrin* (2007). Its basic plot revolves around the curse that Morgoth lays upon the mortal house of Húrin, which allied itself with the Elves in an ill-fated campaign to overthrow the Dark Lord and recover the Silmarils, those precious jewels forged by the greatest of the Elves, Fëanor, and stolen by Morgoth. Following the appropriately named Nírnaeth Arnoediad (Battle of Unnumbered Tears) Húrin is captured while fighting a valiant but doomed rear-guard action. Morgoth, unable to break the human king with conventional torture, sets him on a magical throne that will allow Húrin to witness the realization of the Dark Lord's curse in the suffering and destruction of Húrin's children, Túrin and Niënor.

The very language of this curse carries a reminder of Morgoth's pernicious influence on humanity's relationship with mortality: "But upon all whom you love my thought shall weigh as a cloud of Doom, and it shall bring them down into darkness and despair. Wherever they go, evil shall arise. Whenever they speak, their words shall bring ill counsel. Whatsoever they do shall turn against them. They shall die without hope, cursing both life and death" (*CH*, 64). Still undaunted, Húrin rejects Morgoth's claims to sovereignty over humanity and reminds him that he has no power beyond "the Circles of the World" where he cannot pursue those who "refuse" the dark lord (*CH*, 65).

Morgoth, knowing the truth of this assertion but determined to break Húrin's spirit, adopts the posture of a materialist nihilism (an admittedly dubious posture for a formerly disembodied spirit) by denying the existence of any realm outside of this one: "'Beyond the Circles of the World I will not pursue them,' said Morgoth. 'For beyond the Circles of the World there is Nothing. But within them they shall not escape me, until they enter into Nothing'" (65). This is the essence of Morgoth's corrupting philosophy of death. Knowing full well that Ilúvatar rules both Arda and the realm beyond it, Morgoth seeks to weaken the people resisting him in the former by convincing them that the latter is nothing but a void of nonexistence. Faced in such stark terms, the always-already-flimsy consolations of even the most optimistic brands of atheism—e.g., authentic living, acceptance of absurdity, self-gratification, altruism—feel particularly weak. Tolkien implies that we can only truly cast a cold eye on life and death if we submit to despair and affirm Morgoth's lie that the final end of every life is a meaningless void. As the story of Húrin's children will show, submission to such despair finds its most terrifying realization in suicide.

Most of the ensuing narrative revolves around Túrin, who, following his father's disappearance in the Nírnaeth Arnoediad, is separated from his mother and sister while still a child and grows into a renowned warrior. The story of his life is far too complex and involves far too many obscure character and place names to invite succinct summary here. Suffice it to say that, in spite of his valor, most of what Túrin does bears out Morgoth's curse by turning to bad ends. For example, he gains political influence over the Elven stronghold of Nargothrond and leads a daring campaign against the forces of Morgoth that concludes in the sack of Nargothrond and decimation of its people. He has the especially bad fortune of gaining the enmity of the mighty dragon Glaurung, who corners Túrin's estranged sister, Niënor, erases her memory with his magic, and sends her running madly into the wilderness. Túrin finds her, and, sensing a special connection that they cannot define, the two fall in love, marry, and conceive a child. Glaurung eventually sets out to destroy Túrin's adopted village. In an act of daring cunning, Túrin hides in a ravine and mortally wounds the dragon as it drags its body across the gap. This great victory ends in defeat along the lines of the final act of a Shakespearean revenger's tragedy.

Touched by the venomous dragon's blood, Túrin falls into a swoon. When Niënor arrives seeking her husband, Glaurung uses his final moments of life to call her by her true name, daughter of Húrin. With Glaurung's death, his magic dissipates, and Niënor's memory is restored. Realizing that she has married and conceived a child with her brother, Niënor casts herself from a cliff. As with many events in Tolkien's legendarium, Niënor's suicide is presented without any of the narration of internal thought process more common in *The Lord of the Rings*. This state of affairs is reasonable given the distinct fictional frame of *The Silmarillion*'s narrative. We are reading a story written down by the Elves, who cannot die as mortals can. We must glean a sense of Tolkien's thoughts from how his fictionalized, immortal narrator frames events. Often, following a major event in *The Silmarillion* and those longer texts derived from it, the narrator concludes by commenting on place names, a convention borrowed directly from the Old Testament. In this case, we learn that the river gorge into which Niënor throws herself was, up to that point, known as Cabed-en-Aras ("Leap of the Deer" because a deer once made the amazing jump while fleeing a hunter). Following her suicide, the name changes, displacing the former event, a daring escape, with the new event, a despairing defeat: "The waters of [the river] Teiglin flowed on, but Cabed-en-Aras was no more: Cabed Naeramarth, the Leap of Dreadful Doom, thereafter it was named by men; for no deer would ever leap there again, and all living things shunned it, and no man would walk upon its shore" (*CH*, 244). While the narrative conveys a clear sense of pity for Niënor, it also, like most Greek tragedy,

treats her suicide as a defeat, a horrifying fate that inspires fearful commemoration among the living thereafter.

Túrin fares no better. He eventually learns the truth of what has
happened and has his sister's identity unwittingly confirmed by the Elf
Mablung, who knew Nïenor in the Elven stronghold of Menegroth. Túrin
responds with a wild and mad despair: "I am blind! Did you not know?
Blind, blind, groping since childhood in a dark mist of Morgoth! Therefore leave me! Go, go! Go back to Doriath, and may winter shrivel it! A
curse upon Menegroth! And a curse on your errand! This only was want-
ing. Now comes the night!" (255). Túrin does not simply rage against
the injustice of a cursed life; he actively seeks to enlarge the scope of
that curse by laying it upon the imperfect but essentially good people of
Menegroth, who at least attempted to protect his mother and sister from
danger. Despair, Tolkien implies, amplifies evil because it ceases to think
of right action in response to evil as a possibility.

Returning to the place of Nïenor's death, Túrin falls upon his sword.
Mablung and his companions, who have followed close behind, find the
body, weep at the tragedy, and bury Túrin in a mound topped with a
grey stone bearing his name and declaring him as the dragon's slayer.
Here we receive a clear indication that Tolkien's world is pre-Christian
in the strictest sense (i.e., Christ has not yet come there to conquer
death and spread the good news of the conquest). As a Catholic in the
primary world, Tolkien would know that the Church has historically
denied Christian burial to suicides. In the pre-Christian Middle-earth
the inhabitants must make sense of suicide as best they can. For all its
horror, the act, like that of Dante's Cato, does not define a life singularly.
Túrin and Nïenor still merit commemoration, but it is an awful kind of
remembrance. When Morgoth finally releases a bent and broken Húrin,
the defeated man makes his way to the tombstone of his children. There,
he finds his grieving wife, who promptly dies in his arms. Without a
doubt, evil has befallen his house, and despair has marked it. So, what
do we make of this study in suffering? What does it tell us about Tolkien's view of suicide?

Tolkien refuses to throw the baby of pre-Christian virtue out with
the bathwater of pre-Christian heathenism, even if that includes tragic
suicide; instead, he seeks through the implicit lessons of his narrative to
bring those virtues within the embrace of a more complete, and undeniably Christian, worldview. He makes this point abundantly clear in his
groundbreaking lecture "Beowulf: The Monsters and the Critics" (1936).

There, Tolkien draws a distinction between the incomplete but admirable pre-Christian warrior code embodied in the poem's hero and the fullness of truth latently contained in the poem's nascent Christianity. Bradley Birzer sums up Tolkien's main points succinctly:

> *Beowulf*'s greatest strength, Tolkien believed, lay in the author's understanding that the theme should be implicit rather than explicit. . . . For Tolkien, the Beowulf poet beautifully intertwined pagan virtues with Christian theology. . . . Most certainly a Christian, the author used the poem to demonstrate that not all pagan things should be dismissed by the new culture. Instead, the Christian should embrace and sanctify the most noble virtues to come out of the northern pagan mind: courage and raw will.[14]

Birzer links this sanctification of pagan virtue to a tradition dating back to Augustine and places Tolkien convincingly within that tradition. Like the Beowulf poet, Tolkien puts the monsters front and center because he knows that, with the baptizing of pagan virtue "the understanding of the nature of 'the good' changes . . . the nature of evil remains the same."[15] Tolkien admired northern pagan heroism. We can clearly see this admiration in the story of Túrin, who, in spite of his evil *wyrd* or doom or fate, does great deeds that win him admiration and renown. Two ages after his death, Túrin is named in the council of Elrond as one of the "mightiest Elf-friends of old" (*LOTR*, 270). But Tolkien also understood the limitations of such heroic virtue, and his work rejects ancient heathenism as firmly as modern atheism, especially in their respective attitudes towards death. As we will see later on in the case of Denethor, this rejection of heathen attitudes towards death goes hand in hand with Tolkien's condemnation of suicide. Túrin's heroism is real and worthy of commemoration, but his final act of despair is a warning.

Ralph Wood argues convincingly that Túrin's unhappy end expresses Tolkien's belief in the harsh realities of evil and suffering even within a providential world overseen by a benevolent deity. According to Wood, Tolkien rejected the notion that our lives can be the "sum total of decisions rightly or wrongly made" because we make those decisions within a world of seemingly random, and often evil, forces outside of

---

14. Birzer, *J. R. R. Tolkien's Sanctifying Myth*, 34–35.
15. Birzer, *J. R. R. Tolkien's Sanctifying Myth*, 36.

our control.[16] Rather than promoting the nihilism of Morgoth, Tolkien affirmed providence by creating a secondary world in which God asserts his will by making possible a "right human response" to the chaotic and sometimes downright evil forces of the world.[17] Consequently, human flourishing depends on our ability to accept suffering at the hands of those forces with courageous humility.

I believe this insight about accepting suffering extends to Tolkien's treatment of suicide. As with most twentieth-century Christian writers who tackle the problem of suicide, Tolkien denies the false, saccharine assertion so common at times of tragedy that all things are somehow part of God's plan. Quite the opposite. God's plan is temporally subverted by evil at every turn, and human lives are especially vulnerable. However, the subversive effects of evil are demarcated by our response to it. Túrin is literally cursed by a demon, and he repeatedly seeks to escape his fate by means of his own strength and cunning, going so far as to name himself Túrin Turambar (master of fate). Tolkien the medievalist found in the early encounter between northern European paganism and Catholicism a blending of notions of fate/doom/*wyrd* with the Christian notion of divine providence. As Richard Whitt notes, "It is such a blend, a harmonious blend, that one finds in *The Silmarillion* as well. Sometimes, there appears to be a force controlling men's destinies independent of divinity, while not detracting from this divinity's power."[18] Túrin's desire to master his doom through his own actions instead of reconciling himself to fate and hoping in providence finds its ultimate realization in his despairing suicide. Refusing to accept the extreme and inventive sufferings accorded him by Morgoth, Túrin plays into the Dark Lord's hands by realizing the curse through his own self-slaughter. Morgoth cannot force a free being to steal the gift of Ilúvatar. When Túrin does so under his influence, he has achieved Morgoth's greatest and most horrific victory.

The second noteworthy suicide of Tolkien's First Age comes at the conclusion of the long and disastrous labors of Fëanor and his seven sons to reclaim the Silmarils, and it affirms Tolkien's implicit warning against attempts to master "doom" by seizing death. After losing the Silmarils to Morgoth, Fëanor, disdaining the aid of the Valar, binds his sons to an unbreakable oath, sworn on the name of Ilúvatar himself, that they will recover the gems for themselves and destroy any who

16. Wood, "Confronting the World's Weirdness," 148.

17. Wood, "Confronting the World's Weirdness," 148.

18. Whitt, "Germanic *Fate* and *Doom* in J.R.R. Tolkien's *The Silmarillion*," 116.

withhold them. This same oath calls "the Everlasting Dark upon them" if they fail to keep it (*S*, 83). Not surprisingly, such an audacious covenant bears evil fruit. While Morgoth holds the Silmarils, the sons of Fëanor fight beside the other free peoples of Middle-earth to unseat the Dark Lord; however, once Beren and Lúthien recover a Silmaril and deliver it to the Elves of Doriath, their pledge forces Fëanor's sons to turn their swords on their erstwhile allies. Even after the Valar overthrow Morgoth, Fëanor's two remaining sons, Maedhros and Maglor, find themselves bound to steal the gems from the very people who have liberated Middle-earth. Maglor attempts to convince his brother to abandon the plot and seek the judgment of the Valar, but Maedhros insists that even the Powers of Valinor cannot release them. Together, the brothers sneak into the camp of Eönwë, banner-bearer to the lord of the Valar, and murder the guards set to watch the Silmarils. Refusing to shed more blood, Eönwë declares that the cornered brothers should be allowed to leave with their ill-gotten treasure. Far from being contented, Maedhros and Maglor find that, like Morgoth, they cannot handle the Silmarils without unbearable pain because they have shed innocent blood. Maglor casts one of the stones into the sea and spends the rest of his days wandering the coast "singing in pain and regret beside the waves" (*S*, 254). His brother chooses a darker path.

Maedhros, the most persistent adherent to the evil oath, finally realizes the hopeless nature of the snare he has created for himself: "he perceived that it was as Eönwë had said, and that his right thereto [to the Silmarils] had become void, and that the oath was vain. And being in anguish and despair he cast himself into a gaping chasm filled with fire, and so ended" (*S*, 254). Like Túrin, Maedhros attempts to bend fate to his will, first by means of his own martial prowess and cunning, and finally by claiming sovereignty over his own existence. The major difference, of course, is that Maedhros, like all Elves, is bound within "the Circles of the World." His spirit will leave his body and go to the Halls of Mandos in Valinor and await the end of all time. Elves, we could say, are incapable of suicide in the strictest sense. They are so thoroughly a part of the natural world of Arda that they cannot be fully separate from it. Nevertheless, as a rule, Elves do not destroy their own bodies.[19] Maedhros's act seems like a desperate attempt to end the tragedy of the oath by claiming

19. The closest parallel is Maedhros's grandmother, Miriel, who, following the birth of Fëanor, is consumed by extreme weariness to the point that her spirit leaves her body. But her passing was not caused by despair or her own action.

sovereignty over his own bodily existence, a pursuit at least similar enough to suicide to deserve attention. His submission to despair receives no comment from the narrator of *The Silmarillion*, but it stands out as a profound aberration that serves as the climactic transgression in the long history of transgressions linked to Fëanor's oath.

We know that the suicides of Túrin and Maedhros were part of Tolkien's design from its earliest inception. We also know that he sought to find some way to redeem those noble characters, who had taken the gift of Ilúvatar before their time. In 1926, Tolkien wrote a radically condensed sketch of what would become the posthumously published *Silmarillion*. Also known as the "Sketch of the Mythology" this text concludes by describing an apocalyptic last battle and the healing of Middle-earth. Surprisingly, two of the most prominent heroes in this apocalypse are also the most conspicuous suicides in the narrative of *The Silmarillion*: Túrin and Maedhros, spelled Maidros in the sketch:

> When the world is much older, and the Gods weary, Morgoth will come back through the Door, and the last battle of all will be fought. Fionwë [Eönwë] will fight Morgoth on the plain of Valinor, and the spirit of Túrin shall be beside him; it shall be Túrin who with his black sword will slay Morgoth, and thus the children of Húrin shall be avenged.
>
> In those days the Silmarils shall be recovered from sea and earth and air, and Maidros shall break them and Belaurin [Yavanna] with their fire rekindle the Two Trees, and the great light shall come forth again, and the Mountains of Valinor shall be levelled so that it goes out over the world, and Gods and Elves and Men shall grow young again, and all their dead awake.[20]

There are profound implications to making two suicides (Túrin and Maedhros) instrumental in the overthrow of Morgoth, the healing of Arda, and the resurrection of all the righteous dead.

Perhaps this is the ultimate expression of The One's providence: "But Ilúvatar knew that Men, being set amid the turmoils of the powers of the world, would stray often, and would not use their gifts in harmony; and he said: 'These too in their time shall find that all that they do redounds at the end only to the glory of my work'" (*S*, 42). Could it be that, within this framework, suicide is not a serious offense, that it is turned to providential ends so completely that it is as if it never happened? I think not, for several reasons: first, and most obviously, Tolkien

20. Tolkien, *Shaping of Middle-Earth*, 46.

seems to have set aside this conclusion to the mythology. Christopher Tolkien's published version of *The Silmarillion* leaves the apocalypse as an unknown. There are clear indications that humanity will play a key role in the "Second Music of the Ainur" (42), but the fates of Túrin and Maedhros remain unknown. *The Silmarillion* concludes with a clear disclaimer about future events: "If any change shall come and the Marring [of Arda] be amended, Manwë and Varda may know; but they have not revealed it, and it is not declared in the dooms of Mandos" (S, 255). Second, and more importantly, even in the events related in the "Sketch of the Mythology," Tolkien brings back his suicides in order that they might redress their renunciation of life and duty. Túrin seeks just retribution against Morgoth for the wrongs done to his parents, his sister, and himself. Seen from this vantage, Túrin's reemergence in Tolkien's draft apocalypse highlights the wrongness of his suicide by showing us the rightness of its alternative. Had he not killed himself, had he, as Tolkien suggests he should have, humbly accepted the vicissitudes of fate and responded with right action, Túrin might have used his life to continue the fight against Morgoth. Likewise, Maedhros reemerges in order to do what he should have done while alive. Rather than casting himself, along with the Silmaril, into a fiery pit, he could have undone much of the evil caused by his family by returning the stone to Valinor, helping to regrow the Two Trees, and accepting the just punishment of the Valar. In order to more fully appreciate Tolkien's rejection of suicide as an appropriate response to suffering and his elevation of self-sacrifice as a fitting alternative, we must turn now to *The Lord of the Rings*.

Stealing the Gift in *The Lord of the Rings*

Unlike the often tragic *Silmarillion*, *The Lord of the Rings* provides a transparently and indisputably providential plotline. In spite of this overall difference in tone, the two works exist within the same world, and the latter does not shy away from contemplating the darker facets of Tolkien's secondary reality. Suicide stands out as one of darkest but has received surprisingly little sustained attention from Tolkien scholars. *The Lord of the Rings* takes up *The Silmarillion*'s fascination with suicide and develops that fascination into a more coherent ethic. This development is possible largely because Tolkien drops the style of *The Silmarillion*, which favors the semi-detached, historical recounting of events from a perspective of incomplete Elvish knowledge, and replaces it with a more novelistic style, which prioritizes the semi-omniscient recounting of both events and characters' internal conflicts and thought processes. A character's decision to commit suicide can no longer be related in one or two sentences, as it is in the former text. Instead, Tolkien forces himself to enter into a more profound encounter with the motivations of those who are tempted to steal the gift of Ilúvatar.

As if to highlight the pernicious attraction of death to all feeling people, even the most constitutionally sturdy and optimistic, Tolkien plunges the simplest and most stouthearted of simple stouthearted Hobbits into the bleak abyss of suicidal thought in a chapter fittingly titled "The Choices of Master Samwise." Betrayed to Shelob by Gollum, Frodo is struck down by the daughter of Ungoliant, that light-consuming figuration of starving nothingness and ravenous nonexistence who aided Morgoth in destroying the Two Trees of Valinor in the First Age. In one of his finest moments, Sam, calling on the name of Elbereth and wielding both the Phial of Galadriel and the elven blade Sting, has just faced down the monster over the body of his fallen master. Here, we see Sam at his best: loyal, indomitable, brave in the face of almost certain death. Upon defeating Shelob and finding what appears to be Frodo's lifeless corpse, however, Sam falls from the heights of heroism into his spiritual nadir.

Sam responds to what he believes to be the loss of his master with rage and despair, followed by a desire first for vengeance, and then for oblivion. At first, we are told, "anger surged over him, and he ran about his master's body in a rage, stabbing the air, and smiting the stones, and shouting challenges" (731). Then "black despair came down on him, and Sam bowed to the ground, and drew his grey hood over his head, and night came into his heart, and he knew no more" (731). When Sam finally emerges from this state of catatonic loss, the narrator reveals the true depths his cheeriest character's darkest hour: "how many minutes or hours the world had gone dragging on he could not tell. . . . The mountains had not crumbled nor the earth fallen into ruin" (731). Even the persistence of the outside world can come as a shock in the face of personal despair. Left with the reality of existence, Sam realizes that he must make a choice, but flounders in indecision. It is worth noting that Sam's contemplation of suicide, almost certainly a first in his simple and good-natured life, truly begins with thoughts of revenge against Gollum.

Tolkien repeatedly associates hatred and vengeance with the desire for oblivion. Like Fëanor and his sons, who bound their lives to one of two fates—revenge or "Eternal Darkness"—Sam initially feels that he must choose a life devoted to vendetta or no life at all: "Now he tried to find strength to tear himself away and go on a lonely journey—for vengeance. If once he could go, his anger would bear him down all the roads of the world" (732). Unlike so many literary avengers before him, Sam immediately sees the limitation of such action and decides that death would be better: "It would not be worth while to leave his master for that. It would not bring him back. Nothing would. They had better both be dead together. And that too would be a lonely journey" (732). What follows is one of only two instances of suicidal ideation in *The Lord of the Rings*: "He looked on the bright point of the sword. He thought of the places behind where there was a black brink and an empty fall into nothingness. There was no escape that way. That was to do nothing, not even to grieve. That was not what he had set out to do" (732).

Sam rejects the temptation to simply end his life or resign himself to what we might call suicide by Orc in a heroic last stand over Frodo's dead body. What saves him, aside from his predominant good Hobbit sense, is, strangely enough, the Ring. Rather, we might say that he is saved by the certain knowledge that if he throws away his life the Ring will fall into enemy hands and all the beauty of the world will be extinguished: "If we're found . . . the enemy will get it. And that's the end of all of us, of Lórien, and Rivendell, and the Shire and all. . . . No, it's sit here till they come and kill me over master's body, and gets It; or take It and go" (732). Sam makes no claims to sovereignty over his own life. Unlike Túrin, he fosters no delusions about mastering his own fate or escaping doom by falling on his sword. He recognizes that his life is not his own. It belongs, instead, to all of Middle-earth. Self-destruction would not mean an escape from suffering; it would mean a rejection of all creation and his duty to serve all that is good in a world that often seems unredeemable. Sam overcomes the temptation to fall on his sword, as Túrin did, so that he might continue to struggle against the shadow, as Túrin failed to do.

As a champion of life, Sam recognizes the ultimate good of that struggle against the shadow and demonstrates the necessity of a real and intelligible *telos* or right end. In his seminal book *After Virtue*, Alasdair MacIntyre identifies at the heart of Aristotelian ethics a distinction between "human-nature-as-it-happens-to-be (human nature in its untutored state" and "human-nature-as-it-could-be-if-it-realized-its-*telos*."[21]

---

21. MacIntyre, *After Virtue*, 53.

Ethics ideally guides us in those practices that lead us from the former state to the latter. In a world that often seems governed by inhospitable *wyrd*, people need an ultimate goal of right action that exists objectively outside the self and that ennobles life. Sam's innate sense of duty to serve beauty and goodness in spite of personal distress rests on an implicit, internalized ideal of, to abuse MacIntyre's formulation, Hobbit-nature-as-it-could-be-if-it-realized-its-*telos*. Wedded to this Aristotelian sense of the good, derived form his own nature, is a keen awareness of a divine hierarchy. Sam's invocation of Elbereth in the fight with Shelob marks him as, ethically, something very close to a Thomist, someone who combines a sense of species *telos* derived from reason and experience to what MacIntyre calls "a divinely ordained law" founded on a hierarchy of authority that both limits and expands the range of right action.

Of course, honestly pursuing our *telos* does not guarantee that we will attain it perfectly, or at all. Sam immediately blunders. As is not uncommon in cases of literary suicide, he has mistaken Frodo's temporary paralysis for death. Like Romeo beside the body of Juliet or Niënor beside the body of Túrin, Sam assumes death. Because of this assumption, Frodo is captured by the Orcs. In this sense "The Choices of Master Samwise" could be seen as a story about making the wrong choice at a crucial moment, but Sam, unlike Romeo and Niënor, has made the only choice that really matters; he has opted for life. By making this one difficult decision, he has left the door open to hope, right action, and the workings of providence. Had he given in to the desire for the solace offered by "the bright point of the sword," Sam would have left Frodo to the enemy, handed over the Ring, and transformed eventual eucatastrophe—Tolkien's term for seemingly hopeless situations that turn to the good—into immediate catastrophe. Here Sam emerges as the practitioner of a comedic ethic of life largely missing from the essentially tragic warrior-hero culture of *Beowulf* and almost totally absent from the subjective emotivism identified by MacIntyre as the dominant paradigm of our time. What ultimately saves Sam is a humble acknowledgment of his own subservience to a greater good and an audacious belief in his own ability to serve that good with a life that is not ultimately his own.

Not long after this heroic choice of life over death, hope over despair, humility over pride, Tolkien fashions a vision of its obverse in "The Pyre of Denethor." With Sauron's army at the gates of Gondor, and his last remaining son seemingly mortally wounded, the once mighty Denethor succumbs to despair when his people need him most. Using the magical seeing stone, the Palantir, he believes that he has witnessed enough of unfolding events to know the outcome of the war. Just as Morgoth broke Húrin by forcing him to watch the downfall of his children, Sauron breaks Denethor by twisting the Palantir so that it shows only the evidence of certain defeat. Tolkien, as we know by now, abhors such dire certainty. Not only is certainty about the future usually a delusion, it most often results in despair. No future lacks for suffering, and our minds are ill-equipped to face suffering without the aid of hope.

Denethor explicitly abjures hope. Rather than fight and lose, he decides to master fate by choosing and enacting his own destruction: "Better to burn sooner than late, for burn we must. . . . I will go now to my pyre. To my pyre! No tomb for Denethor and Faramir. . . . We will burn like heathen kings before ever a ship sailed hither from the West. The West has failed" (825). When Pippin tells him of Denethor's plan, Gandalf immediately associates suicide with the evil will of Sauron: "Even in the heart of our stronghold the Enemy has power to strike us: for his will it is that is at work" (850). He then confronts Denethor, reminding the Steward that his "part is to go out to the battle of your city, where maybe death awaits you" (852). Gandalf stresses death as a possibility, even a likelihood, but Denethor holds to his despairing certainty: "Battle is vain. . . . Why should we not go to death side by side?" (853). Gandalf is not a suicide hotline worker doing the important but medicalized and secularized work of keeping citizens alive so that they can serve the state. He doesn't attempt to make Denethor think that he has "so much to live for" or convince him that life isn't all that bad. In his ordained role as servant of the Valar and Ilúvatar, he speaks the plain truth—Denethor should not kill himself because his life is not his own. His response provides Tolkien's most explicit and unambiguous argument against suicide as a right or privilege available to the individual: "'Authority is not given to you, Steward of Gondor, to order the hour of your death,' answered Gandalf. 'And only the heathen kings, under the domination of the Dark Power, did this, slaying themselves in pride and despair, murdering their kin to ease their own death. . . . We are needed. There is much that you can yet do'" (853). Suicide, understood in this light, both abnegates responsibility and, more importantly, asserts false sovereignty over individual existence.

Denethor is not merely ending lives by attempting filicide-suicide. As a warrior and ruler, he has doubtless had to take many lives that fell within his ordained authority. At the core of this self-destructive desire lies a kind of mutiny, a rebellion against a higher authority. To highlight the metaphysically transgressive nature of his revolt, Denethor conducts the act in a manner meant to symbolically reject the practices of the good Númenóreans of the Second Age, who brought with them the wisdom of the Valar and Ilúvatar. John R. Holmes makes much of Tolkien's use of the word "heathen," which occurs only in "The Pyre of Denethor." Like the *Beowulf* poet before him, who condemned "the heathen practice of burning the dead," Tolkien identifies Denethor's choice of pyre over burial with a pagan transgression and raises the stakes by making Faramir a living victim.[22] We are clearly meant to associate Denethor's despair and suicide with paganism; however, the scene may be read as an equally fierce condemnation of modern notions of unrestricted human license and sovereignty over death. Denethor's argument for suicide could be framed within current discussion of "quality of life." He has decided that Gandalf's "hope" is a vain illusion. Denethor laments the current state of things and says that he would "have things as they were in all the days of my life. . . . But if doom denies this to me, then I will have *naught*: neither life diminished, nor love halved, nor honour abated" (854). Are these not the words of the enlightened modern antinatalist and rational epicurean? If nothing awaits us after death and life has become more pain than pleasure, why shouldn't the wise man choose oblivion now rather than oblivion later? Why should we not choose this benevolent nonexistence for all humanity? In the competing arguments of the Wizard and the Steward, we find the continuing competition between Tolkien's comic Christianity, on the one hand, and the amalgamated visions of tragic paganism and absurd modernity, on the other.

    Gandalf's confrontation with Denethor, with its insistence on limited authority over death, calls to mind his famous speech to Frodo concerning Bilbo's decision not to kill Gollum when he had the chance. Frodo laments Bilbo's mercy and insists, with ample justification, that Gollum "deserves death" (59). Gandalf seems to lose his temper at this offhanded remark: "Deserves it! I daresay he does. Many that live deserve death. And some that die deserve life. Can you give it to them? Then do not be too eager to deal out death in judgment. For even the very wise cannot see all ends" (59). Tolkien scholars have spent more than a little time unpacking these lines, but I would like to point out two ways in which these words specifically anticipate the tragedy of

---

22. Holmes, "'Like Heathen Kings,'" 122.

Denethor's suicide. First, Gandalf makes clear that certainty about the future is always illusory and often dangerous. Suicide in Tolkien's work is always bound up with the desire to master fate and realize doom ahead of its time. Second, without lengthy references to Elvish myths about Ilúvatar's gift to men, Gandalf makes clear that, like life itself, death is something beyond the proper authority of mortals. Gandalf's shock at Frodo's callous talk of death no doubt comes in some part from his faith in good Hobbit sense. Hobbits, as a rule, do not take life except under the most dire circumstances. Frodo's wish that Bilbo had killed Gollum hints at the malicious influence of the Ring already at work in his mind. In a broken world, we may be forced to kill, as the Hobbits must reluctantly do when they return to the Shire at the end of their quest, but, Gandalf reminds his pupil, death can never justly be the sovereign domain of human will because we cannot redress death once we have doled it out. He reiterates this point under a different aspect and in different terms when confronting Denethor. Authority over our own death has not been granted to us. Our lives are not of our own making and, therefore, cannot be ours to unmake.

Modern medical discourse around suicide as a manifestation of a clinical mental disorder is slowly giving up ground to those who would treat suicide as a right within the domain of individual authority. Tolkien had great sympathy for those struggling with what his fiction imagines as the palpable pressure of exterior, demonic will. We need only look to Frodo, who suffers under and ultimately succumbs to the malign influence of the Ring. However, the truly wise people of his fictional world have no patience for those who would overreach their natural authority by claiming absolute sovereignty over the lives of others or their own lives. Tolkien calls the animating essence of being "the Secret Fire" or "flame imperishable." It is a gift given to Arda, the world that is, at the beginning of time by Eru Ilúvatar. In his battle with the balrog, Gandalf identifies himself as "a servant of the Secret Fire" (330). His is a life dedicated to the service and protection of life. So is Tolkien's. The author's investment in external moral authority, though common enough through most of human history, also marks him as distinctly anti-modern. It's one thing to counsel people that life is, in general, worth living; it's another kettle of stewed rabbit entirely to insist that they *must* live because the ordering intelligence that granted them the spark of life demands they not extinguish it.

Tolkien's sympathetic but emphatic rejection of suicide does not finally amount to pious condemnation. Instead, he affirms the essential and incalculable importance of the individual life in the ongoing conflict between good and evil. Just as we can go wrong by attempting to seize death before it is offered, we can go right by offering our lives up for others. Boromir and Sam, though both imperfect in their own ways, stand out as two of the most powerful examples of this self-donative approach to right action. Both eventually receive the gift of Ilúvatar, but it is a gift earned and not taken. Tolkien claimed that death is the overarching concern of his work. Peter Kreeft lays out Tolkien's vision of good death plainly:

> We could call this theme "good death versus bad death," death of the self (ego) versus death of the soul. . . . The point . . . is that he who voluntarily loses his life, gives up his life, for others, *will save it*, and he who chooses to cling to his life will lose it. When we try to be the lords of our own life, the life we cling to as our own is a miserable shadow of the true life that the true Lord wants to give us.[23]

Postmodern suicide discourse cannot account for authority over human life derived from outside of individual or state sovereignty.

This failure to articulate the essential nature and value of human existence in relation to a higher, permanent, and benevolent creator makes suicide not only permissible, but logically desirable for the individual. States and corporations may have a vested interest in preventing mass citizen-consumer suicide, but neither anti-suicide nets around Chinese manufacturing buildings nor suicide prevention programs in American high schools can hope to achieve much without providing a vision of life that not only denies the individual right to suicide, but also affirms the individual obligation to a heroic life of right action. We are all, in Denethor's fatalistic sense, doomed to die. Any civilization that affirms individual sovereignty over that doom, that makes Turambars of its citizens, will soon find itself illuminated by pyres. Tolkien's contemporary, Graham Greene, who opted for gritty realism over sub-creative fantasy, knew all too well the temptation to master life by controlling death. Far more than Tolkien, he attempted to bring us into the mind of the suicide in order that we might better understand the mysteries of both the human will and divine mercy.

23. Kreeft, *Philosophy of Tolkien*, 98.

5

Graham Greene's Pseudo-Suicides

Leon Bloy comes to see us. "There are no sinners in Hell," he tells us, "for sinners were the friends of Jesus. There are only the wicked."—Jacques Maritain, *Notebooks*

A suicide is a man who cares so little for anything outside him, that he wants to see the last of everything.—G. K. Chesterton, *Orthodoxy*

EMPLOYING G. K. CHESTERTON's definition of the suicide as "a man who cares so little for anything outside him, that he wants to see the last of everything," there are no obvious suicides in the novels of Graham Greene. The same could not be said of any of the other authors discussed so far in this book. Houellebecq, Moore, Benson, Tolkien: they all present us with characters who desire oblivion for its own sake. Not so, Greene. Unlike Florent-Claude Labrouste, Mike Fletcher, Mabel Brand, and Túrin Turambar, Greene's suicides do not desire death or particularly wish "to see the last of everything." They are more like pale shadows of Dante's Cato, who died for love of freedom and directs souls at the base of Mount Purgatory, than Pier della Vigne who despaired of embodied life itself in his fall from political grace and languishes as a thorny tree in the seventh circle with the other suicides separated from "the flesh we robbed from our own souls."[1] Of course, Dante neither admits the pagan Cato to paradise nor provides any example of a Christian suicide who has found salvation. Greene often seems to wish to do just that

---

1. Alighieri, *Inferno*, XIII.105.

by presenting us with what I would call "pseudo-suicides," characters who undoubtedly take their own lives but whose motives and innermost movements of soul are not necessarily defined by the desire to reject life or God.[2] Action and intention, the two necessary elements of a particular sin, are not cleanly aligned in Greene's pseudo-suicides. Though anxious to preserve for the pseudo-suicide the possibility of salvation, I will argue, Greene never allows his pity to blind him to the persistent reality of sin, a reality largely forgotten in the modern discourse around the problem of suicide. Greene maintains that self-killing always involves some kind of moral failure, but it may not always be the particular moral failure of Chesterton's suicide.

Greene, Pieper, and Sin

Greene's insistence on exploring the limits of pardonable exceptions in cases of suicide clearly has roots in his biography. Always prone to bouts of depression followed by euphoric activity, Greene was eventually diagnosed as manic depressive or bipolar. Biographer Richard Greene notes that the young Graham Greene "was experimenting with methods of suicide" from an early age.[3] Such experimentation continued in his teenage years when a distraught Greene, plagued by what he simply termed "boredom"—the same spiritual malady that would drive him to seek out excessive risks his whole life—infamously engaged in a solitary game of Russian roulette. Though biographers have since raised doubt about the complete veracity of his version of things, Greene recounted the incident memorably in his autobiography, *A Sort of Life* (1971). Interestingly, he insists on treating the incident not as a suicide attempt but as a kind of risk-taking meant to draw him out of his depression, not end his life:

> Unhappy love, I suppose, has sometimes driven boys to suicide, but this was not suicide, whatever a coroner's jury might have said: it was a gamble with five chances to one against an inquest. The discovery that it was possible to enjoy again the visible world by risking its total loss was one I was bound to make sooner or later. . . . I put the muzzle of the revolver to my right

2. I am not using the term *pseudo-suicide* in the clinical sense. There are, within medical literature, case studies of people who have harmed themselves or ended their own lives while in an unconscious state of sleep. See, for example, Mahowald et al., "Parasomnia Pseudo-Suicide." That is not the subject of this chapter.

3. Greene, *Unquiet Englishman*, 15.

ear and pulled the trigger. I remember an extraordinary sense
of jubilation, as if carnival lights had been switched on in a dark
drab street. My heart knocked in its cage, and life contained an
infinite number of possibilities.[4]

Green describes the event as a kind of rite of passage, like the first experience of sex. He went on to repeat the experiment a handful of times over
the next few years. Continuing the sexual metaphor, he notes that the
once climactic feeling became merely a "crude kick of excitement" more
akin to lust than love. Though he put the revolver away for good before
the end of his Oxford days, Greene continued to think of his pseudo-
suicidal experiment with Russian roulette as the prototype for a lifetime
spent warring against boredom with the weapon of risk.

If we are willing to risk credulity by taking Greene fully at his word,
then it seems clear that suicide qua suicide was never something he particularly desired. Rather, he exposed himself to the extreme danger of
harm, either from himself or others or the natural world, as a means of
combatting the ennui of his existence. Put more simply, he risked death
in order to cling to life. Joseph Pieper, a German Catholic philosopher
and Greene's contemporary, will have much to say in this chapter about
sin, and his insights into the nature of sloth, or *acedia*, may help us in
making sense of Greene's account of his early flirtation with suicide. In
his groundbreaking *Leisure the Basis of Culture* (1948), Pieper identifies
acedia as the hallmark vice of the modern age, not because we moderns
have become less industrious but because we have attempted to cope
with our alienation from the core of our being through frenetic activity
and increasingly desperate ploys to escape the ennui that comes with
that alienation. In the deepest sense, the idle man "does not want to be
as God wants him to be, and that ultimately means that he does not wish
to be what he really, fundamentally, *is*." "*Acedia*," Pieper insists, "is the
'despair from weakness' which Kierkegaard analyzed as the 'despairing
refusal to be oneself.'"[5]

What better description of Greene's predicament? For many people,
acedia manifests itself in daily bustle and work in service to the common
vices that separate them from the fearful task of being what God wants
them to be. For the introspective and sensitive Greene, the boredom
of *acedia* leads to contemplation of a more permanent solution to the

4. Greene, *Sort of Life*, 130–31.
5. Pieper, *Leisure the Basis of Culture*, 24.

perpetual problem of the "despairing refusal to be oneself." Much like Walker Percy, as we will see in the final chapter of this book, Greene's serious contemplation of suicide, of the possibility of permanently ending life, allows him a viable escape from despair. Finding that life contains an "infinite number of possibilities," Greene becomes open to the possibility of life, of a liberation from *acedia* into his true being, or at least onto the road leading to that consummation. It should come as little surprise that a man attracted to the possibilities afforded by suicidal ideation would write several novels in which suicide plays a key role. It should also come as no surprise that the motivations of Greene's suicides are complex and demand close attention. When we add in his conversion to Catholicism, what emerges is a quintessentially modern attempt to make sense of the problem of suicide within what was for Greene, and a growing number of people, the essentially alien conceptual framework of sin.

A certain segment of Greene scholars will doubtless shy away from this explicitly "Catholic" treatment of a novelist whom secular scholars have been claiming as a kind of subversive ally and double agent for decades. In the most recent book attempting to deal with Greene's Catholic fiction from a more or less secular and deconstructionist perspective, *Between Form and Faith: Graham Greene and the Catholic Novel* (2021), author Martyn Sampson argues that "Greene's novels should not be defined as Catholic in a narrowly religious sense."[6] This is fair enough, as Greene himself rejected the label of Catholic novelist, preferring to think of himself as a novelist who happened to be Catholic and write about Catholics. As Greene points out in his preface to *The Comedians* (1966), he saw writing about his coreligionists as almost demographically inevitable and warned against reading the protagonist of that novel as an alter ego:

> Ah, it may be said, Brown [the protagonist] is a Catholic and so, we know, is Greene . . . It is often forgotten that, even in the case of a novel laid in England, the story, when it contains more than ten characters, would lack verisimilitude if at least one of them were not Catholic. (*C*, xxi)

The reasoning is a bit frail and feels disingenuous. Greene does not write about Catholics the way he does about any other group. He devotes substantial attention to what it means to live within and struggle with Catholic dogma; nevertheless, Sampson is well within his rights to ask readers to avoid defining Greene's novels "as Catholic in a narrowly religious

---

6. Sampson, *Between Form and Faith*, 39.

.sense." Why one would choose to define anything in a "narrowly reli-gious" sense is beyond me, but it confuses me less than Sampson's insis-tence that we should instead read Greene's novels as texts "characterized by their implication within multiple individualist and collectivist notions of meaning."[7] As often happens with critics of Catholic literature who want to distance themselves from its Catholicity, Sampson must reject a "narrowly religious" definition of meaning in favor of oppressively broad and obfuscatory definitions of meaning.

While I appreciate that much of the expansive critical conversation surrounding Greene's fiction, which I will labor to avoid rehearsing too tediously, chooses to look past the larger, and sometimes tenuous, truth claims inherent in his work in favor of discussing it on an abstracted level of form or historical context, I intend to take a more direct ap-proach. I propose to make sense of Greene's suicides as he does, that is, in relation to Catholic teaching about sin, which, as Greene repeatedly reiterates, is far more nuanced than most people grasp. My main re-source for this discussion of sin, aside from Greene's works themselves, will be Pieper's *The Concept of Sin* (1977).[8] Pieper links our modern reticence to speak at all about sin to the radical modern philosophical project of expunging the theological dimension of reality from human discourse, a project that found its clearest expression in Nietzsche's command in *The Dawn of Day* (*Morgenröte*, 1881) to "Get rid of the concept of sin from the world!"[9] Suffice it to say that Greene, unlike many of his critics, was never content to get rid of the concept of sin, but he did wish to interrogate it, especially as it relates to the "mortal," the deadly, the seemingly unforgivable sin of suicide.

Before moving on to a consideration of this interrogation, we need a clear definition of "mortal" sin. This definition from Pieper, derived from Thomas Aquinas, will be foundational for my consideration of Greene's pseudo-suicides:

> To sin "mortally" means: deliberately to apply the most intense valuation and love of which one is capable not to God but to oneself.

7. Sampson, *Between Form and Faith*, 39.

8. I am not, here, arguing for something like influence. I find no evidence that Greene read Pieper or vice versa. Instead, Pieper will serve as the philosophical repre-sentative of a highly nuanced and orthodox Catholic understanding of sin that will help us better grasp the ideas Greene is exploring in a more oblique manner in his fiction.

9. Quoted in Pieper, *Concept of Sin*, 12.

To qualify as truly "deadly," this decision against God must go all the way to the roots and shirk from nothing. It must be a decision so radical that its only analogue at the opposite pole would be the decision of the martyr or blood-witness: in both cases it is a matter of life and death. Whoever loves something to the fullest limits wills to have it *forever*. Which means that mortal sin, when realized to its ultimate consequence, likewise "wills eternity."[10]

As a necessary consequence of this "decision against God," the sinner loses that which he has renounced. Whether in the work of Dante, Dostoevsky, C. S. Lewis, or Jean Paul Sartre, this renunciation results in self-imposed imprisonment—Sartre's inclusion may seem like a stretch, but even he in *No Exit* (1944) puts the souls of the damned together in a room with a wide-open door whose threshold they cannot bear to cross. The condemned person holds the key to the door he has placed between himself and God and locked with his own hand. Since the suicide's act cannot help but be final and cannot in any obvious way admit of redress, its finality marks it as one of the most serious of the mortal sins.

As definitive as this formulation sounds, Pieper reminds us from the beginning of his treatise that sin "really refers to that place where each human being lives in the innermost secret cell of his person, a place to which no one else has any access whatever."[11] Greene's novels repeatedly treat the sin of suicide as something inaccessible from the outside even as his characters attempt to sit in judgement of those who have taken their own lives. In spite of his flirtations with heresy—including a latent and semi-ironic Manichean streak in his darker moments—Greene's imaginative treatment of suicide, and sin in general, never directly contravenes Catholic orthodoxy. Rather than rejecting the idea of suicide as a sin, Greene rejects hasty damnations of suicides, since, due to the very inaccessible nature of sin, they risk missing the true movement of soul at the heart of the matter.

From a Catholic perspective, the first of Greene's pseudo-suicides presents the fewest stumbling blocks, though the same cannot be said for those approaching Greene's work from a purely secular perspective. The unnamed "whiskey priest" of *The Power and the Glory* (1940), one of Greene's earliest "Catholic" novels, lives and dies in obscurity as so many did during the oppression of Catholics in Mexico in the 1930s. As

10. Pieper, *Concept of Sin*, 89.
11. Pieper, *Concept of Sin*, 9.

martyrs go, he leaves much to be desired. An alcoholic, father of an illegitimate child, and, most damning in the eyes of Greene and the Church, serial committer of sacrilege, the whiskey priest seems less destined for martyrdom than death by cirrhosis. Furthermore, the circumstances of his death have led at least one critic to lump him in with Greene's suicides, a misreading I will address at the end of this chapter.

Having fled and almost escaped the lieutenant who wants his life, the whiskey priest allows himself to be drawn back into danger by a peasant Judas figure who has sold the priest out to the forces of the state. Knowing full well that he is being led into a trap set by his enemies, the priest goes to the deathbed of an American gunman because the man wrote a note asking for last rites. Even this attempt to save a soul is seemingly a failure. The dying fugitive cannot make a good confession, and the priest is reduced to offering a prayer for conditional absolution, a desperate prayer: "At the best, it was only one criminal trying to aid the escape of another—whichever way you looked, there wasn't much merit in either of them."[12] Following this failure, the priest is arrested, interrogated, and executed. Though a faithful woman records his name in the role of martyrs, the priest seems less assured of the nobility of his death. "Martyrs," he tells the lieutenant, "are not like me. They don't think all the time—if I had drunk more brandy I shouldn't be so afraid."[13] Rebuking himself for his past failures, the priest confesses to the lieutenant that his life has been dominated by the foundational sin of pride: "Pride's the worst thing of all. I thought that I was a fine fellow to have stayed when the others had gone. And then I thought I was so grand I could make my own rules."[14] This is not the stuff of triumphant hagiographies, but it highlights Greene's investment in testing the boundaries of sin. Following *The Power and the Glory*, Greene would turn his attention to a series of pseudo-suicides, characters who take their own lives, but whose conflicted motivations call into question our own impulses to judge their acts as mortal sins.

The Heart of the Matter (1948) takes the dividing line between the sinner and the saint as its primary subject of inquiry. The novel's epigraph, taken from Charles Péguy, makes that clear from the beginning: "Le pécheur est au cœur même de chrétienté. . . . Nul n'est aussi compétent que le pécheur en matière de chrétienté. Nul, si ce n'est le saint" [The

---

12. Greene, *Power and the Glory*, 191.
13. Greene, *Power and the Glory*, 197.
14. Greene, *Power and the Glory*, 197.

sinner is at the very heart of Christianity. . . . No one knows as much as the sinner about Christianity. No one, except the saint]. The novel's protagonist, Major Scobie, stands out as the most notable of Greene's pseudo-suicides because he so maladroitly fumbles his way between the competing desires of the sinner and the saint. Nowhere in Greene's corpus does the problem of suicide receive more attention and analysis than in this novel. Because it is so well known in this respect and critics have spilled so much ink in analysis of Scobie's suicide, I will limit myself to a briefer assessment than the novel deserves. For the purposes of this chapter, it suffices to point out that Scobie presents the most extreme case of the pseudo-suicide. A more or less practicing Catholic with full understanding of the deadly nature of his sins, Scobie initiates an adulterous relationship, then engages in a series of increasingly serious crimes to keep knowledge of the affair from his wife, including collusion with a criminal in the death of a faithful servant. Scobie's moral descent reaches its nadir when he commits sacrilege by receiving Holy Communion in a state of mortal sin and then compounds the offense by taking his own life in an elaborately premeditated and unquestionably voluntary suicide. Neither his sacrilege nor his suicide result from a disbelief in or hatred of God. Scobie dies of despair, a sin which Greene knew well and sought to better understand, and perhaps defend, through Scobie.

In the *Summa*, Thomas Aquinas devotes several questions to despair, and, perhaps surprisingly to some, compares it to pride. Just as people may pride themselves on their virtues and thereby turn what is good (virtue) towards a sinful end (pride), "fear of God or horror of one's own sins may lead to despair, in so far as man makes evil use of those good things, by allowing them to be an occasion of despair."[15] Horrified by his adultery and sacrilege, Scobie embraces suicide as the only means of (1) protecting his wife from knowledge of his infidelity and securing her financial future, (2) protecting his mistress from the pain of abandonment, and (3) protecting God from the repeated desecration of his sacrilegious participation in the sacrament of Communion. Put in these plain terms, his suicide becomes, like most sinful acts, clearly *contra rationem*. Scobie's wife is no fool and knows full well about his infidelity. His death leaves his mistress utterly distraught and at the mercy of a cad. And God? Who could be safer from harm? This failure of reasoning on Scobie's part led some early critics, including George Orwell, to write

15. Aquinas, *Summa Theologiae*, II–II, q. 20, art 1.

off the character as unbelievable. As Joseph Hynes points out, however, readers like Orwell miss the fact that "Scobie, for all his thoughtfulness and sensitivity, is not a reader of books. What needs adding is that he is not intellectual and not even especially intelligent."[16] When assessing Scobie's suicide, we must keep in mind that his reasoning is almost bound to be rather fuzzy. At the heart of this death is an irrational loss of hope, one that, in spite of Greene's persistent reminders of the limitlessness of God's mercy, provides a profound reminder of why the Church has historically condemned suicide so categorically.

Thomas identifies despair as one of the greatest sins, since it involves turning away from one of the theological virtues (faith, hope, and love) by "ceasing to hope for a share in God's goodness."[17] Though, according to Thomas, despair is strictly speaking less grievous than disbelief in or hatred of God, it is more dangerous to the life of the soul because it effectively saps our will to move towards the good by convincing us of the impossibility of the task. This analysis maps well onto Greene's imaginative representation of Scobie's despair and resonates with the modern psychological interest in perceived burdensomeness, the notion that many suicides result in large part from the person's sense that those around them would be better off if they were dead. Despair makes doing what is right seem nearly impossible and thereby tempts us into viewing our very existence as pointless or even vile. Of course, Thomas does not assert that despair, for all its gravity, results necessarily in damnation. In fact, his assertion that loss of hope is less grievous than loss of faith or love may help us to understand better the hope that Greene clearly holds out for Scobie's salvation, even if Greene's attempt to depict Scobie as a pseudo-suicide is ultimately unconvincing to some.

The novel concludes with a discussion between Mrs. Scobie and the family priest, Fr. Rank. Baiting the priest into sharing her resentment of her late husband, whose attempt to stage his suicide as a natural death has fooled no one, she maintains that "he must have known that he was damning himself."[18] Fr. Rank reminds her that the Church "doesn't know what goes on in a single human heart"; he also makes the somewhat unexpected claim that Scobie "really loved God."[19] Despite Fr. Rank's defense, Scobie's suicide rubbed many the wrong way, and not just among his Catholic

---

16. Hynes, "'Facts' at The Heart of the Matter," 717.

17. Aquinas, *Summa Theologiae*, II–II, q. 20 art. 3.

18. Greene, *Heart of the Matter*, 254.

19. Greene, *Heart of the Matter*, 255.

readers. For example, when the novel was adapted for film, the suicide was omitted altogether. Unlike today, the Hollywood of the 1950s shrank from depicting suicide, and the screenwriters for the adaptation of *The Heart of the Matter* chose to have Scobie die unexpectedly at the hands of a criminal. Greene wrote to director Sir Alexander Korda about the proposed changes and implored him to keep the suicide by having Scobie leave his revolver home and intentionally take a bullet in the line of duty. Then, surprisingly, Greene argued that such an ending would be happier than the accidental death planned by the screenwriters:

> We then have the priest's commentary and rebuke of Mrs. Scobie as at the end of the book. Not only does the film become more controversial and more interesting, but the ending is far less melancholy than if we simply leave it at the death.[20]

It seems clear that, at least in 1952, Greene considered the conclusion of his novel to be, if not happy, at least happier than an ending that saw Scobie die with no commentary on the mystery of God's mercy.

As many Catholic readers have pointed out, Greene's tentative apologia for Scobie via Fr. Rank risks glossing the fact the Scobie has chosen to express his love for God in an undeniably deficient way. When Evelyn Waugh reviewed *The Heart of the Matter*, he, guided by the epigraph from Péguy quoted earlier, tentatively posited that Greene was setting Scobie up as a kind of saint. Rejecting this reading out of hand in a personal letter to Waugh, Greene wrote that "I did not regard Scobie as a saint, & his offering his damnation up was intended to show how muddled a mind full of good will could become when once 'off the rails.'"[21] Authorial intent aside, Greene's assessment of his own character is true to the text itself. Scobie is indeed muddled by the novel's conclusion; nevertheless, Fr. Rank's defense of Scobie rings true in two senses. First, we must remember Pieper's insistence that sin "really refers to that place where each human being lives in the innermost secret cell of his person, a place to which no one else has any access whatever." Second, it is undeniable that God's mercy extends beyond the bounds of our meager knowing. Michael Brennan concludes that Greene "went to considerable lengths in the final scene to ensure that the fate of Scobie's soul, in accordance with Catholic teaching, was not a matter upon which any reader could

20. Greene, *Graham Greene*, 201.

21. Greene, *Graham Greene*, 160.

pass ultimate judgement."[22] Still, it's no accident that Greene's Catholic readers have been repeatedly alarmed by the extent to which the novelist takes his presumption, his almost scandalous reliance on God's mercy. Ultimately, what saves Greene's novel and prevents it from degenerating into a quasi-nihilistic defense of suicide is his insistence on retaining the concept of sin in this and later works.

As if unsatisfied with his imaginative exploration of suicide in *The Heart of the Matter*, Greene reenacted Scobie's death under a different guise five years later in his play *The Living Room* (1953). The drama inverts the dynamics of the novel. The play focuses on Rose, a young Catholic engaged in an affair with an older, married psychologist named Michael. Unfettered by Scobie's Catholic scruples regarding marriage, the atheist Michael leaves his neurotic wife to run off with his young mistress. Rose does not fare so well. Following an encounter with Michael's wife in which the woman threatens to commit suicide with a handful of pills, Rose can no longer evade the disastrous consequences of her affair. In a tumultuous conversation with her uncle, the crippled Fr. Browne, Rose rejects his somewhat unconvincing pleadings that she end her affair and take comfort in prayer and the Mass. After an even more unconvincing declaration of her disbelief in God, she attempts to pray the Our Father while swallowing the pills left behind by Michael's wife. Rose's failed prayer calls to mind Scobie's attempts to say a Hail Mary and Act of Contrition while dying. Likewise, the play's final scene recapitulates the denouement of *The Heart of the Matter*. In it, Michael confronts Fr. Browne with the Church's condemnation of suicide, to which the old priest responds, "We aren't as stupid as you think us. Nobody claims we can know what she thought at the end. Only God was with her at the end."[23] Echoing Fr. Rank, Fr. Browne rejects what he sees as an oversimplification of Church teaching by drawing attention back to the nature of sin as something unknowable occurring, to revert to Pieper's phrase, in "the innermost secret cell of his person." The danger of such an assertion, of course, is that it invites misreading by critics who would like to recruit Greene as a nihilist in papist's clothing undermining the very notion of sin, which is just what happened.

Following the first performances of *The Living Room*, Greene sat down with *The Paris Review*, and the interviewer clearly stated his

22. Brennan, *Graham Greene*, 90.
23. Greene, *Living Room*, 124.

intention to explore "unknown things" about the author. The ensuing conversation had nothing to do with biography, narrative form, or
sex. It focused immediately on Greene's faith. Attempting to frame his
"Catholic" works as heterodox, the interviewer emphasized the subject of
suicide, implying that Greene's compassionate treatment amounted to a
denial of the reality of sin. The exchange is worth quoting in full:

> Interviewer: Scobie in *The Heart of the Matter* committed sui-
> cide too. Was it your purpose when you wrote *The Living Room*
> to show a similar predicament and to show that suicide in cer-
> tain circumstances can almost amount to an act of redemption?
>
> Greene: Steady, steady. Let's put it this way. I write about situ-
> ations that are common, universal might be more correct, in
> which my characters are involved and from which only faith can
> redeem them, though often the actual manner of the redemp-
> tion is not immediately clear. They sin, but there is no limit to
> God's mercy and because this is important, there is a difference
> between not confessing in fact, and the complacent and the pi-
> ous may not realize it.[24]

Though far from the most articulate theologian, Greene is clearly not on
an antinomian crusade against Catholic morality. He believes in sin but,
because he understands the limits of our apprehension of sin, maintains
his reluctance to condemn sinners.

Greene does not absolve his character of sin. Scobie has gone "off
the rails," in Greene's own words, and done terrible things. What's worse?
He has made any practical redress of his sins effectively impossible by
ending his life. Without a doubt, Scobie is conflicted. He does not seem to
desire suicide as an end; he thinks that he is damning himself to save two
women he loves. Scobie's despair may well be outweighed by his clearly
imperfect but real faith in and love of God, but we cannot help pitying
him for his loss of hope in a situation that could have been avoided.

At the risk of simplifying the problems of a complex character in a
great work of art, it is tempting to point out that Scobie's main failure may
be reduced to his fear of speaking openly and on mutual terms with the
women in his life because of his pathological "pity," a distorted version
of what ought to be a moral virtue. Devoted as he is to protecting them
from themselves and him, Scobie cannot achieve anything like mature
intersubjectivity of the kind that, as we will see in the final chapter of this

---

24. Greene, "Art of Fiction No. 3."

book, Walker Percy insists we need to overcome the temptations of despair. Michael Brennan sums up the predicament nicely: "Scobie's marital dilemma focuses on the psychological 'sin' of pity and its inevitable consequence, a fascination with the real Catholic sin of suicide as the only available release from personal crisis."[25] It's hard to imagine someone who wouldn't succumb to despair if he truly felt, as Scobie seems to, that only he could be counted on to set everyone's lives right without the aid of those very people. Only God has both the power and authority to miraculously intervene in the lives of created beings. Scobie doesn't want to die; he just doesn't know how to live in a world of love that not only extends out to others but also back onto the self.

But what wisdom can be taken from this insight? If we accept that the modern epidemic of suicide stems at least in part from the loss of a shared cultural abhorrence of suicide as a sin, as I do, doesn't Greene's counsel of reliance on God's mercy come all too close to our own popular paradigm? Should we treat suicide more like an unfortunate accident than a sin? Should we pity the sinner so much that we cease to even call sinful actions by their name for fear of misreading them? Following the lead of Thomas Aquinas, Pieper (no feel-good universalist himself) draws our attention to one of the core difficulties of the concept of sin. Starting from the premise of the essential goodness of the world, Thomas finds that the orthodox belief in "the ontological goodness of the creature" applies to ourselves and our actions, which "means that we must ascribe essential good to *every* act of will in the inmost cell of our freedom" including the "sinful deed."[26] So, if all creation is good on the level of being, and no created being can will something purely evil, how do we make sense of the sin as a willed act against God's order and treat it with proportional opprobrium?

In short, and in a manner that I fear will be all too short for the liking of actual theologians, we may put it this way: reason, not the castrated logic of the Enlightenment but the integrated *ratio* and *intellectus* of Christendom, includes the inescapable reality of conscience and provides us with a vision of the order of God's creation. We could, of course, deny the created nature of nature and insist with the atheist existentialists that reason is a fantasy that gives birth to the fantasy of sin. Since, as I discuss in a later chapter, Walker Percy addresses this literal absurdity at some

---

25. Brennan, *Graham Greene*, 83.

26. Pieper, *Concept of Sin*, 58.

length, I will leave it to one side for now. Greene, for all his vacillations of faith, continued to see God's created order in the universe. Within this order, as Pieper notes, our *cupiditas*, our "*already corrupted* desire to have and to enjoy," stems from our *superbia* or pride, that "well spring of all sin."[27] If we accept, as Greene's work implies, that no one can act purely on the intention to turn away from God because our wills are also always turning toward something else that is good, at least ontologically good, then a pure act of pride becomes seemingly impossible for anyone except a being of pure intellect, such as Satan.

From this vantage point, it is tempting to join Greene's interviewer from the *Paris Review* in perversely calling suicide an "act of redemption" since it appears to be more rooted in despair than pride and, especially in the cases of Scobie and Rose, still involves some love of God, however imperfect. Yet we must recall the novelist's cautionary response of "Steady, steady." We cannot close the door on the reality of sin so easily. Just because an outsider should not hope to know the inmost movements of another person's soul toward or away from God's mercy does not mean that reason cannot shed light on actions and separate minor peccadilloes from deadly sins with some hope of accuracy. We cannot pass ultimate judgment on the suicide any more than on the penny pincher, as either could theoretically be turning more radically away from God than the other in their actions. But any attempt to equate the two acts would remain abhorrent to our reason. Sin exists. Even while arguing for the possible redemption of his pseudo-suicides, Greene repeats that "They sin, but there is no limit to God's mercy." The fact that sin occurs in the innermost spaces of the soul, spaces often mysterious to even the sinner, allows Greene to entertain the possibility that his suicides have not finally turned away from God but toward him even in their despair. We can, and should, dare to hope for the ultimate salvation of any suicide, but that hope only makes sense if there is something to hope for, if we recognize that even the most pitiable acts of the will can be greeted with fear and trembling.

Politics and Suicide in *The Comedians*

Seeking to add clarity to his definition of mortal sin, Pieper provides a political analogy. We can easily imagine one polity ruled by just laws

27. Pieper, *Concept of Sin*, 62.

that are simply not observed or enforced strictly enough. Reestablishing order in such a state simply requires better adherence to the "healthy principle of the reigning laws."[28] Likewise, the merely venial sinner need only adhere better to a correctly ordered conscience, something that can be achieved more or less by the sinner's internal resources. However, the truly corrupt polity, like the mortal sinner, cannot hope to reform itself using its own internal resource. The Nazi regime, Pieper reminds us, was incapable of reform toward justice because its disorder emerged from fundamentally unjust laws, laws that made atrocities not only tolerable but necessary. In the latter state, the "evil lurks not in the 'conclusion' but in the 'principle.'"[29] Greene was fascinated by the moral lives of individuals within dysfunctional political regimes until the end of his career. We see the intersection of this fascination and his obsession with suicide notably in *The Power and the Glory*, and it emerges again in *The Comedians* (1966).

The novel takes place in Haiti under the nightmare regime of François Duvalier, better known as "Papa Doc." Its narrator, Mr. Brown, was abandoned by his mother at an early age and left in the care of a Jesuit school in Monaco. Though initially thought of as a prime candidate for the religious life, Brown left the Jesuits in order to pursue a number of failed business ventures, including a luxury hotel in Haiti inherited from his estranged mother. At the novel's beginning, Brown is returning by boat to Port-au-Prince after failing to find a buyer for his hotel in the capital. The story opens with two suicides separated by time but unified in the place of his hotel and in his memory. The first occurs in the narrative present as a direct consequence of Papa Doc's tyranny and may be, at least according to one character, the only truly venial of Greene's pseudo-suicides. The second suicide, brought to Brown's mind by the first, occurred before the ascent of Papa Doc and comes closer to a bona fide suicide than anything else in Greene's corpus. As if to highlight the moral shortcoming of both acts, Greene concludes his novel by presenting us with an example of suicidal heroism from the comedy's seemingly least heroic character.

Upon arrival at his now-vacant hotel, the tourists having been chased off by Papa Doc's feud with the United States, Brown finds the body of Dr. Philipot, a government minister targeted by the dictator's

28. Pieper, *Concept of Sin*, 69.
29. Pieper, *Concept of Sin*, 69.

hit men, in the deep end of his empty pool. The man has slit both wrists as well as his throat for good measure. Rather than obsessing over this suicide, as Scobie obsesses over the suicide of Pemberton, the apostate Brown readily accepts it as part of the regular course of affairs in the new Haiti, and quickly takes action to hide the body in a shallow grave outside of town with the assistance of the Haitian communist physician, Dr. Magiot. While waiting for Dr. Magiot, Brown's narrative slips to the past and another suicide.

Before the reign of Papa Doc, Brown came to Haiti in response to a letter from his mother, the self-styled Comtesse de Lascot-Villiers. He finds her ensconced in her own hotel and engaged in an affair with her much younger employee, Marcel. Soon after Brown's arrival, his mother succumbs to a heart condition exacerbated by her evening activities with Marcel. Though Brown is mostly unaffected by his mother's death, Marcel blames himself, descends into a drunken despair, and hangs himself in the room he used to share with the Comtesse. Brown tells us that Marcel "must have had great resolution, for he had only to swing a few inches to land his toes on the end of my mother's great bed" (C, 83). Unlike his other suicides, Greene has very little to say about Marcel's death. Brown fears that news of the suicide will hurt the hotel's bottom line but seems otherwise unaffected. In spite of the muted description of Marcel's suicide, Greene invites us to compare it to that of the novel's other suicide, Dr. Philipot.

Dr. Philipot's suicide receives substantially more analysis, not from Brown but from Dr. Magiot, the most philosophically sophisticated character in the novel.

> Doctor Magiot pronounced a short carefully phrased discourse over the dead. "However great a man's fear of life," Doctor Magiot said, "suicide remains the courageous act, the clear-headed act of the mathematician. The suicide has judged by the laws of chance—so many odds against one that to live will be more miserable than to die. His sense of mathematics is greater than his sense of survival. But think how a sense of survival must clamour to be heard at the last moment, what excuses it must present of a totally unscientific nature." (C, 92)

A communist who has lost faith in both Catholicism and voodoo, Dr. Magiot has embraced the materialism of Marx. When Brown appeals to religion and expresses surprise at the doctor's seeming admiration for the dead man's resolve, Magiot reminds his fellow ex-Catholic about the distinction between mortal and venial sin. He insists that Dr. Philipot did not take his life because of theological despair: "In this despair, there was nothing theological. Poor fellow, he was breaking a rule. He was eating meat on Friday" (*C*, 92). In what should be an unsurprising move at this point, Greene both undercuts the purely materialist account of suicide by introducing sin into the discourse, and refuses to label the suicide in question as a mortal sin. Fearing not only the unimaginable torture sure to be inflicted on him by Papa Doc's men, but also desperate to save his family from the same fate, Philipot took his life.

Once again, Greene makes intent the thin edge of the wedge of salvation by suggesting that Philipot's suicide ought to be considered a venial act because it did not emanate from any desire to reject God; however, in doing so, he, intentionally or otherwise, reminds us of the danger of the purely materialist account of suicide. If, like Dr. Magiot, we treat suicide as the courageous "clear-headed act of the mathematician," then life becomes reduced to the level of a hedonic calculus. Dr. Philipot took his life so that the Tonton Macoute would not butcher his family. Marcel took his life to end the pain of lost love and the shame and guilt of having precipitated that loss. Both acts required formidable determination. Neither act was, as far as we know, motivated by a theological despair.

It is tempting once again to treat Greene as a would-be relativist so intent on forgiving his characters that he abandons distinctions between good and evil. While he consistently wishes to justify his pseudo-suicides, he also consistently holds up examples of flawed characters actively pursuing a higher good in a vicious world. In *The Power and the Glory*, he gives us the whiskey priest. In *The Comedians*, he gives us the unlikely figure of "Major" Jones, a surprisingly lovable Anglo-Indian con artist who attempts first to defraud and then to overthrow Papa Doc's government. Jones has two dreams. One is to own a luxury golf course. The other is to be the war hero he has long pretended to be. Though risible because of his compulsive lying and boasting about his imagined military campaign in the Pacific theater, Jones ultimately resembles the whiskey priest in his willingness to die for a higher ideal, even if that ideal remains vague and almost absurd in his case. Jones's death invites comparison with the novel's suicides and suggests a higher calling for human fortitude than the willingness to overcome the animal "sense of survival."

When Jones's plan to swindle Papa Doc collapses, so does his dream of the luxury golf course. Brown helps him find shelter in the South American embassy. The ambassador's wife, with whom Brown has been carrying on a lengthy affair, takes such a liking to Jones that Brown talks the fake war hero into joining the guerilla insurgency against Papa Doc. Misadventure ensues when they attempt to rendezvous with the guerillas, and Brown eventually confesses that he has no jungle fighting experience. He does have flat feet, a condition that excluded him from military service in the past and will prove fatal in the near future. Huddled together in a dark cemetery hiding from the authorities and waiting for daybreak, Brown and Jones engage in an extended confession in which the phony major reveals his inner self to the might-have-been priest. Jones, to no one's surprise, confesses that he served no military function in the war but merely arranged entertainment for the troops back at base. But, in that environment, Jones felt the pull of a vocation:

> You know, there had been times in Imphal when I almost wished the Japs would reach us. The authorities would have armed even the camp-followers then. . . . After all I had a uniform. A lot of unprofessionals do well in war, don't they? . . . You can feel a vocation, can't you, even if you can't practice it? (C, 169)

On one level, Jones's sense of vocation to military service seems utterly absurd, but, compared to Brown's lifelong devotion to profit and evasion of anything like a vocation, as a priest, a husband, a father, Jones's calling appears more comic, in the Christian sense, than absurd, in the existentialist sense. He is attempting to conform his life to something higher in the essence of his being, not flailing aimlessly in a meaningless world.

Brown deposits Jones with the guerillas, who are led by young Philipot, nephew of the same Dr. Philipot who committed suicide in the pool at the novel's opening. Brown then flees to the Dominican Republic. There, some time later, he meets the broken remnants of the guerillas as they limp across the border. From Philipot, he learns of Jones's death. After weeks in the bush, their group suffered an ambush and had to flee. Jones, practically crippled by his flat feet, "found what he called a good place. He said he'd keep the soldiers off till we had time to reach the road" (C, 287). Philipot dreams of raising a monument to Jones and writing to the Queen of England about his bravery; however, aware of Jones's dicey past and dubious military credentials, Brown cannot share Philipot's blind admiration of the man.

Jones's death could run the risk of seeming utterly farcical were it not for the sermon of a young priest at the collective funeral for the dead—though not a Catholic, Jones is included "out of courtesy" (C, 287).

The homily focuses on St. Thomas the Apostle's assertion, "Let us go up to Jerusalem and die with him." Greene does not provide the context for this line, but I will. Jesus has decided to go to Jerusalem to tend to his dying friend Lazarus. Knowing that their leader will likely face death at the hands of his enemies if he goes to the city, Thomas encourages his fellow disciples to follow Jesus into mortal danger. The priest's homily is worth quoting at some length, as it helps to frame the seeming absurdity of Jones's life within the larger comedy of the Gospels:

> The Church is in the world, it is part of the suffering of the world, and though Christ condemned the disciple who struck off the ear of the high priest's servant, our hearts go out in sympathy to all who are moved to violence by the suffering of others. The Church condemns violence, but it condemns indifference more harshly. Violence can be the expression of love, indifference never. One is an imperfection of charity, the other the perfection of egoism. (C, 288)

Unable to actually condone violence, the priest nevertheless draws a clear distinction between violence done in service to some greater good and the apathy of "the cold and the craven" (C, 288), a position not wholly inconsistent with Catholic teaching but certainly controversial.

This sermon helps in understanding Greene's sympathy for his pseudo-suicides. For all their failings, they cannot be said to have gone the way of Dante's lukewarm neutrals denied access to either heaven or hell because they would not commit to either good or evil. They are wholly unlike T. S. Eliot's "Hollow Men" who say this of themselves:

> Those who have crossed
> With direct eyes, to death's other Kingdom
> Remember us—if at all—not as lost
> Violent souls, but only
> As the hollow men
> The stuffed men.[30]

Marcel, Dr. Philipot, and Jones, for all their failings, are not hollow men. The same cannot necessarily be said for Brown, who, at the novel's conclusion, finds himself bereft of the faith needed to pursue a cause larger than himself and making his way in the world as a mortician. Ultimately, Greene undoubtedly favors faith and action, however flawed in content

30. Eliot, *Complete Poems and Plays*, 56.

and expression, over self-concerned apathy; however, we should not be tempted to draw a moral equivalence between all those characters whose actions lead to their own deaths, as some critics have done.

Martyrs

In his book *Fictional Death and the Modernist Enterprise* (1995), Alan Friedman correctly identifies the larger contours of Greene's artistic project by asserting that the novelist defined his early fiction in opposition to the dominant aesthetic and religious tendencies of high modernism. Unlike many modernist writers, such as Virginia Woolf, Greene chose to tell stories in a more conventional, less avant-garde and experimental narrative form. He also put religious concerns front and center in his novels, judging his characters' actions and deaths "by Catholic rather than worldly criteria."[31] In his examination of death in Greene's work, Friedman attempts to reverse the novelist's process, judging his characters by worldly rather than Catholic criteria. This inversion leads him to lump in the whiskey priest with Scobie, Rose, and Greene's other suicides since they all "desperately seek death."[32] Aside from the fact that the whiskey priest, as we have seen, was a particularly reluctant martyr who did not want to die, such conflation of characters' motivations and acts, though understandable from a secular perspective, threatens to strip Greene's fiction of its moral nuance. For all his attempts to forgive pseudo-suicides, such as Scobie and Rose, Greene cannot help elevating even the most imperfect martyr to a very different moral level. The whiskey priest walks into the hands of his killers attempting to right his past wrongs by hearing the confession of a dying criminal. Even critics specially invested in the deep ironies of the novel and its subversion of conventional hagiographies can see in it a "record of spiritual triumph."[33] Though I doubt that a critic as astute as Friedman intended to create a total moral equivalence between Greene's suicides and his most prominent martyr, it is hard not to conclude that because sin does not exist for the critic as it did for the artist, suicide becomes an effectively neutral term in Friedman's assessment of Greene's work.

31. Friedman, *Fictional Death*, 230.
32. Friedman, *Fictional Death*, 232.
33. Grob, "'Power and the Glory,'" 1.

From the purely secular perspective, any person who acts in a way that precipitates his or her own death may be considered a suicide. We could be forgiven for wondering if, given the gray materialism of such a perspective, a life lived for its own temporary preservation before inevitable death is preferable to suicide in any meaningful sense, a theme taken up by Houellebecq in an earlier chapter. Calling the martyrdom of the whiskey priest and deaths of Greene's other pseudo-suicides by the same name may be legitimate in a world devoid of any possibility of sin or redemption, but it certainly demonstrates the poverty of a worldview that not only can't distinguish between the martyr and the suicide, but also cannot hope to grasp Greene's larger project of defamiliarizing suicide by presenting it to a modern audience within the context of the reality of sin. Greene attempts to save his pseudo-suicides, first, by demonstrating that their motivation was not to "see the last of everything" (in Chesterton's words) and, second, by stressing the mystery of God's mercy; however, he never attempts to pass off mortal sin as what Pieper identifies as its opposite, "the decision of the martyr or blood-witness."[34] A civilization that loses consciousness of that distinction should show no surprise when its citizens turn to suicide with the fervor of the ancient Christian martyrs, and it has little hope of dissuading them without recourse to a shared understanding of the reality of sin.

Greene is concerned with narrative's ability to cast doubt on what constitutes the sin of suicide as opposed to the act of taking one's own life. Any suicide, he seems to suggest, could be a pseudo-suicide, a person driven to self-destruction, but not by a desire for oblivion or by theological despair. Behind acts of self-killing, we find real people with often complex and contradictory motivations. Likewise, our martyrs may prove to be better witnesses to their faith than daily practitioners of it. Muriel Spark, who received material assistance from Greene when beginning her career as a writer, also sought to highlight the difficulty of distinguishing between the suicide and the martyr. Her work will be the subject of my next chapter.

34. Pieper, *Concept of Sin*, 89.

6

The Misunderstood Martyrs
of Muriel Spark

One man flung away his life; he was so good that his dry bones
could heal cities in pestilence. Another man flung away life; he
was so bad that his bones would pollute his brethren's.—G. K.
Chesterton, *Orthodoxy*

The Church of the first centuries, although facing considerable
organizational difficulties, took care to write down in special
martyrologies the witness of the martyrs. . . . In our own century
the martyrs have returned, many of them nameless, "unknown
soldiers" as it were of God's great cause.—St. Pope John Paul II,
Tertio Millennio Adveniente

IN HIS INFLUENTIAL APOLOGETIC work *Orthodoxy* (1908), G. K. Chesterton complains of a flippant "free thinker" who "said that a suicide
was only the same as a martyr."[1] Such free thinking was very much in
the air at the time. This baffling equation of martyr and suicide had recently found its most prominent academic expression in the work of
Émile Durkheim (1858–1917), a founding father of modern sociology.
Durkheim's 1897 book *Suicide: A Study in Sociology* cuts against the
grain of centuries of Western thought by defining suicide as "all cases of
death resulting directly or indirectly from a positive or negative act of
the victim himself, which he knows will produce this result."[2] Intent on

1. Chesterton, *Orthodoxy*, 131.
2. Durkheim, *Suicide*, 44.

adopting a purely scientific approach to his subject, Durkheim rejects the consideration of individual motive and insists that "an act cannot be defined by the end sought by the actor"; consequently, he lumps together the soldier facing death to save his comrades, the merchant hanging himself to avoid financial ruin, and the "martyr dying for his faith."[3] Blinkered by his own fascination with the measurable, Durkheim produces a definition of suicide that lumps together St. Thomas More, the Catholic martyr who opposed Henry VIII knowing that it would result in execution; Kurt Cobain, the front man for grunge rock group Nirvana who shot himself in 1994; and Michael Murphy, a Navy lieutenant who died saving the lives of his fellow soldiers in Afghanistan in 2005.

Not surprisingly, Chesterton has little time for such reductive thinking. Demurring with his usual gusto from any equation of martyrdom and suicide, he launches into a forceful distinction between the two:

> Obviously a suicide is the opposite of a martyr. A martyr is a man who cares so much for something outside him, that he forgets his own personal life. A suicide is a man who cares so little for anything outside him, that he wants to see the last of everything. One wants something to begin: the other wants everything to end. In other words, the martyr is noble, exactly because (however he renounces the world or execrates all humanity) he confesses this ultimate link with life; he sets his heart outside himself: he dies that something may live. The suicide is ignoble because he has not this link with being: he is a mere destroyer; spiritually, he destroys the universe.[4]

Chesterton is, in the ultimate sense, right; however, as we saw in our discussion of sin in the previous chapter, the human inability to read with certainty the interior lives of others limits the easy applicability of this definition. What if, for example, a missionary placed himself in the way of death in a foreign land when he could have stayed comfortably at home? What if a vicious husband staged a public martyrdom out of envy for his wife's worldly success? Muriel Spark, the often controversial writer at the heart of the Catholic literary revival of the mid-twentieth century, composed novels that force readers into narratives in which characters question the boundary between martyrdom and suicide. Though the epistemological challenge presented by these novels would strike Durkheim as immaterial, it matters a great deal to Spark. She

3. Durkheim, *Suicide*, 43.
4. Chesterton, *Orthodoxy*, 131.

rejects our all-too-common deterministic understanding of suicide as a pure product of mental illness, a death caused by an emotional-chemical imbalance rather than cancer or a brain aneurism. Acknowledging the reality and horror of volitional self-destruction, she elevates its opposite, volitional self-sacrifice, even while testing the limits of the liminal space between the two. In doing so, she adds clarity to our vision of what a martyr is, can be, and ought to be.

Martyrdom as Theo-drama in *The Girls of Slender Means*

Spark's first substantial exploration of the boundaries between martyrdom and suicide came in 1963 in *The Girls of Slender Means*. The novel follows the lives of the poor ladies of the May of Teck club, a social support organization for young women forced to leave their families in the country and work in London, in the months between VE Day and VJ Day in 1945. On this level, the book presents a quintessentially Sparkian tableau of young women in an economically depressed post-war England, who must attempt not only to survive on scarce rations but to do so while avoiding the carbohydrates and fats that will ruin their chances of landing desirable boyfriends. The ladies lend dresses, barter for soap, cultivate American GIs for good times and extra provisions. They live in a kind of worldly cloister and demonstrate the profound difference between poverty and want: "As they realized themselves in varying degrees, few people alive at the time were more delightful, more ingenious, more movingly lovely, and, as it might happen, more savage, than the girls of slender means" (*GSM*, 4).

Charming and humorous as this main narrative is, the novel would lack any deeper metaphysical consequence were it not for the framing narrative, which begins in 1963. A former member of the club turned columnist, Jane Wright, telephones various people from her past with news of the apparent martyrdom of Nicholas Farringdon, in Haiti. Jane, a bit dubious about the affair since she knew Fr. Farringdon in her youth as a handsome, bisexual anarchist poet who snuck the beautiful but vapid Selina out of the upper window of the May of Teck club for rooftop assignations, reaches out to her former housemates for clues and context as she composes a column about and tries to make sense of the apparent martyr. As Spark's biographer points out, the author was "appalled" when her publisher attempted to market the novel as a "light-hearted comedy of manners," overlooking this framing narrative, which infuses the book with "an aspect of eternity."[5] Over the course of the novel, as we learn about the events of 1945, we see the Jane of 1963 slowly shift her thinking. She begins with healthy skepticism, opining that those attempting to make a martyr out of Farringdon will have to cover up his past: "I knew him well, you know, in those days. I expect they'll hush it all up, about those days, if they want to make a martyr story" (5).

From the outset, Jane and Spark's other characters betray their belief that martyrs are, at least some of the time, manufactured—that the Church and press collaborate to whitewash lives in order to turn people into martyrs, even those who may have sought death intentionally. In the primary 1945 narrative, the young Jane Wright works for a publisher interested in lowballing Nicholas for the publication rights to his forthcoming work of political philosophy, *The Sabbath Notebooks*. Jane turns to Rudi Bittesch, a mutual acquaintance, for a psychological account of Nicholas that might help her to direct the negotiations. According to Rudi, Nicholas's work, though purportedly radical, "smells religious" and emanates from the mind of a confused man who will "finish up a reactionary Catholic" (57). Even before the outbreak of war, Nicholas, the misfit son of a respectable English family, was torn between religion and his own death drive: "he could never make up his mind between suicide and an equally drastic course of action known as Father D'Arcy. Rudi explained that the latter was a Jesuit philosopher who had the monopoly for converting the English intellectuals" (63). Like so many characters in modern Catholic fiction, Nicholas finds himself torn between the foot of the cross and the barrel of the gun. Spark, clearly aware of this dilemma, feints toward a faux resolution. She invites readers to resolve the dilemma by treating Nicholas' future martyrdom as a kind of religiously sanctioned suicide.

We are alerted to the danger of this too-tidy resolution by one of Spark's favorite ploys: she puts the misguided interpretation in the mouth of an eminently respectable English person. In this case, the faulty interpretation comes to Jane from Lady Julia Markham, head of the management committee for the May of Teck Club. Lady Julia's contact at the Foreign Office unofficially relates that Nicholas was "making a complete nuisance of himself, preaching against the local superstitions" (149). Her source reports that the priest "had several warnings" and "got what he

---

5. Stannard, *Muriel Spark*, 294.

asked for" (149). We could be forgiven for questioning the reasons for Nicholas's decision to continue to preach his faith in the face of death. Martyrdom, after all, ought not to be sought for the sake of fame or oblivion, but for the sake of witnessing to God. T. S. Eliot's play *Murder in the Cathedral* draws this conundrum into stark relief.

Spark admired Eliot as a poet and dramatist. One of her published *Pensées* from 1953 credits him with having the power to liberate the language of younger poets "from a cramped and narrow range of poetic possibility."[6] That same year, in a review of Eliot's *The Confidential Clerk*, she identified it as "a Catholic play, meaning that it presents situations which are wholly true, and they are everywhere and always true."[7] In words that could equally be applied to *Murder in the Cathedral*, she concludes by claiming that the "play gives a renewed life to some points of Christian teaching which seem irrelevant to the modern world."[8] This is certainly the case with Eliot's treatment of martyrdom in *Murder*. The play's central figure, Thomas Becket, soon to be murdered by the king's knights for defending the rights of the Church against the power of the state, wrestles with a series of demonic tempters. They approach Becket with offers of pleasure, power, wealth, fame, and security, all of which he scorns with seeming ease. But the final tempter offers him an enticing vision:

> King is forgotten, when another shall come:
> Saint and Martyr rule from the tomb.
> Think, Thomas, think of enemies dismayed.
> Creeping in penance, frightened of a shade.[9]

What greater triumph than to force all of one's enemies and their descendants to venerate one as a saint? The allure of a false martyrdom becomes the central agon of the rest of the drama, and the glory of Thomas's true martyrdom becomes the play's central glory. More on this later. For now, it is enough to note that Eliot's concern with true and false martyrdom helps to shed light on a tension at the center of Spark's *The Girls of Slender Means*, which begins and ends with contemplation of the motivations behind Nicholas's death.

---

6. Spark, *Informal Air*, 87.
7. Spark, *Informal Air*, 90.
8. Spark, *Informal Air*, 91.
9. Eliot, *Murder in the Cathedral*, 37.

Several characters link Nicholas's conversion from suicidal anarchist to missionary to the climactic event of the main 1945 narrative. In late July, as the allies prepare to drop the first atomic bombs on Japan and the world stands partly in ruins, an unexpected explosion and fire at the club leave several girls, including Jane, trapped on an upper floor. Nicholas assists with the rescue effort, but they are unable to save Joanna Childe, the daughter of a country curate living in London to become an elocution teacher. Joanna's perfect voice emerges throughout the novel spouting bits of Coleridge, Shakespeare, the Bible, and the Book of Common Prayer. On the night of the fire, she begins compulsively reciting the psalms from that day's liturgy. As the house burns, she proclaims Psalm 127: "*Except the Lord build the house: their labour is but lost that build it. Except the Lord keep the city: the watchman waketh but in vain. It is but lost labour that ye haste to rise up early, and so late take rest, and eat the bread of carefulness: for so he giveth his beloved sleep*" (164). The last one on the escape ladder, Joanna dies as the house collapses.

When Nicholas, clearly rattled by the experience, attempts to relate some of it to Joanna's father, the respectable Anglican clergyman seems surprised by his daughter's behavior and betrays prim embarrassment when Nicholas praises Joanna for her religiosity:

> Nicholas said, "She was reciting some sort of office just before she went down. The other girls were with her, they were listening in a way. Some psalms."
>
> "Really? No one else mentioned it." The old man looked embarrassed. He swirled his drink and swallowed it down, as if Nicholas might be going on to tell him that his daughter had gone over to Rome at the last, or somehow died in bad taste.
>
> Nicholas said violently, "Joanna had religious strength."
>
> "I know that, my boy," said the father, surprisingly.
>
> "She had a sense of Hell. She told a friend of hers that she was afraid of Hell."
>
> "Really? I didn't know that. I've never heard her speak morbidly." (171–72)

Blaming Joanna's restlessness for drawing her out of the rural idyll of her youth and into the disturbed life of the metropolis, he declares that real Christianity can only be found in small country parishes. Here, the elderly clergyman sounds strikingly like the good but jejune Edmund of Austen's *Mansfield Park*: "We do not look in great cities for our best morality. It is not there that respectable people of any denomination can do most good; and it certainly is not there that the influence of the clergy can be most felt."[10] Nicholas internally rejects this assertion, comparing it to a psychologist friend who revealed his plans to leave America because of the superabundance of neurotics. The physicians of the soul want only healthy souls on which to practice and salutary environments in which to save the already saved.

Spark's critique seems clear at this point. Christianity cannot be safely tucked away in little, respectable enclaves because it is a missionary religion that demands true fervor at least from some of its members. It demands martyrs in a world more suited to suicide. Her poignant dialogue between the elder Anglican clergyman and the young Catholic in anarchist's clothing calls to mind the aphorism popularly attributed to Gustave Mahler: "Tradition is the handing down of the flame and not the worshipping of ashes." Rather than carrying the metaphorical flame of Christianity forward in time, secular humanity has invented new world-engulfing munitions, city-eating bombs prepared to drop on Japan while a home for girls of slender means burns in Kensington.

By the end of the novel, Jane connects Nicholas's conversion and eventual martyrdom to the incident of the fire and quotes one of the maxims from *The Sabbath Notebooks* to make sense of Nicholas's dual nature, encapsulated in his spiritual attraction to the saintly Joanna and his love affair with the utterly worldly Selina: "He's got a note in his manuscript that a vision of evil may be as effective to conversion as a vision of good" (180). This may be the closest Spark comes to direct philosophizing in a humorous novel aesthetically opposed to such didacticism. Nicholas has seen plenty of evil. Suicidal even before the war, he witnesses enough of human suffering (the fire, a public stabbing during the VJ day celebrations) to make him thoroughly aware of the need for its opposite.

Nicholas's pre-conversion intuition that "a vision of evil may be as effective to conversion as a vision of good" encapsulates the power of martyrdom. The martyr provides a vision of the good in action, but his martyrdom is not self-imposed. The martyr does not destroy himself but is destroyed by the evil in the world made manifest through the actions of essentially normal people. The martyr's seeming fanaticism appears extreme because it rejects evasion. It may even seem at first, as it does

---

10. Austen, *Mansfield Park*, 77.

in Jane's case, like just another kind of suicide; however, conflation of martyrdom and suicide demonstrates a radical and dangerous misunderstanding of the two diametrically opposed acts.

Suicidologist Edwin Shneidman produced the research that gave birth to the now cliché idea that the suicidal person is seeking a permanent solution to a temporary problem. His famous list of ten "psychological commonalities of suicide" begins with the assertion that "The common *purpose* of suicide is to seek a *solution*. Suicide is not a random act. It is never done without purpose."[11] The martyr is likewise in search of a permanent solution. In this case, however, the problem is not personal mental anguish but the universal problem of sin and damnation. The object of the martyr's attention is, on one level, personal salvation, but also, on another level, the salvation of other souls. This is especially true with missionary martyrs like Nicholas, who are willing to endure the extremes of human suffering. The suicide chooses death, not desirable in itself, as the permanent solution to temporary suffering. The martyr accepts death, the unnatural child of original sin, as a temporary consequence of witnessing to a truth that promises eternal salvation.

To better frame this distinction between martyr and suicide, we may root it in one of the primary insights of Swiss theologian Hans Urs von Balthasar, the notion of "Theo-drama." Balthasar, in the second part of his expansive theological trilogy, lays out a theory of the theological act moving from aesthetics to dramatics to logic. Theology finds a beginning in the aesthetic experience of God, a Theo-phany in which we "encounter and perceive the phenomenon of divine revelation in the world."[12] The perception of that Theo-phany should rightly lead to a Theo-praxy, in which we are drawn into active participation in the drama that is God's action on the world and the world's response to that action. Theo-logy emerges when, "having examined this dramatic interplay," we "reflect on the way in which this action is expressed in concept and word."[13] Vital theological contemplation, therefore, must be inspired by aesthetics and animated by right action. Drama serves as von Balthasar's artistic analogy for the Theo-praxy whereby we actively play our roles in salvation history:

11. Shneidman, *Suicidal Mind*, 130.
12. Balthasar, *Theo-Drama*, 15.
13. Balthasar, *Theo-Drama*, 15.

The *good* which God does to us can only be experienced as the *truth* if we share in *performing* it . . . not only in order to perceive the truth of the good but, equally, in order to embody it increasingly in the world, thus leading the ambiguities of world theater beyond themselves to a singleness of meaning that can come only from God.[14]

In this dramatic arena, as Balthasar scholar Medard Kehl points out, "human beings do not stand there as spectators or puppets, they are drawn as partners of a dialogical event of love"; we only properly play our role when we freely allow ourselves "to be 'chosen' and 'sent' to 'perform' consistently the 'play' of God and his love."[15]

Within this Theo-dramatic framework, Balthasar looks to theater, both ancient and modern, to help make sense of death in general and the self-sacrificial death of the martyr in particular. Death, he tells us, "stands, unuttered, behind every play, and often enough it becomes its explicit subject matter. . . . For it is simultaneously the unavoidable end to which all are obliged to come, and the concluding event that a man can arrange—in suicide—and shape in manifold ways."[16] Though death presents itself as the "ultimate humiliation," it may also become "something most precious and noble" if the character in the drama "accepts it as the total offering and final form of his existence."[17]

Balthasar singles out the suicide and the martyr as those who express their "existential will" by either seeking out or enduring death and sees in their acts an attempt to "imprint a meaning, retrospectively" on a "whole existence."[18] The suicide may seek to assert his will through death. In contrast, the properly Christian martyr has a clearer sense of his death as a witness to a truth that exists independent of his will. Such a witness is a participatory act made possible by grace. Earlier in his contemplation of the distinctly Christian dramatic hero, Balthasar asserts that such a hero is always "situated in the discipleship of the Lord." In Balthasar's view, Eliot's Becket exemplifies such a hero. He demonstrates that "the testimony of the Christian life is a dramatic mode of the presence of his Lord."[19] This Christian approach to life transforms the suffer-

14. Balthasar, *Theo-Drama*, 20.

15. Kehl, "Introduction," 49.

16. Balthasar, *Theo-Drama*, 369–70.

17. Balthasar, *Theo-Drama*, 370.

18. Balthasar, *Theo-Drama*, 370.

19. Balthasar, *Theo-Drama*, 118.

ing of tragedy into a comedic suffering, and a "new dramatic dimension" emerges from the life and death of the Christian hero. Such a person can lay down his life not only to resist state injustice or secure the good of another but as a testament to the goodness of reality itself. Such a person perceives the glory of God and chooses to accept the call to witness to the truth of that glory by enduring death. Of course, the Christian faces a temptation unknown to others. The Christian can desire martyrdom out of pride and turn the greatest act of self-abnegation into the greatest act of self-aggrandizement. Becket crystalizes this dilemma in the most memorable line from *Murder in the Cathedral*: "The last act is the greatest treason: / To do the right deed for the wrong reason."[20] The climax of the martyr's Theo-drama comes when he or she submits to self-sacrifice for the right reason, fidelity to God's will.

On the contrary, suicide is perhaps the most spectacular manifestation of ego-drama, that false reality in which the individual asserts an all-encompassing personal will. The antihero of the ego-drama imagines himself the sole subject in a world of objects, the singular speaker of Macbeth's "tale told by an idiot." Balthasar takes an explicitly anti-Freudian position by rejecting the psychoanalyst's conception of the person as ego "doomed to be the locus of anxiety caught between the three superior sinister powers that conspire against it: the id, the super-ego, and the external world."[21] But this Freudian position, as I discuss in the introduction to this book, has become the dominant mode of self-understanding in the modern world. Can it come as any surprise, therefore, that suicide has become such a defining feature of the post-Christian West, and martyrdom has become incomprehensible to most? Stripped of God, or, in some sects, at least stripped of anything traditionally identifiable as the Christian God, the inescapably immanent self remains and either demands that the drama of life revolve around its will or despairs of an existence governed by anything less capricious than the freedom to which it is cursed.

Ego-drama defines the world of Spark's *Girls of Slender Means*. Each charming and "vicious" girl spends her days pursuing the fleeting goals of the undefined and ill-defined self, whether it be Selina's quest for sexual gratification from her many boyfriends or Pauline Fox's mad attempts to maintain her imaginary relationship with the famous

20. Eliot, *Murder in the Cathedral*, 44.
21. Balthasar, *Theo-Drama*, 513.

actor Jack Buchanan. Only Joanna and Nicholas glimpse the larger
Theo-drama of their existence. Joanna witnesses to this larger reality by
reciting the psalms as the house burns around her. Nicholas, exposed
to the awesome glory of God's revelation by Joanna's death, eventually
takes on his role in the Theo-drama forgotten by all those around him.
He does so by preaching against the pagan superstitions of the Haitians
who kill him for his troubles. Nicholas becomes one of the many "'unknown soldiers' . . . of God's great cause" of whom Pope John Paul II
speaks in *Tertio Millennio Adveniente,* his apostolic letter to the faithful
in preparation for the Jubilee Year 2000.[22]

Two things threaten to transform the Christian martyr's Theo-
dramatic act from a noble self-sacrifice into an absurd act of self-destruction. The first threat, most obviously, is atheism. If God is dead, then
the drama becomes a farce, though it may still point to reality by way of
a kind of inverted theology. Godot never comes, and the curtains close
on an even worse scene of absurd degradation than the one on which
they opened. But, at the time Spark was writing—and this applies to a
lesser extent even today—thoroughgoing atheists remained a minority
and nominal Christianity held a majority status in England in terms of
raw demographics. In *Girls,* we meet few committed atheists, but most
common people clearly live and think in a manner hardly indicative of
any religious commitment. The second threat to a clear understanding of
the martyr comes, less obviously, from a domesticated, respectable Christianity exemplified by nice country vicars.

Girls of Slender Means stands apart from the other novels explored
in this book in part because of its deft representation not of martyrdom,
but of the ambivalent response to martyrdom from supposed Christians.
By 1963, the "girls" of the May of Teck club have become the respectable
women of modern England. For them, as for so many today, suicide is
easier to grasp and make sense of than martyrdom, so they simply equate
the two and treat Nicholas's self-sacrifice as, at worst, a suicide by other
means, and, at best, an act of fanaticism. Jane's early conversation with
Lady Julia reveals the former attitude. Her last conversation with her old
friend Nancy, "the daughter of a Midlands clergyman, now married to
another Midlands clergyman," reveals the latter attitude (180). Unable
to grasp Nicholas's motivations, she writes them off: "I don't understand
these fanatics" (181). This is surely the language of modernity, a time

22. John Paul II, *Tertio Millennio Adveniente.*

in history when even Christians, adherents to a religion founded on the crucifixion and renewed throughout history by the blood of martyrs and missionaries, cannot comprehend the difference between the tragic ego-drama of the suicide and the comic, in the truest sense, Theo-drama of the martyr. They cannot comprehend anyone who, to return to Chesterton's definition of a martyr, "cares so much for something outside him, that he forgets his own personal life."

Martyrdom as Ego-drama in *The Public Image*

Five years after the publication of *Girls*, Spark returned to the subject of suicide and martyrdom in *The Public Image* (1968). Her inspiration for the book came in part form a disturbing dream about a baby, a suicide, and her despised ex-lover Derek Stanford. On first rehearsal, the plot of *The Public Image* sounds like a somewhat sensational critique of the celebrity industry. After years of minor roles, Annabel Christopher has become a successful actress living and working in Rome and navigating a world of paparazzi and gossip. Part of this success stems from her ability to cultivate and maintain her public image as the English "tiger lady," a woman of ferocious private passions concealed in public under detached and proper English manners. Key to the success of this facade is the fiction that Annabel and her husband, Frederick, are the ideal couple with a passionate love life, a fiction they attempt to maintain by having a baby. In reality the two are engaged in an unfaithful marriage of mutual distrust and resentment held together by the thinnest strings of codependence. Frederick, a failed actor and self-hating screenwriter, cannot stand his wife's success and decides to demolish her public image by committing suicide and orchestrating a series of events to pin the blame for his tragic death on Annabel. Attempting to paint her as a party girl and neglectful wife and mother, Frederick arranges for a large group of young bohemians to appear at Annabel's new apartment for a raucous party at the precise time he intends to kill himself. He also leaves behind him a series of suicide notes condemning his wife for participating in orgies and driving him to despair. In the wake of Frederick's death, Annabel spends the remainder of the novel attempting to control the narrative in the papers and save her career.

This melodramatic plot does little to convey the experience of reading the novel or the Catholic inflection of a narrative set in the central city of the Church. Though set in Rome, *The Public Image* makes little use of its surroundings. The majority of the interactions, with the exception of the description of Frederick's orchestrated party, take place between a couple of characters in closed rooms. As if to reflect the banality and shallowness of her subject, the false face that celebrities present to a world hungry to glut itself on the spectacle of gossip, Spark refuses to let the color, charm, and vibrancy of Rome penetrate the narrative and animate its characters—with one important exception. To make himself a martyr in the eyes of the public, Frederick chooses to kill himself by jumping to his death in the excavated catacombs beneath the Basilica of Saints John and Paul. In a suicide note addressed to his mother but meant for public consumption (an especially cynical move given that his mother has been dead for some years), Frederick attempts to write himself into a larger martyrology: "Pray for me. . . . Unworthy, I die with the Holy Martyrs in the hope of attaining Peace."[23] Near the Colosseum and built over the bones of two early Christian martyrs, the church stands as a monument to those who chose to live and give their lives within God's richer Theo-dramatic universe. Frederick's suicide note attempts to draw this larger Theo-drama into the infinitely smaller ego-drama of his life, a reduction made all the more ridiculous since the ego-drama is repackaged as a melodrama for the tabloids. Embittered by his failure to make himself the center of public attention and Annabel's success in that same realm, he intentionally reduces his life to a lie. This travesty of his "martyrdom" demonstrates the vacuity of egocentric conceptions of life and contrasts them with the vital substance of real martyrdom.

Unlike other suicides in Spark's work, Frederick inspires little immediate sympathy; however, I contend that much of the novel is dedicated to instructing its readers in a kind of rightly ordered pity that grasps the enormity of suffering and painful nullity that undergirds sin itself. Though we are tempted to treat Frederick's suicide as primarily an attack on his wife and her career, Spark repeatedly provides subtle reminders that Annabel's inability to pity her husband indicates an extreme failure to treat other people not as objects or characters on the self's stage but as other subjects, other persons involved in a reality given by God rather than fashioned by the entertainment industry.

Annabel first learns of the suicide from her physician, Dr. Tommasi, who brings his wife and daughter to the actress's flat to help comfort her

23. Spark, *Public Image*, 97.

and care for baby Carl. Dr. Tommasi takes Annabel to the hospital to identify her husband's body. Quickly realizing that Frederick's death will undermine their carefully crafted public image as the perfect celebrity couple, Annabel organizes a 2:00 AM press conference to counter the narrative that what happened was a suicide. When the doctor's wife learns about the impending press conference, she states the obvious: "This is ridiculous, for an actress to think of the public when there is a private tragedy. . . . It's unnatural."[24] Annabel responds that her husband would have wanted her to carry on with her career. Hearing this, the Tommasis's daughter, an ugly girl with an unspecified mental impairment, asks one simple, cutting question: "If that's what he wanted why did he commit suicide and make a scandal for you?"[25] The simple women of the Tommasi family are the only characters capable of confronting Annabel with the truth. The maintenance of her image and her career has played a part in her husband's descent into despair.

Though Frederick's suicide is perhaps the most malicious in modern literature, we are subtly reminded that both his act and his wife's attempted cover-up are sins. Both acts are *contra naturam* and *contra rationem*. As Pieper points out in *The Concept of Sin*, and as I noted in my earlier discussion of Greene, the sinner works against the right order of created human nature, and, thus, works against reason and against God. Whatever our surface rationalizations, we commit the most serious anti-rational and anti-natural sins because of pride, which often masks the turning away from God as a turning towards "freedom" or some other masking ideal. C. S. Lewis, one of Pieper's sources for *The Concept of Sin*, devotes a chapter of *Mere Christianity* (1952) to "The Great Sin" of pride. There, he reminds us that pride is "the complete anti-God state of mind" that places the self at the middle of a vast competition with the rest of humanity.[26] Because of pride, even the practicing Christian can forget about God completely by thinking only of how much more pleasing he must be to God. Frederick presumably would say that his suicide is serving justice by unmasking a sham actress and destroying the career that should have been his. Annabel would claim that she is perverting the truth to combat the injustice of Frederick's envy. Morally speaking, he and Annabel are playing analogous games, and both are losing.

24. Spark, *Public Image*, 72.
25. Spark, *Public Image*, 73.
26. Lewis, *Mere Christianity*, 122.

Like Chesterton, Spark sought to clarify the difference between Christian martyrdom and suicide for a modern world that was all too ready to conflate the two. The common grasp of this difference has not improved in the intervening decades. The early years of the twenty-first century muddied the concept of the martyr in the popular Western consciousness by tying the word to increasingly common suicide attacks by radical Islamic terrorists. More recently, Christian martyrdom has also been conflated with self-destructive acts of political protest. When, in 2024, US airman Aaron Bushnell set himself on fire in front of the Israeli embassy in Washington, DC to protest the Israel-Hamas war, a *Time* article on "The History of Self-Immolation as Political Protest" shockingly traced the practice back to early Christian martyrs: "Self-immolation was also seen as a sacrificial act committed by Christian devotees who chose to be burned alive when they were being persecuted for their religion by Roman emperor Diocletian around 300 A.D."[27] In order to make the obvious clear, the website Catholic Answers responded with an article titled simply "No, Christians Didn't Light Themselves on Fire." Unafraid to challenge her readers by presenting them with martyrs treated as suicides and suicides treated as martyrs, Spark helps to clarify the stakes of this distinction. Never a bland moralist, she invites us into a Theo-dramatic reconsideration of our lives through stories infused with a biting wit and dark humor that would have delighted the subject of my final chapter, Walker Percy, who confronted the modern crisis of suicide with his own dark humor, rooted in a particularly Christian existentialism.

27. Burga and Shah, "History of Self-Immolation."

7

Walker Percy: Suicide and Christian Existentialism

I tie the noose on in a knowing way
As one that knots his necktie for a ball;
But just as all the neighbours—on the wall—
Are drawing a long breath to shout "Hurray!"
The strangest whim has seized me. . . . After all
I think I will not hang myself to-day.

—G. K. Chesterton, "A Ballade of Suicide"

But, as was pointed out above, the degree of consciousness po-
tentiates despair.

—Søren Kierkegaard, *The Sickness Unto Death*

ARGUABLY NO WRITER WHO has died of natural causes can claim a more
intimate acquaintance with suicide than Walker Percy (1916–1990). Paul
Elie tells the tragic Percy family story succinctly:

> Percys were melancholy people, and their prominence seems to
> have compounded their sadness. There was a suicide in nearly
> every generation. One Percy man dosed himself with laudanum;
> another leaped into a creek with a sugar kettle tied around his
> neck. John Walker Percy—Walker Percy's grandfather—went up
> to the attic in 1917 and shot himself in the head. LeRoy Pratt

Percy—Walker Percy's father—committed suicide in 1929 in precisely the same manner.[1]

It should come as no surprise that this legacy left a lasting impression on Percy's life and work. After immersing himself in the works of the great existentialist thinkers of his day, along with a healthy dose of Aquinas, while recovering from tuberculosis, Walker Percy eventually turned to writing and the Catholic Church. All of that writing, from his first successful novel, *The Moviegoer* (1961), to his 1983 mock–self-help book, *Lost in the Cosmos*, took up, in one way or another, the problem of suicide. Percy, a self-proclaimed "ex-suicide," managed to break the cycle of self-inflicted death in his own family, and his work provides clues as to how other alienated souls trapped in the general malaise of a modern anti-culture might do the same.

Writing about the modern "Depressed Self" in *Lost in the Cosmos*, Percy begins by noting that "The suicide rate among persons under twenty-five has risen dramatically in the last twenty years."[2] This increase seems especially provoking to Percy given that young Americans live in a world of incredible prosperity.[3] He poses a question based on this propensity for self-destruction among the young and accompanies that question with several possible explanations. Here is a sample:

> *Question* (I): Are people depressed despite unprecedented opportunities for education, vocations, self-growth, cultural enrichment, travel, and recreation
>
> (a) Because modern life is more difficult, complex, and stressful than it has ever been before? . . .

1. Elie, *Life You Save*, 10.

2. Percy, *Lost in the Cosmos*, 73. Percy would not be surprised to find that this trend has only gotten worse in the succeeding four decades. In 2020, the Centers for Disease Control and Prevention reported that the overall US suicide rate increased by 35 percent between 1999 and 2018. Suicide now "ranks as the second leading cause of death for ages 10–34." See Hedegaard et al., "Increase in Suicide Mortality in the United States, 1999–2018."

3. Here, I should repeat a set of illustrative statistics cited in this book's Introduction. According to the most recent World Health Organization data, South Korea, one of the world's most prosperous countries, also boasts both one of its highest suicide rates, with about fifty-seven deaths per 100,000 people, and one of its highest rates of psychiatrists working in the mental health sector, with about six psychiatrists per 100,000 people. Syria, one of the world's most war-torn and least prosperous countries has fewer than four suicide deaths per 100,000 people and almost no mental health infrastructure. See World Health Organization, "Suicide Mortality Rate (per 100 000 Population)" and "Psychiatrists Working in Mental Health Sector (per 100,000)."

(d) Because, for young people, education is more inferior than ever, leaving one unprepared to face the real world? . . .

(e) Because belief in God and religion has declined and with it man's confidence in the place of the self in the Cosmos, in the Chain of Being, and in its relation to others?[4]

As he often does in *Lost in the Cosmos*, Percy saves the most devastating answer to his proposed question for last: "(h) Because modern life is enough to depress anybody? Any person, man, woman, or child, who is not depressed by the nuclear arms race, by the modern city, by family life in the exurb, suburb, apartment, villa, and later in a retirement home, is himself deranged."[5]

So, what are we to do with all this depression? Percy casually proposes, "The only cure for depression is suicide."[6] This solution smacks of satire, which is not to say that the author isn't in earnest, only that he has not yet shown his whole hand. Suicide as a cure for depression is an immodest proposal, but, unlike Swift, Percy isn't really joking. As he goes on to clarify, Percy is not suggesting the act of suicide as a cure for depression; rather, he presents earnest suicidal ideation, the authentic consideration of self-annihilation, as a wholly reasonable response to an absurd modernity in which our abstracted and autonomous selves lumber about the cosmos without tether or purpose. This darker version of Pascal's wager asks us to truly entertain the possibility of oblivion as a means of opening new vistas of understanding and, perhaps, renewing our connection to the God who is the source and end of all cosmic meaning.

Could this really be the argument of one of the great Catholic writers of the twentieth century? How could any Catholic recommend suicidal ideation as a solution to the problem of suicide? What had become of the ontological certainty of Benson's death-defying apocalypse or Tolkien's life-affirming Middle-earth? Had good old-fashioned nineteenth-century pessimism taken such root in the twentieth-century soul that even the luminaries of Christian literature worshiped at thanatotic altars? Walker Percy was, indeed, haunted, and perhaps even possessed (a key word in his semiotics of the self) by the longing for death. I cannot say in all earnestness that I would recommend his writing to those contemplating self-harm, because it often walks such a fine line

4. Percy, *Lost in the Cosmos*, 74.
5. Percy, *Lost in the Cosmos*, 74–75.
6. Percy, *Lost in the Cosmos*, 75.

between hope and despair. It is, in the final estimate, this almost conju-
gal (i.e., deadly serious and flirtatiously playful) relationship with death
that makes Percy the profoundest literary interpreter of suicide in the
most suicidal age in human history so far.

Marcel and Camus: Varieties of existentialism, varieties of suicide

Before we can appreciate Percy's theory of suicide and the various manifestations of that theory in his fiction—he is so much a novelist of ideas
that the distinction can be hard to draw at times—we must first attempt
to understand him within the larger tradition of philosophic existentialism. This will take some time and, necessarily, draw us away from Percy's
fiction for a while; however, a detailed discussion of Percy's existentialist
foundations will give us the vocabulary we need to better understand the
treatment of suicide in his novels.

Within the loosely associated group of modern "existentialist"
thinkers, none provides a more illuminating contrast to Percy than
Albert Camus (1913–1960). Though Camus was born just three years
before Percy, he died one year prior to the publication of Percy's first
novel, *The Moviegoer*. Notably, both Camus and Percy forcefully rejected
the title "existentialist" at different points in their careers. In a famous
1945 interview in *Les Nouvelles Littéraires*, Camus insisted that he not be
called an existentialist and referred to his *Myth of Sisyphus* (1942) as an
explicit rejection of existentialism. Percy, asked late in life what he would
prefer to be called rather than an "existentialist," responded with a typical
blend of laconic self-mockery and evasiveness: "God knows."[7] In another
interview, he defines existentialism, quite helpfully I think, as "exploring
man's predicament."[8] If this definition holds any water, then both men
would surely qualify as existentialists. Both can trace their thinking back
to that great investigator of man's predicament, Kierkegaard (albeit affir-
matively in Percy's case and oppositionally in Camus's). Both responded
to Sartre and rejected his famous dictum "existence precedes essence"
with its negation of any shred of essential human nature. They are linked,
furthermore, by their investment in suicidal ideation as a starting point
for philosophical inquiry. The Platonist, Taoist, Aristotelian, Thomist,

7. Leary, "Surviving His Own Bad Habits."
8. Gulledge, "Reentry Option," 300.

Marxist, or Stoic may take up the question of suicide by-the-by. Even the neo-hedonist, neo-pessimist, antinatalist philosophers of the twenty-first century write about suicide merely as a potential (mostly undesirable) means of avoiding the unpleasantness of existence. Only the existentialist philosopher turns to angst, despair, and suicidal ideation as a potential basis for all other philosophical inquiry. Camus infamously begins *The Myth of Sisyphus*, as we noted earlier, declaring that there "is but one truly serious philosophical problem, and that is suicide. Judging whether life is or is not worth living amounts to answering the fundamental question of philosophy."[9] Percy would agree.

Both Percy and Camus exist at least within the penumbra of existentialism and should not be allowed to shake off the term entirely. There, we may say, is where the similarities end. Though both writers take suicidal ideation as a starting point for existential philosophical inquiry, Camus embraces a positive absurdism that is contained within but ultimately rejected by Percy's idiosyncratic brand of Christian existentialism. Percy's vexed Christian rejoinder to Camus's existentialism, with its ultimately lame answer to the problem of suicide—"One must imagine Sisyphus happy"—cannot be fully appreciated without first grasping his substantial debt to the work of French Christian existentialist Gabriel Marcel (1889–1973), whose philosophy also employs suicidal ideation as a starting point for inquiry into the human condition.

John F. Zeugner's "Walker Percy and Gabriel Marcel: The Castaway and the Wayfarer" (1975) provides an important overview of Percy's debt to Marcel, especially regarding the notion of intersubjectivity—essentially, the love between two subjective beings that takes them out of the self and directs them ultimately towards the possibility of ascent to the transcendent.[10] Zeugner touches on the subject of suicide in passing and gives it only glancing attention. In his book *Fyodor Dostoevsky, Walker Percy, and the Age of Suicide* (2019), John F. Desmond undertakes a detailed investigation of the two authors' shared fascination with suicide as a signal malady of the modern age and explores the various ways in which suicides in the novels of Dostoevsky and Percy are "linked directly or indirectly to the major ideological issues—religious, philosophical, and political—of the times."[11] Desmond's study, though authoritative, touches only briefly on the influence of Marcel. This influence provides

9. Camus, *Myth of Sisyphus*, 3.
10. Zeugner, "Walker Percy and Gabriel Marcel," 23–4.
11. Desmond, *Fyodor Dostoevsky, Walker Percy, and the Age of Suicide*, 2.

distinct insights into Percy's theorization and novelization of suicide. Percy's biographer Jay Tolson describes Marcel as the novelist's "closest *semblable* among the French existentialists."[12]

Like Percy, Marcel was a late convert to Catholicism raised by a close relative after the death of his mother. He found intellectual sparring partners among contemporary atheistic existentialists, most notably Jean-Paul Sartre (1905–1980). Tolson describes Percy's attraction to Sartre in a manner that could serve equally well for Marcel: "Percy's enthusiasm for Sartre may seem strange. After all, Sartre's militant atheism could not have been more different from Percy's convinced fideism. But Percy found the difference a tonic and a challenge."[13] Marcel knew Sartre personally and found opportunities to place laurels on his opponent's head while simultaneously heaping coals.

In his essay "Existence and Human Freedom" (1946), Marcel places Sartre in the same influential company as Marx and Nietzsche and repeatedly praises his intellect and originality. This acknowledgment of Sartre's power and importance does not prevent Marcel from denouncing the former's brand of existentialism as a philosophy that threatens to drive the modern world further into the abyss of an "eschatological age," in which "at every level of being, a clearly traceable process of self-destruction is taking place."[14] At the heart of this self-destructive philosophy is the existential experience of *nausea* that emerges when I "apprehend myself as a *prey* of existence."[15] The abundance of being that overwhelms and inspires the poet or the pantheist becomes, in Sartre's estimation, an "obscenity."[16] The obscenity of existence helps Sartre to understand his nauseous response to the experience of being as proof of the fundamental absurdity of life. This revelation spawns what Marcel calls a "negative-enlightenment" or "philosophy of non-being" that rejects all attempts to illuminate an absurd existence.[17] All we can know for certain is that we are condemned to freedom, condemned to choose, and that "the choice is always absurd, since it is beyond all reasons, and since it is impossible not to choose."[18] What, according to Marcel, emerges from

12. Tolson, *Pilgrim in the Ruins*, 238.

13. Tolson, *Pilgrim in the Ruins*, 238.

14. Marcel, "Existence and Human Freedom," 48.

15. Marcel, "Existence and Human Freedom," 51.

16. Marcel, "Existence and Human Freedom," 55.

17. Marcel, "Existence and Human Freedom," 56.

18. Marcel, "Existence and Human Freedom," 81.

Sartre's foundational realization of the absurdity of existence? A long list of antipathies. His existentialism is anti-order, anti-family, anti-love, and anti-hope. Freedom is a life sentence; hell is other people; love is sadism or masochism or both or simply hate by another name.

Despite his repeated assertions of respect for Sartre, Marcel cannot help pointing out the fundamental chink, perhaps the gaping hole, in Sartre's nihilistic armor. Namely, Sartre's certainty of the absurdity of existence rests on his certainty of God's nonexistence. This certainty, paradoxically, requires that Sartre fall back on base materialist rationalism by asserting, roughly, that God doesn't exist because I cannot prove his existence with my five senses. As a consequence, according to Marcel, Sartre drops out of the existentialist project altogether: "he [Sartre] must take up his stand on the traditional ground of objective thought and declare that *there is no God*, as one might say that there are no people on Mars; but in that case he must give up the plane of existentialism and fall back on the most obsolete positions of traditional rationalism."[19] The importance of Marcel's insight here cannot be overstated. Using materialist rationalism as the basis for an existential metaphysics seems to me not unlike pretending that a nineteenth-century English classroom might serve as a twentieth-century Parisian café. It would be, to appropriate Sartre's own language, inauthentic in the extreme.

Marcel goes on to demonstrate that Sartre's confused atheistic, materialist, rationalist existentialism has dire consequences. Most notably, it undergirds a paradox of values. If there is no transcendent principle in reality, or if the transcendent is shrunken to the level of the attainment of a freedom that is inescapable anyway, then nihilism triumphs. This insight leads Marcel to question how Sartre can simultaneously deny "the existence of values or at least their objective basis" and still value, as he clearly does, any action over any other action. The contradiction is inescapable even with recourse to sophisticated word games about the difference between authentic and inauthentic being—terms which become equally devoid of meaning once we accept that we are condemned to a freedom the outcome of which is ultimately meaningless. Marcel affirms a very different position in relation to values. "I do not," he insists, "'choose' my values at all, but I *recognize* them and then posit my actions in accordance."[20] Sartre often speaks as if this were true even though

19. Marcel, "Existence and Human Freedom," 85.
20. Marcel, "Existence and Human Freedom," 88.

his philosophy denies the possibility of such truth by flatly denying the possibility of a divine foundation for such recognition.

It is worth noting that Sartre's position on the divine clearly shifted later in life to the extent that claims have been made for both his conversion to Judaism and even a deathbed conversion to Catholicism. Though both claims, particularly the latter, are disputed, we should keep in mind that the early Sartre whom Marcel critiques may not represent the philosopher's final word on God. Nevertheless, by insisting on the objective reality of existential absurdity in his most important writings, Sartre denies not only God but the whole project of existentialism and devolves into a pseudo-Nietzschean pseudo-rationalism. Marcel takes another approach.

According to Marcel, the solution to Sartre's practical denial of existentialism must be a transcendence of existentialism.

> [Existentialism] transcends itself . . . when it opens itself out to the experience of the supra-human, an experience which can hardly be ours in a genuine and lasting way this side of death, but of which the reality is attested by mystics, and of which the possibility is warranted by any philosophy which refuses to be immured in the postulate of absolute immanence or to subscribe in advance to the denial of the beyond and of the unique and veritable transcendence.[21]

To put it another way, existentialism must reject a crass materialism in favor of a more humble and more ambitious investigation of the mystery of transcendence or, to use a key phrase in Marcel's lexicon, "the ontological mystery." What makes the contemplation of this mystery possible? Suicide, of course.

Like Kierkegaard before him and Percy after, Marcel approaches the transcendent by the dark road of despair in his important early work "On the Ontological Mystery" (1933).[22] The modern person, in Marcel's estimation, has been largely reduced to his or her function. Our world "conspires to identify . . . man with his functions," both in terms of his individual social roles ("as worker, as trade union member, or as voter") and in terms of the general regimentation of his existence.[23] Not surpris-

21. Marcel, "Existence and Human Freedom," 88.

22. In Marcel's own estimation, these early principles remained consistent for the rest of his career. See Marcel, Introduction to *Philosophy of Existentialism*, 5.

23. Marcel, "On the Ontological Mystery," 11.

ingly, life "in a world centered on function is liable to despair."[24] At the core of this despair lies an "ontological need" that cannot be satisfied by the "degraded rationalism" that informs the "functionalist world."[25] This despair manifests itself in the emergence of the philosophy of pessimism, which holds, in essence, that being is really nothing. But, according to Marcel, despair, and even suicidal ideation, can serve as a springboard for pursuing the mystery at the heart of being: "The deathly aspect of the world may, from a given standpoint, be regarded as a ceaseless incitement to denial and to suicide. It could even be said in this sense that the fact that suicide is always possible is the essential starting point of any genuine metaphysical thought."[26] Here we see the common thread that connects Marcel, Camus, and Percy. All three understand the contemplation of suicide as an existential touchstone. Thinking of the ultimate act of despair calls us into radical contact with the stakes of our own existence. For Marcel, suicidal ideation makes possible one approach to the ontological mystery. The approach is perilous. We can give in to despair and become part and parcel with the "era of despair" in which we live.[27] Yet, the realization of despair leaves us open to the virtue residing in the heart of the ontological mystery, hope.

Hope, in Marcel's estimation, springs from humble acceptance that we must draw strength and sustenance from something outside of ourselves. Humanity increasingly places its reserves of optimism in the realm of "technical progress," but "speaking metaphysically, the only genuine hope is hope in what does not depend on ourselves."[28] Such hope is grounded in humility. Pride rejects hope and establishes a "principle of destruction" that inevitably comes to be directed both outward and inward. Here I speak for myself in saying that Marcel's investment in humility seems to stem from his belief in the importance of the experience of "ontological need" as an invitation to exploration of the ontological mystery. Were we to draw all sustenance from the self (a relatively shallow well even in the case of the genius), we could not open ourselves to ontological need and truly pursue the ontological mystery. Despair, then, comes from reliance on the self and rejection of the hope that comes as a gift from the transcendent.

24. Marcel, "On the Ontological Mystery," 12.
25. Marcel, "On the Ontological Mystery," 11.
26. Marcel, "On the Ontological Mystery," 26.
27. Marcel, "On the Ontological Mystery," 30.
28. Marcel, "On the Ontological Mystery," 32.

It should come as no surprise that, unlike Marcel (and Percy), both Sartre and Camus revile hope. Camus goes so far as to identify hope as a kind of religious trickery and rejects it as an alternative to despair and suicide, preferring a positive absurdism that, in a process surely understood by no one other than Camus, who provides only the most elliptical explanations of its inner workings, results in happiness without the aid of hope: "One must imagine Sisyphus happy."[29] Camus may be able to square the circle of a hopelessness without despair; Marcel prefers to view hope as a kind of grace that makes both testament to the transcendent and communion with others (self-gift) possible. In "Testimony and Existentialism" (1946), Marcel makes a point of noting that his ideas about grace need not necessarily rely on the word's Christian connotations.[30] In other words, affirmation of grace need not necessarily be limited to believers. One of Sartre's greatest failings, accordingly, is his inability to grasp the grace of self-gift as anything other than pathology. Sartre suffers from an "inability to grasp the genuine reality of what is meant by *we* or of what governs this reality, that is precisely our capacity to open ourselves to others."[31] By recognizing the importance of gift, we make ourselves receptive to the existential possibility or "presence" and inoculate ourselves against despair and the suicidal ideation that led us to a contemplation of the ontological mystery.

Presence is an ontological state. Marcel defines it as a mystery but attempts to give it clearer shape by contrasting it with "unavailability (indisponibilité)," an alienation from others that is directly linked to despair.[32] Presence is a quality of reciprocity that cannot be reduced to a principle. It must be expressed existentially; it is "something which reveals itself immediately and unmistakably in a look, a smile, an intonation or a hand shake." As a consequence or expression of presence, the soul may become consecrated to others and, in effect, insulated from despair. Here I reach the summit of Marcel's thinking about suicide in "On the Ontological Mystery":

> [T]he soul which is at the disposal of others is consecrated and inwardly dedicated; it is protected against suicide and despair, which are interrelated and alike, because it knows that it is not

29. Camus, *Myth of Sisyphus*, 8–9; 123.
30. Marcel, "Testimony and Existentialism," 98.
31. Marcel, "Testimony and Existentialism," 100.
32. Marcel, "On the Ontological Mystery," 40.

its own, and that the most legitimate use it can make of its freedom is precisely to recognize that it does not belong to itself; this
recognition is the starting point of its activity and creativeness.[33]

Note that freedom is not a condemnation for Marcel, as it is for Sartre.
On the contrary, freedom is the experience of escape from unavailability
by means of true presence with and for other free beings.

Rather than identifying with a function or with possessions, the
free, present self participates in its existence by being for others: "The
most legitimate use [the soul] can make of its freedom is precisely to
recognize that it does not belong to itself."[34] In short, we penetrate the
mystery of our existence by loving. Marcel is quick to note that a prin-
cipled or dogmatic belief in something like an abstracted golden rule
cannot stand in for this vital, loving presence. Likewise (and here I'll
make a point not presented by Marcel but, I believe, in perfect keeping
with his existentialism) a base philanthropy won't cut it. The billionaire
who gives abundantly to humane causes but cannot abide most human
individuals, the scientist who strives to cure cancer as a concrete service
to an abstracted human species, are both perhaps more alienated than
the honest pessimist, whose radical proximity to despair and suicide
might yet inspire a turn to hope and presence.

Binx Bowling, protagonist of Percy's *The Moviegoer*, notices this
false presence, this pale imitation of love, at work in the testimonia of
the "nice," uniform contributors to the radio show "This I Believe": "On
This I Believe they like everyone. But, when it comes down to this or
that particular person, I have noticed that they usually hate his guts"
(*MG*, 109). Ultimately, the way of the free and present soul, the way into
the ontological mystery, is intimately social and "undiscoverable except
through love."[35] Anticipating the objection that his recourse to love finally reveals that his philosophy is nothing more than Christian teaching dressed up as existential insight, Marcel again insists that none of
his conclusions depends on Christianity as a necessary postulate, in the
way, we will recall, that he accuses Sartre of depending on a materialist
atheism as a postulate for his supposed existential discovery of the absurd
as the defining principle of reality. Marcel admits that "it is quite possible
that the existence of the fundamental Christian data may be necessary *in*

33. Marcel, "On the Ontological Mystery," 43.
34. Marcel, "On the Ontological Mystery," 43.
35. Marcel, "On the Ontological Mystery," 43.

fact to enable the mind to conceive" some of his notions; nevertheless, he insists that the development of his ideas took place some twenty years before he even considered conversion to Catholicism.[36] What matters, for our discussion, is that Gabriel Marcel found that suicidal ideation could be taken as one starting point for the development of an existential philosophy that affirms hope and love.

Marcel's existentialism explicitly defined itself in opposition to that of Sartre. Percy's existentialism, as I have already suggested, finds its inspiration in Marcel and its dark opposite in the work of Camus. Among the existentialists, Camus stands out as the signal philosopher of suicide. As we have already noted, Camus identifies suicidal ideation as the starting point of modern philosophical inquiry. He ultimately rejects the suicidal act; however, the path of reasoning leading to this conclusion proves so convoluted and contradictory that it is hard to imagine anyone prone to considering self-annihilation deriving much guidance or comfort therefrom. Nevertheless, we must follow the path of Camus's thought, if only to understand better the alternative road paved by the Christian existentialism of Marcel and Percy.

Camus rejects the idea that the meaninglessness of life necessarily entails that life is not worth living. "Does," he asks, "[life's] absurdity require one to escape it through hope or suicide . . . Does the absurd dictate death?"[37] His answer: certainly not. Hope or suicide is a false dichotomy. One can embrace the absurdity of existence without rejecting existence. Furthermore, the absurd man can, like the imagined Sisyphus of Camus's title, find a kind of joy in a life of the perpetual present. Sartre, Camus's sometime antagonist, sums up the point neatly in his review of Camus's novel *The Stranger* (1942): "The absurd man will not commit suicide; he wants to live, without relinquishing any of his certainty, without a future, without hope, without illusion, and without resignation either. He stares at death with passionate attention and this fascination liberates him. He experiences the 'divine irresponsibility' of the condemned man."[38] The absurd man will not follow existentialists such as Søren Kierkegaard, one of Percy's most enduring philosophical masters, by sacrificing logic for hope. Faced with the absurdity of existence and wracked by despair—an emotion that Camus insists (unconvincingly to my mind) we ought not feel in the face of life's meaninglessness—Christian existentialists make a

36. Marcel, "On the Ontological Mystery," 44, 45.
37. Camus, *Myth of Sisyphus*, 8–9.
38. Sartre, *Literary and Philosophical Essays*, 29.

"leap" by dressing up the absurd as the inscrutability of God and thereby affirming that "the very thing that led to despair of the meaning and depth of this life now gives it its truth and its clarity." By making this leap, Camus claims, "Kierkegaard calls for . . . the third sacrifice required by Ignatius Loyola, the one in which God most rejoices: 'The sacrifice of the intellect.'"[39] What results from this "existential attitude" is a form of "intellectual suicide" by which "god is maintained only through the negation of human reason."[40] Camus conveniently overlooks his own "leap," the one that brings him to absolute certainty about the absurdity of existence, the one that allows him to demand airtight reasoning from other thinkers while simultaneously denying the reasonability of the cosmos. He also overlooks the fact that his absurdism is vulnerable to Marcel's critiques of Sartre. Like Sartre, Camus relies on a materialist rationalism to provide the key postulate upon which his philosophy depends: the nonexistence of God.

Camus demonstrates the limits of his absurdism most profoundly in his discussion of Dostoevsky. Seeking to further illustrate his absurdist philosophy, Camus turns to Dostoevsky, one of the greatest literary analysts of suicide and the man who served as Percy's guide to that particular ring of hell.[41] Camus praises Dostoevsky for representing the absurd man brilliantly in his fiction but also derides the Russian novelist for crafting art that ultimately rejects the reality of the absurd for the illusory consolations and hope (the blackest four-letter word in Camus's lexicon) offered by religion. Because of this recourse to hope, Dostoevsky becomes yet another Christian existentialist in the mold of Kierkegaard, who must leap to God because he cannot abide the reality of the absurd.

This critique is, of course, painfully shortsighted. Because the absurd is the only *a priori* he can admit, Camus cannot engage seriously with any theistic existentialism even when he marshals the objective clarity to represent its claims accurately. Such is the case with his treatment of Dostoevsky, whose argument for the immortality of the soul Camus summarizes quite clearly: "If faith in immortality is so necessary to the human being (that without it he comes to the point of killing himself), it must therefore be the normal state of humanity. Since this is the case, the

---

39. Camus, *Myth of Sisyphus*, 37.

40. Camus, *Myth of Sisyphus*, 39–40.

41. Percy's debt to Dostoevsky regarding suicide has been exhaustively demonstrated in Desmond, *Fyodor Dostoevsky, Walker Percy, and the Age of Suicide.*

immortality of the human soul exists without any doubt."[42] As pure syllogistic reasoning, this line of thought may leave something to be desired; however, rejecting suicide as contrary to man's nature, a nature endowed in him by a supreme if understandably inscrutable creator, seems vastly more reasonable than convincing others of the meaninglessness of life only to turn around and insist that they heroically suffer the slings and arrows of outrageous fortune because they are capable of imagining a mythical figure (Sisyphus) doing so with a smile on his face. In short, Camus's faith in the absurd blinds him to all but the absurd. Having had the benefit of reading deeply in both Christian existentialism and its atheistic absurdist counterpart, as well as a mind humble enough for the task of synthesis, Percy responded to Camus's "one truly serious philosophical problem" by developing his theory of the ex-suicide.

Like Dostoevsky before him, Percy believed that ideas have consequences and that the modern age is tormented by the kinds of ideas that abstract us from reality. In this state of abstraction, we risk self-destruction out of pure disorientation. For example, Raskolnikov, the protagonist of *Crime and Punishment*, finds himself contemplating suicide when his attempts to transcend traditional notions of good and evil result in utter failure. Suffice it to say that Dostoevsky wrote about the death-drive attendant upon radical modern philosophies and ideologies at a time when such intellectual contagions were still primarily a disease of a particular intellectual class. Writing the better part of a century later, Percy concerns himself less with the pernicious effects of nihilistic philosophy on university students and would-be revolutionaries. His novels explore the mass cultural fallout from the triumph of these ideas.

This observation is not novel. John F. Desmond distinguishes Percy's interest in despair as a quotidian reality from that of both Dostoevsky and Camus, who explore suicide as a mode of revolt against the metaphysical order. Percy's protagonists "are more in revolt against the tawdry culture they inhabit, the absurdity of a culture obsessed with satisfying fleeting desires, while seemingly oblivious to concern for the ultimate meaning of life and human destiny." Their suffering stems "as Percy said, from 'ontological deprivation,' an unawareness of metaphysical reality, though they do experience, often subconsciously, a growing sense of spiritual malaise that is only intensified by the diversions they use to try

---

42. Camus, *Myth of Sisyphus*, 104.

to escape it."[43] As instructive as the intertextual relationship between Dostoevsky and Percy can be, I agree with Desmond that the latter's concerns are markedly different. By comparison, I would argue, Marcel's brand of Christian existentialism, with its emphasis on the mostly unmet "ontological need" of our self-destructive age, provides more insight into Percy's understanding of and response to the problem of suicide than the work of Dostoevsky. Percy's protagonists are not, like Raskolnikov, Christians corrupted by reading radical philosophy; they are born into a world already permeated by spiritual dysfunction to the point that nearly all his characters experience Raskolnikov's sense of divided self and his consequent psychosomatic manias, as it were, naturally. We need only think of the liberals (Leftpapas) and conservatives (Knotheads) in *Love in the Ruins* (1971), with their endemic impotence and constipation respectively. In Percy's world, the psychosomatic traces of metaphysical dysfunction can be found in nearly everyone, but only the sensitive have the sense to contemplate ending it all.

Percy faces this broken world of endemic despair, a world that he personally inhabits, from the perspective of a particularly Christian existentialism that both embraces and transforms Camus's absurdist philosophy. Camus's absurdism falls flat in both comprehending and refuting the Christian existentialism of Kierkegaard and Dostoevsky. Their theism acknowledges the seeming absurdity of existence without jettisoning God as the ultimate principle of reality; his absurdism cannot acknowledge God even as a remote possibility without jettisoning the absurd as the ultimate principle of reality. Fully aware of this tension, Percy repeatedly presents us with ex-suicides, people saved from suicide by the contemplation of suicide, who have unflinchingly confronted the seeming absurdity of existence. Rather than accepting that absurdity or fleeing from it into an anesthetized and inauthentic orthodoxy, they move tentatively, imperfectly, and painfully away from the existential naught of modernity and toward something like faith. None of his characters is finally saved—even his nuns and priests are wracked by demons and doubts—but neither are his characters who truly seek as lost as the damned souls of Sartre's *No Exit* or the absurd antihero of Camus's *The Stranger*.

Might the ex-suicide still conclude that the world is absurd? Surely. At that point he might decide, like Camus, to find joy by divesting himself of hope (somehow). Or the ex-suicide, awaking on the beach to

---

43. Desmond, *Fyodor Dostoevsky, Walker Percy, and the Age of Suicide*, 143–44.

a realization of God, or the possibility of God, may turn to hope, faith, and love. The absurdist's joy without hope, the Christian existentialist's hope beyond reason: serious contemplation of suicide makes both possible, or neither.

Keeping Quentin Compson Alive

Percy deals with suicide at least in passing in nearly all his novels and at greatest length in *The Second Coming* (1980), which focuses on a now middle-aged Will Barrett, protagonist of *The Last Gentleman* (1966), as he wrestles with a profound depression. It opens with Will's decision to end his life and then follows him as he wrestles with the memory of his father's suicide, attempts to disprove the existence of God by starving himself to death in a cave, and then finds himself saved by a toothache and the love of a girl escaped from a mental hospital. Relevant as *The Second Coming* is to the subject or this chapter, *The Moviegoer* strikes me as the more appropriate starting point for anyone interested in Percy's surprisingly consistent philosophical vision, and it provides the most succinct literary elaboration of his existential engagement with suicide.

In a 1984 interview, Percy places his first literary success squarely within the tradition of continental existentialist literature: "It was one of the first times that an American novel did what the European novels had been doing for many years—talking about alienation."[44] He compares his novel's protagonist, Binx Bolling, to Dostoevsky's Raskolnikov and Camus's Meursault. In addition to acknowledging his participation in this European tradition, Percy clearly outlines his debt to Southern literature's most famous suicide, Quentin Compson, the troubled scion of the degenerating family at the heart of Faulkner's *The Sound and the Fury* (1929):

> I would like to think of starting where Faulkner left off, with the Quentin Compson who didn't commit suicide. Suicide is easy. Keeping Quentin Compson alive is something else. In a way, Binx Bolling is Quentin Compson who didn't commit suicide.[45]

Faulkner's young Southern aristocrat is less an existentialist than a deeply disappointed romantic. Unable to realize a chivalric ideal of old-world honor and gentility in the face of his sister's sexual exploits and his father's

44. Gulledge, "Reentry Option," 298.
45. Gulledge, "Reentry Option," 300.

apathetic nihilism, Quentin does the "easy" thing, from the perspective of narrative, by drowning himself.

Binx, in contrast, possesses no lofty ideals capable of denigration by a callous modernity. Thoroughly a creature of his age, Binx is possessed by a despair predicated on nothing in particular and everything in general, a state of affairs terribly common among the increasingly depressed inhabitants of postmodernity. Today, we would be hard-pressed to find a young person contemplating suicide because his sister violated his notion of family honor by having sex before marriage. But it would be tragically easy to find men and women of all ages succumbing to the generalized malaise and despair that characterize Binx's life. As we will see, this despair leads to the morbid contemplation of death, but that very contemplation serves as the basis for his "search," his groping attempt to justify living. Ultimately, I argue, this search results in an imperfect attempt to address the unfulfilled ontological need that Marcel identifies at the heart of modernity.

Percy knew this need intimately and realized that few people in the post-religious, scientistic, materialist West are capable of meeting it by traditional means. He makes this point clear in *Lost in the Cosmos* when discussing the difficulty of what he calls "reentry"—the attempt by the modern person (be he artist, scientist, or "any person in the culture") who feels alienated from immanent existence.[46] In an "age of faith," humanity "perceived a saving relationship with God" and, therefore, "the self did not feel displaced, or if it did, it understood its displacement."[47] In our age, most displaced selves must attempt reentry with the aid of booze or sex or travel or shoddily appropriated Eastern spirituality. An increasing number turn to what Percy calls "reentry refused," suicide: "Suicide, strangely enough, though the direst of options, is often the most honest, in the sense that the suicide may have run out of the other options and found them lacking."[48] Reentry by means of what he calls "the direct sponsorship of God" remains at least "theoretically possible, if practically extremely difficult" thanks to the triumph of materialism and the obnoxiousness of most professed believers.[49] In *The Moviegoer*, Percy attempts to keep his suicidal protagonist alive without relying directly on faith in God, a thing mostly inaccessible to so many moderns.

46. Percy, *Lost in the Cosmos*, 145.
47. Percy, *Lost in the Cosmos*, 145.
48. Percy, *Lost in the Cosmos*, 155.
49. Percy, *Lost in the Cosmos*, 156.

He does so by drawing Binx into an existential quest that culminates in the seemingly simple but ultimately heroic act of what Marcel would call "presence" with another broken person. This experience of loving presence becomes the basis of hope in a hopeless world and may even serve as a first step towards a reconciliation with life and a genuine realization of the transcendent.

Binx Bolling may be trapped in a metaphysical malaise, his very self may be abstracted from the world, but he's unlikely to make a fuss about it. His despair lacks any sense of the dramatic but permeates every facet of his otherwise high-functioning life. An unimpressive member of his college fraternity and an undistinguished veteran of the Korean War, Binx resides in the middle-class New Orleans suburb of Gentilly, where, in his words, he sells mutual funds "to widows and dagos" (*MG*, 39). Binx is unexceptional. He pays his taxes, reads the newspapers, and generally drifts along in life. A disappointment to the matriarch of the family, Aunt Emily—"an Episcopalian by emotion, a Greek by nature and a Buddhist by choice" (*MG*, 23)—he has failed to live up to either his father's legacy by dying in war or his uncle's example by conquering life through unshakable affability: "Uncle Jules is the only man I know whose victory in the world is total and unqualified. He has made a great deal of money, he has a great many friends, he was Rex of Mardi Gras, he gives freely of himself and his money. He is an exemplary Catholic, but it is hard to know why he takes the trouble" (*MG*, 31). We should take this description of Uncle Jules as "an exemplary Catholic" with a grain of salt.

At its core, Binx's family adheres to an old Southern stoicism that, for all its nobility, cannot help being essentially at odds with the Gospels. In a 1956 article for *Commonweal*, "Stoicism in the South: Epictetus or the Psalms?," Percy quotes Aunt Emily's favorite line from the *Meditations* of Marcus Aurelius to make his point:

> How immediately we recognize the best of the South in the words of the Emperor: "Every moment think steadily, as a Roman and a man, to do what thou hast in hand with perfect and simple dignity, and a feeling of affection, and freedom, and justice." And how curiously foreign to the South sound the Decalogue, the Beatitudes, the doctrine of the Mystical Body.[50]

In his article, Percy takes aim at the racism entrenched in the hierarchical model of Southern Agrarian stoicism, while also calling Catholics to

---

50. Percy, "Stoicism in the South."

order for their own complacencies.[51] Of course, Percy's rejection of an ossified stoicism in favor of a vital Christianity carries with it profound implications about suicide. In the final analysis, Percy reminds us that the "Christian is optimistic precisely where the Stoic is pessimistic." Michael Cholbi's *Suicide: The Philosophical Dimensions* (2011) highlights the shift from the Stoic to the Christian perspective on suicide as paradigmatic of the larger shift in discussion of the ethics of suicide. Stoics, such as Seneca and Cicero, treated suicide as a rational option for those faced with a life dominated by suffering. For them the question of suicide was "a secular question of personal virtue, well-being, or one's relationship with the larger community."[52] For their Christian inheritors, suicide became less of a social and ethical question and more of a metaphysical one focused on the "significance of suicide for an individual's relationship to God."[53] Because most of his family lives within the earlier Greco-Roman ethical paradigm, treating Christianity more as a porch on which to socialize than a mansion in which to live, Binx's larger existential and metaphysical quest makes him a distinctly black sheep.

Binx's only hope for escape from the almost total spiritual malaise of his culture and the lifeless stoicism of his family comes in the form of what he calls the "search." *The Moviegoer* begins with Binx's recollection of "the possibility of a search," something he first intuited years earlier while injured on a battlefield in Korea: "Six inches from my nose a dung beetle was scratching around under the leaves. As I watched, there awoke in me an immense curiosity. I was onto something. I vowed that if I ever got out of this fix, I would pursue the search. Naturally, as soon as I recovered and got home, I forgot all about it" (*MG*, 11). The German philosopher Josef Pieper, one of Percy's many brilliant Catholic contemporaries, would have identified Binx's epiphany as an experience of wonder. In the second part of his seminal *Leisure the Basis of Culture* (1948), Pieper identifies the experience of wonder as the starting point for the philosophical act, an act which liberates humanity from the quotidian malaise of the world of total work, what Marcel called the "functionalist world."[54] Man may be drawn out of this world of servile existence by stepping "beyond the chain of ends and means, that binds the world of work,

51. For more on the racial dimension of Percy's argument, see Rosenberg, "Walker Percy and the Racist Tragedy of Southern Stoicism."

52. Cholbi, *Suicide*, 40.

53. Cholbi, *Suicide*, 41.

54. Marcel, "On the Ontological Mystery," 11.

in love" or by stepping "towards the frontier of existence, deeply moved by some existential experience, for this, too, sends a tremor through the world of relationships, whatever the occasion may be—perhaps the close proximity of death."[55] As part of his renewed search early in the novel, Binx spends a great deal of time watching TV because he claims "it doesn't distract me from the wonder. . . . not for five minutes will I be distracted from the wonder" (*MG*, 42). The "existential experience" that accompanied his exposure to "the close proximity of death," to use Pieper's language, initiated Binx into a world of wonder that forced him to reevaluate life as a kind of quest. "The search," he insists, "is what anyone would undertake if he were not sunk in the everydayness of his own life. This morning, for example, I felt as if I had come to myself on a strange island" (*MG*, 13). Coming to consciousness of the strangeness of his life, Binx can begin a search and perhaps escape despair.

Percy employs this exact littoral metaphor again decades later in *Lost in the Cosmos* to describe the existential state of the "ex-suicide," the person who has faced the often depressing reality of existence, seriously entertained suicide, yet opted for life. Here's how he describes the experience of deciding against suicide:

> Suddenly you feel like a castaway on an island. You can't believe your good fortune. You are . . . sole survivor of a foundered ship whose captain and crew had worried themselves into a fatal funk. And here you are, cast up on the beach and taken in by islanders who, it turns out, are themselves worried sick. . . . And you, an ex-suicide, lying on the beach? In what way have you been freed by the serious entertainment of your hypothetical suicide?[56]

Aware that he can take his life at any time, the ex-suicide can live his life. Though Binx has this same revelation while near death in Korea, he quickly abandons the search when life asserts itself again. Nevertheless, that one "existential experience" has drawn him into Pieper's philosophical act and made him aware of Marcel's ontological mystery. *The Moviegoer* follows Binx as he reawakens to that mystery.

In Percy's novels it often seems that only the most outwardly broken and death-touched characters recognize and can sweep away some of the malaise of existence. Binx, the survivor of a revelatory

55. Pieper, *Leisure the Basis of Culture*, 68.
56. Percy, *Lost in the Cosmos*, 78.

near-death experience in war, finds one sympathetic fellow searcher, his semi-suicidal stepcousin Kate. The survivor of a car crash that killed her fiancée, Kate, like Binx, awakens to an ontological need because of her experience of death. Both characters pursue the search down many blind alleys before discovering something like genuine hope. Binx seeks reentry into the world of everyday existence by seducing a succession of secretaries. Kate is subjected to the vagaries of one of Percy's favorite targets of satire, modern psychotherapy, which in turn drives her to contemplate and attempt suicide. Under the influence of psychological analysis, Kate experiences a pseudo-revelation that smacks of Camus's brand of existentialism. While meeting with her psychologist, she realizes that his admonitions to "live joyfully and as oneself" are meaningless (*MG*, 114). Tired of searching for the hidden meanings behind her life and actions, Kate concludes that at base "there is nothing" except a radical freedom (*MG*, 115). Not surprisingly, her enthusiasm for this positive absurdism quickly fades. Her momentary philosophical transcendence culminates in a crashing reentry that leaves her groaning under the weight of her self. What happens next is illustrative. Rather than arguing with Kate about her ideas or trying to convince her to "live joyfully," Binx proposes marriage. It's a somewhat lame proposal, but it shows a glimmer of an attempt to achieve Marcel's state of "intersubjectivity," to be for Kate as opposed to just being.

This first proposal fails; nevertheless, it hints at a better alternative to be realized at the novel's conclusion. In the meantime, Kate and Binx's reentry options, soulless sex and soulless therapy, continue to disappoint. Neither can reconcile the self, awakened to its ontological need, with a world dead to that need. In the end, their best hope lies in each other. Only Binx can understand Kate's insistence that "suicide is the only thing keeping me alive" (*MG*, 194). He can support her existence as an ex-suicide because he's essentially in the same boat, or, to stick with Percy's metaphor from *Lost in the Cosmos*, on the same beach. Their decision to marry at the novel's conclusion does nothing to guarantee material happiness. Instead, it offers hope by inviting them into Marcel's world of intersubjectivity; it offers them the opportunity to be truly present to one another, to be "at the disposal of others" as opposed to "captive" souls trapped in the despair that comes of living in contact only with the self.[57] Marcel argues that the soul set at the disposal of the other "is protected

57. Marcel, "On the Ontological Mystery," 43.

against suicide and despair" because it knows that "it does not belong to itself."[58] Presented with the chance to pursue the ontological mystery through an ongoing search and find something like hope in an imperfect but potentially salvific mutual self-giving, Binx and Kate conclude their story by beginning that search in communion.

Even at the novel's conclusion their road ahead is uncertain, and their existential angst remains. What matters is that their nearness to death and realization of despair open them up to the possibility of something more. They refuse to be distracted from or dispossessed of their angst and are therefore capable of confronting it. *The Moviegoer* takes its epigraph from Kierkegaard's *The Sickness Unto Death* and warns the reader that "the specific character of despair is precisely this: it is unaware of being despair." Binx ratifies this sentiment while contemplating his dead father's mistaken belief that a stimulating hobby might help pull him out of his chronic depression. "As for hobbies," Binx muses, "people with stimulating hobbies suffer the most noxious despairs since they are tranquilized in their despair" (*MG*, 86). Percy does not glorify despair, but he would rather not wrestle it in the dark of distraction. Binx and Kate reach an understanding with life because they are acquainted with death and, therefore, capable of doing life honestly and authentically. This is hardly a prospect to cheer the soul. Is realization of despair as a narrow road to hope the best modern humanity can aspire to? Percy does offer us a more inherently hopeful, if nearly unattainable, vision of a life more characterized by hope than despair, a life more present to the ontological mystery, a life (to use the metaphorical language of *Lost in the Cosmos*) in which reentry into the quotidian is made possible though "the direct sponsorship of God" (*LC*, 156).

The clearest example of such a life comes in the form of Binx's sickly, disabled nephew, Lonnie. The most radically dependent and outwardly broken character in the novel, Lonnie comes closest to what Marcel describes as "sanctity," and not because of some Tiny Tim-ish saccharine innocence. If innocence can be conflated with ignorance of sin and death, Lonnie is the least innocent person in all of Percy's corpus. Percy strongly implies that this fourteen-year-old boy manages to achieve self-awareness without becoming mired in the toxic self because of his proximity to death and his awareness of sin and grace as existential realities that can actually be discussed. Lonnie lingers on the doorway of death his whole short life,

58. Marcel, "On the Ontological Mystery," 43.

a state of affairs that offers him the chance to consider the condition of his soul with a ruthless honesty mostly absent in the other characters. When, driven by concern over the boy's poor health and physical weakness, Binx attempts to convince Lonnie not to fast during the Lent, the boy insists that he must fast in order to "conquer an habitual disposition" to envy (*MG*, 163). If what Binx calls "the peculiar language of the catechism" sounds quaint to modern ears, we might attribute this quaintness to the fact that Lonnie's language, unlike so much of what passes for communication in our age, actually signifies something.

Earlier in the novel, Binx connects his growing suspicion that "everyone is dead" (*MG*, 99) to the failure of everyday conversation to signify anything meaningful: "At such times it seems that the conversation is spoken by automatons who have no choice in what they say . . . and I think to myself: this is death" (*MG*, 100). Conversely, "Lonnie's monotonous speech gives him an advantage . . . his words are not worn out" (*MG*, 162). Because he is not dead inside, because he is present in Marcel's sense of the word, Lonnie can ask a real question, like "do you love me?" and elicit a meaningful answer from Binx (*MG*, 162). His proximity to death and awareness of what Catholics call the four last things (death, judgement, hell, and heaven) makes true presence and true love possible.

This essential insight—that love is the way out of despair—sounds far too wholesome and predictable for Walker Percy, the cutting and irreverent satirist who seriously proposed suicidal ideation as a first step to solving the problem of suicide. We must remember that Percy's investment in satire springs from a clear desire to put modernity to shame. But he is no reactionary. Far from retreating to a medieval Thomism (not that a retreat of this kind is such a bad option), Percy sought to wrestle with modernity on its own terms and, if not win, fail better—to misleadingly appropriate Samuel Beckett's memorable phrase. Unlike many of the writers explored in this book, such as Huysmans, Moore, Benson, or Tolkien, Percy is a child of existentialism who could not and would not unlearn the lessons of the nursery. Rather, he found a way to reconcile the seeming absurdity of modern life with Christian faith, hope, and love. In order to understand Percy's notion of the "ex-suicide" as a manifestation of his "Christian existentialism," we must grasp both its debt to European existentialism and its resistance to that philosophy's most popular and soulless propositions.

Coda

At this point, it should come as no surprise that Catholic writers continue to wrestle with the problem of suicide in their writing. Catholic neo-Decadent novelist Donna Tartt's *The Secret History* (1992), a kind of infernal American *Brideshead Revisited*, follows a group of privileged pseudo-pagan classics majors as they descend into deeper and deeper depravities. The novel concludes with a suicide, and Tartt, who explicitly eschews artificially dragging her faith into the lives of her creations, gives no hint that this suicide can be explained away or wiped out by God's mercy. Her characters have no sense that such a thing exists and no inclination to seek it out.

David Foster Wallace, who twice essayed a conversion to Catholicism and took his own life in 2008 after a long struggle with depression, wrote penetratingly about suicide on more than one occasion.[1] Wallace's final collection of short stories, *Oblivion* (2004), contains several stories involving suicide and coalesces around the story "Good Old Neon," which is narrated posthumously by an advertising executive who has driven his car into a bridge abutment. Having realized that his life, for all its material success, is effectively a fraud, and having exhausted the consolations of hedonism, Eastern meditation, charismatic Christianity, and psychological analysis, the narrator commits to suicide after an offhanded joke in an episode of the hit comedy *Cheers* reveals that even his suffering is a risible cliché. The story concludes with a moving address from the narrator to his author, Wallace himself, in which we get a glimpse of the author's desperate desire to understand intimately and

---

1. Andrew Bennett devotes the final chapter of *Suicide Century* to Wallace's work.

sympathetically the suffering of another mind seemingly so unlike his own but still drawn to the same dark place.

Another American author in the postmodern mode, Cormac McCarthy (1933–2023), wrestled with suicidal ideation and dealt with the subject in his fiction. McCarthy, a lapsed Catholic whose religious upbringing continued to animate his novels in subtle ways throughout his career, had little time in his work for redemption and salvation but gave profound attention to humanity's fallen nature and propensity for evil. The mother in *The Road* (2006), which is arguably McCarthy's most religiously preoccupied novel, decides to take her own life rather than face the horrors of the postapocalyptic wasteland her world has become. McCarthy does not condemn her for this act, which he hints may have been partly inspired by a desire to improve the odds of survival for her husband and son, but his novel celebrates the valor of carrying the flame of life and goodness in a seemingly God-forsaken world. The challenge of suicide appeared again at the end of his career in the companion novels *The Passenger* and *Stella Maris* (2022). A suicide serves as the nexus of the two novels about a pair of brilliant but disturbed siblings navigating life in the nuclear age brought about in part by their father.

Catholic author Alice McDermott's 2017 novel, *The Ninth Hour*, opens with the suicide of a working-class husband and father and traces the generational impact of this trauma. Though McDermott effectively rejects orthodox teaching on suicide, and nearly everything else, over the course of the novel, the finally unsatisfactory nature of this heterodox vision is itself instructive. Christopher Beha's equally challenging *What Happened to Sophie Wilder* (2012) provides a more compelling exploration of the mind and personality of a suicidal Catholic. Written prior to Beha's reversion to Catholicism, the novel questions easy pieties about suffering but, I believe, also ratifies the Catholic understanding of suffering and forgiveness. Beha's heroine succumbs to despair in the aftermath of committing a terrible sin and takes her own life. Her friend and sometime lover Charlie Blakeman, a lapsed Catholic and struggling author, concludes the novel with a vision of redemptive hope by reimagining her final decision as a difficult but salvific turn to cloistered religious life.

Both Beha and McDermott, like Greene before them, trouble a perhaps simplistic and overly legalistic understanding of suicide. They dare hope, to borrow from Hans Urs von Balthasar, that all men will be saved. This impulse strikes me as laudable to a point, but I fear that, at least in McDermott's case, it conceals something of a devil's bargain. Without commenting on the mystery of God's particular judgement, we can comment on the dangerous slide from an appropriately tragic sense of pity and fear in the face of grave sin to a perhaps prideful or presumptuous sense of mercy. If we can understand and forgive the suicide, surely God can. Perhaps, but such thinking quickly leads to a sweeping antinomianism. Beha saves his work from this slide by giving the clear impression that such things as God, sin, and salvation exist as more than cultural constructs. I am not sure that McDermott does the same, but both of their novels deserve a fuller treatment than I can provide here.

Furnishing a more detailed reading of the many works of Catholic literature that have taken up this subject of suicide since Walker Percy would take me beyond the scope of this project. My goal was never to provide an exhaustive catalogue; instead, I wanted to bring my readers into contact with those great modern artists whose specifically Catholic vision might offer, if not solutions to our epidemic of self-destruction, at least some wisdom. Wisdom holds out the offer of comfort and consolation; it also guarantees a degree of fear and trembling. Though I'm hesitant to attempt to reduce or paraphrase the wisdom gleaned from the works of art explored in this book, I would like to at least attempt the task before closing.

I began with Houellebecq, whose work is closest to us chronologically, because I believed, and still do, that he has convincingly and truly diagnosed some of the main causes of our suicidal modernity. Particularly, his novels trace our suffering, and our misguided attempts to end or evade that suffering, back to the Western turn away from theism and toward materialism. His novels wallow in the alienation and atomization caused by this shift and reject the idea that we can somehow medicate or engineer our way out of this spiritual malady without ceasing to be human. They also suggest a negative way back to something like wholeness. If a materialist lie about who and what we are brought us to this point, a deeper anthropological truth—that we humans are a unique amalgam of body and spirit with real spiritual needs—can at least point us in the direction of salvation. Hopefully, those seeking a way out of the materialist horror portrayed in his novels, like the character Michel Houellebecq in *The Map and the Territory*, may be tempted to rediscover the religion that animated the Western world for two thousand years. Such a rediscovery may seem impossible in our century, but the truth is that a vital Christianity still exists and can still offer the spiritual sustenance so lacking in postmodern culture.

J. K. Huysmans and George Moore, in many ways Houellebecq's decadent forebearers, provide a helpful reminder that there is nothing particularly new about the content of the modern pessimistic philosophy that implicitly informs the lives of Houellebecq's doomed hedonists and suicidal geniuses. Houellebecq's breakout novel, *The Elementary Particles*, imagines the creation of a post-human world in which humanity has been willingly abolished and replaced by an engineered simulacrum of its own creation. Huysmans and Moore imagine exhausted hedonists espousing a far more comprehensive pessimist philosophy that dreams of an end to all sentient existence, a species suicide that would cleanse the world of individual suffering and the general plague of humanity. Unfortunately, this brand of extreme philosophical pessimism has found its way, however subtly, into the mainstream of our culture and convinced an increasing number of people that life, if not worth ending immediately, is at least not particularly worth continuing. Some have gone so far as to imagine the eradication of humanity as a net gain for global ecology. If we hope to combat the intellectual contagion of despair contained in this antinatalist worldview, we must realize that (individually and as a species) our choice remains that of both Des Esseintes and Mike Fletcher—the choice between the foot of the cross and the barrel of a gun. No third way, however banal or harmless, can hope to satisfy in the ultimate sense.

Intuiting this dilemma and its eschatological ramifications, Monsignor Robert Hugh Benson looked ahead to a dystopian future in which ordinary well-meaning people would espouse euthanasia as a foundational right of a new and demonic political regime. As what John Paul II called the "culture of death" continues its ascendancy and our daily reality comes into closer alignment with Benson's nightmare vision, we should return to his prescient novel for a clearer sense of what it really means to resist such a regime. For Benson, the answer is clear: we must fight the battle at the level of the individual soul, and that soul must turn for its sustenance to the wellspring of the spiritual life, prayer. This forgotten practice, though insufficient as a means of self-willed self-help or a gimmick of therapeutic wellness, offers a meaningful avenue of grace that is open to all, even those who make the tragic choice to take their own lives in a culture that has ceased to value the dignity of the individual soul.

Tolkien also stressed the importance of everyone in the grander narrative of his sub-created world. Unafraid as he was to follow characters like Turin into the depths of despair and tragedy, Tolkien provides a hopeful imaginative response to the problem of suicide. If asked to name one author whose work could help inoculate anyone against despair, I would turn to Tolkien. In our patently unheroic age, his work calls the most normal and unheroic people to reconceive their lives as adventures. The adventure of existence is often fraught with trials, and the seemingly inexorable power of evil can threaten to cause us to abandon hope and counsel despair; however, a moral imagination informed and enlivened by Tolkien's stories cannot help but be more resilient in the face of an often physically and psychologically painful existence. On the cosmic level, he re-presents the core Christian theological insight that one supreme and benevolent God allowed his free creatures to choose good or evil so that, in the fullness of providential time, the greatest and most noble of goods might be realized. On the local level, he envisions common Hobbits who persist through every kind of suffering in service to something larger than themselves. Not all of the stories in Tolkien's legendarium end happily. He understood the pagan sense of tragic existence and, refusing to cast out the good with the bad, drew the pagan notion of heroic excellence into the Christian vision of an ultimately comic worldview. If we want to resist a suicidal culture, we need stories that will instill in the hearts of the young a yearning for such heroism and a surety of such providence.

Having struggled from an early age with suicidal ideation and found some consolation in his conflicted Catholic faith, Graham Greene helps remind us of both the many potential failures of would-be heroes and the limitations of religious consolation to those experiencing the attraction of self-destruction. He also relentlessly stresses the mystery of God's mercy. Few people today are tempted to condemn suicides too quickly or presume to consign anyone to eternal perdition. In fact, our dominant cultural tendency is to refuse to even think of suicide as a sin or of damnation as a possibility. Greene's writing cuts against this grain by stressing the reality of sin and refusing to exempt suicide from that genus; however, his intensive exploration of the motives of his suicidal characters also drives home the needed corrective to this understanding. Sin is real. Suicide is a sin. But, as Dante knew, not every person who takes his own life has committed the sin of suicide, properly understood. Greene's novels repeatedly remind us that we should neither presume upon God's mercy by treating suicide as a tragic accident divorced from volition, nor presume to understand all the inmost working of the souls of those who make the terrible decision to end their own lives. Any wishing to heal our suicidal culture must be willing to unapologetically condemn the act as a violation of an objective moral order while ceaselessly reminding themselves of the mysteries of the human heart and appealing to God's fathomless mercy.

Greene also helps to draw attention to the martyr as a positive counterexample to hold up against that of the suicide. Martyrs, including the absurdly fallen whiskey priest, willing to lose their lives in service to God and others can help us to understand better the proper orientation towards death as something neither to be feared nor sought out. As we saw, Muriel Spark makes a profound contribution to this conversation by repeatedly highlighting the differences between the suicide and the martyr. Her work frames the former in terms of a perverse ego-drama that places the often vicious self at the center of a tiny cosmos. The latter, by contrast, emerges as part of a Theo-drama that understands the self as just one participatory actor in a much larger cosmic play. Spark, like most modern Catholic authors, tends to focus on the former, but she also reminds us that those living properly Theo-dramatic lives will seem strange and incomprehensible to us because they have aligned their lives with a supreme value that has become alien to most of our self-seeking, self-interested souls. Though her sardonic wit never allows Spark to embrace Tolkien's unapologetically heroic vision of human existence—you wouldn't really wish to be anyone in a Muriel Spark novel—she too offers to draw her readers into a much more consequential and meaningful sense of their own existence. Such a sense of meaningfulness remains one of our most likely defenses against despair.

Not everyone can be a martyr, of course. For most of us, the potential malaise of day-to-day existence presents a far more immediate adversary than any physical persecution at the hands of others. Reading Walker Percy will not make anyone feel better about the modern condition. He knew and gave voice to the quiet desperation experienced by so many in our age of abundance, license, and accompanying neurosis. Unwilling to submit to his seemingly predestined suicide, Percy went to the heart of our shared existential crisis and found God. That discovery didn't make him a saint, but it kept him alive. It also enabled him to compose novels that can take us to the edge of the abyss without, like so many works of the existentialist imagination, leaving us there to fight dragons without sword or armor. These novels remind us that we cannot simply pretend that modernity never happened. We are inheritors of our culture and must learn to engage authentically with its very real angst. The good news is that, like so many of Percy's characters, we are called to quest for a meaning that actually exists and to fulfill our ontological need with a hope that can be found in loving self-donation to other struggling selves.

Lame as these sweeping assertions are in relation to the works of art that inspired them, I hope that they may help some to internalize and articulate better the distinct and profoundly right Catholic response to the problem of suicide. Of course, even sympathetic readers of this book, readers who still think that art can both delight and instruct, would be justified if they questioned the efficacy of literature as a vehicle for wisdom. After all, does anyone even read any of these books? Admittedly, the impact of Catholic literature on our broader culture will always be limited, but, even in a society that has less and less time for books, it's encouraging to note that a kind of literary revival has taken place in the last two decades. New presses have emerged to give voice to new and profoundly gifted Catholic authors. At least one new MFA program in the United States has been designed explicitly to help emerging writers find a voice through and in the Catholic tradition.

Alongside this artistic revival, we are experiencing a global rebirth of classical education. As classical Catholic, Christian, and charter schools gain in popularity among parents and gain greater support from politicians who truly wish to promote the good of their people, increasing numbers of students of all backgrounds find themselves in schools that foreground great literature as a mode of knowing. These students are being trained to understand literature as an important ingredient in the examined and purposeful life, and many are also learning to disdain the oppressive vulgarities of mass culture, the products of which likely do more to increase societal depression than any economic or political factors. We may yet hold out hope that these grassroots cultural movements could lead to a larger cultural rebirth.

We also shouldn't kid ourselves. Even in the most healthy and integrated society, there will be those who decide that the only solution to life is to end it. In our fallen world, sin and suffering can never be wholly overcome by our efforts, but we should do what we can to foster a culture capable of providing all people with a sense of their fundamental importance. To achieve this, we must be willing to reject any mass culture that would reduce the human person to less than the image and likeness of God or attempt to replace traditional conceptions of the good life with banal fantasies born of the pleasure principle. Great literature (heck, even plain good literature) still offers the promise of helping to form individuals in wisdom toward such a good life. No one is saved by art; however, if it provides a momentary stay against despair and draws us into a vision of true, cosmic meaning and hope, however tinged with the raw realities of our suffering world, then we should cherish it. We should celebrate such art, share it with our loved ones, teach it in our schools, and find times in our own lives to contemplate it. If this small book can aid anyone in that process, then I am grateful.

Bibliography

Alighieri, Dante. *The Inferno*. Translated by Robert Hollander and Jean Hollander. New York: Anchor, 2002.

The American Foundation for Suicide Prevention. "What We've Learned Through Research." https://afsp.org/what-we-ve-learned-through-research.

Aquinas, Thomas. *Summa Theologiae*. Translated by Fathers of the English Dominican Province. New York: Benziger Brothers, 1911–1925.

Arendt, Hannah. *The Human Condition*. Chicago: The University of Chicago Press, 2018.

Austen, Jane. *Mansfield Park*. London: J. M. Dent and Sons, 1922.

Balthasar, Hans Urs von. *Theo-Drama: Theological Dramatic Theory Vol. I*. Translated by Graham Harrison. San Francisco: Ignatius, 1988.

Beckson, Karl. "Moore's *The Untilled Field* and Joyce's *Dubliners*: The Short Story's Intricate Maze." *English Literature in Transition, 1880-1920* 15:4 (1972) 291–304.

Benatar, David. *Better Never to Have Been: The Harm of Coming into Existence*. Oxford: Oxford University Press, 2006.

———. *The Human Predicament: A Candid Guide to Life's Biggest Questions*. Oxford: Oxford University Press, 2017.

Bennett, Andrew. *Suicide Century: Literature and Suicide from James Joyce to David Foster Wallace*. Cambridge: Cambridge University Press, 2017.

Benson, Robert Hugh. "Catholicism and the Future." In *A Book of Essays*, 1–16. Freeport, NY: Books for Libraries, 1968.

———. "Preface." In *Lord of the World*. London: Sir Isaac Pitman & Sons, 1907.

———. *Lord of the World*. London: Sir Isaac Pitman & Sons, 1907.

Betty, Louis. *Without God: Michel Houellbecq and Materialist Horror*. University Park: The Pennsylvania State University Press, 2016.

Birzer, Bradley J. *J. R. R. Tolkien's Sanctifying Myth: Understanding Middle-Earth*. Wilmington, DE: ISI, 2002.

Boer, Theo A., Ronald E. Bolwijn, Wim Graafland, and T. Theo J. Pleizier. "Legal Euthanasia in Pastoral Practice: Experiences of Pastors in the Protestant Church in the Netherlands." *International Journal of Public Theology* 14:1 (2020) 41–67.

Bogost, Ian. "What is Object-Oriented Ontology? A Definition for Ordinary Folk." http://bogost.com/writing/blog/what_is_objectoriented_ontolog/.

Brennan, Michael G. *Graham Greene: Fictions, Faith and Authorship*. New York: Continuum, 2010.

Burga, Solcyré, and Simmone Shah. "The History of Self-Immolation as Political Protest." *Time*, February 26, 2014. https://time.com/6835364/self-immolation-history-israel-hamas-war/.

Calfas, Jennifer, and Anthony DeBarros. "U.S. Fertility Rate Falls to Record Low." *The Wall Street Journal*, April 25, 2024. https://www.wsj.com/us-news/america-birth-rate-decline-a111d21b

Camus, Albert. *The Myth of Sisyphus*. Translated by Justin O'Brien. New York: Vintage, 2018.

———. *The Rebel: An Essay on Man in Revolt*. Translated by Anthony Bower. New York: Vintage, 1991.

The Centers for Disease Control. "Emergency Department Visits for Suspected Suicide Attempts Among Persons Aged 12–25 Years Before and During the COVID-19 Pandemic—United States, January 2019–May 2021." https://www.cdc.gov/mmwr/volumes/70/wr/mm7024e1.htm?campaign_id=9&emc=edit_nn_20220104&instance_id=49344&nl=the-morning&regi_id=120330962&segment_id=78602&te=1&user_id=3676184f5ce616ad2c6661dc96fd5392.

———. "Facts About Suicide." https://www.cdc.gov/suicide/facts/index.html.

———. "Suicide Data and Statistics." https://www.cdc.gov/suicide/suicide-data-statistics.html.

Chance, Jane. *The Lord of the Rings: The Mythology of Power*. Lexington: The University Press of Kentucky, 1992.

Chesterton, G. K. "A Ballade of Suicide." In *The Collected Poems of G. K. Chesterton*, 180. New York: Dodd and Mead, 1932.

———. *Orthodoxy*. New York: John Lane, 1909.

Cholbi, Michael. *Suicide: The Philosophical Dimensions*. Peterborough, ON: Broadview, 2011.

"David Benatar." The Exploring Antinatalism Podcast, March 2020. https://open.spotify.com/episode/3OSAJJTeQfkT2jxSU4PMFB.

Desmarais, Jane, and David Weir, eds. *Decadence and Literature*. Cambridge: Cambridge University Press, 2019.

Desmond, John F. *Fyodor Dostoevsky, Walker Percy, and the Age of Suicide*. Washington, DC: The Catholic University of America Press, 2019.

Dostoyevsky, Fyodor. *The Brothers Karamazov*. Translated by Constance Garnett, Random House, 1950.

Dreher, Rod. "France's Master Of 'Materialist Horror.'" *The American Conservative*, August 25, 2019. https://www.theamericanconservative.com/dreher/michel-houellebecq-master-materialist-horror-louis-betty/.

Durkheim, Émile. *Suicide: A Study in Sociology*. Translated by John A. Spaulding and George Simpson. Glencoe, IL: Free Press, 1951.

Eagleton, Terry. *Culture and the Death of God*. New Haven: Yale University Press, 2014.

Eakin, Emily. "Michel Houellebecq: Le Provocateur." *The New York Times*, September 10, 2001. https://www.nytimes.com/2001/09/10/magazine/michel-houellebecq-le-provocateur.html.

Edelman, Lee. *No Future: Queer Theory and the Death Drive*. Durham, NC: Duke University Press, 2004.

Elie, Paul. *The Life You Save May Be Your Own: An American Pilgrimage*. New York: Farrar, Straus and Giroux, 2004.

Eliot, T. S. "Baudelaire." In *Selected Prose of T. S. Eliot*, edited by Frank Kermode, 231–36. New York: Farrar, Straus and Giroux, 1975.

———. *The Complete Poems and Plays: 1909–1950*. New York: Harcourt Brace, 1971.

———. "Frances Herbert Bradley." In *The Selected Prose of T. S. Eliot*, edited by Frank Kermode, 196–204. New York: Farrar, Straus and Giroux, 1975.

———. *Murder in the Cathedral*. New York: Harcourt, Brace and Company, 1935.

Engelhart, Katie. *The Inevitable: Dispatches on the Right to Die*. New York: St. Martin's, 2021.

Exit International. "Exit Vision, Mission, and Values." https://www.exitinternational.net/about-exit/our-philosophy/.

Felski, Rita. "Suspicious Minds." *Poetics Today* 32:2 (2011) 215–34.

Fraizer, Adrian. *George Moore: 1852–1933*. New Haven: Yale University Press, 2000.

Freud, Sigmund. "Contributions to a Discussion on Suicide." *The Standard Edition of the Complete Psychological Works of Sigmund Freud*, Vol. 11, edited and translated by James Strachey, 231–32. London: Hogarth, 1974.

Friedman, Alan Warren. *Fictional Death and the Modernist Enterprise*. Cambridge: Cambridge University Press, 1995.

Gayle, Damien. "More People Not Having Children Due to Climate Breakdown Fears, Finds Research." *The Guardian*, November 9, 2023. https://www.theguardian.com/environment/2023/nov/09/more-people-not-having-children-due-to-climate-breakdown-fears-finds-research.

Girard, René. "The Gospel and Globalization." *New Perspectives Quarterly* 22:3 (2005) 59–64.

Greene, Graham. *The Comedians*. New York: Penguin, 2005.

———. *Conversations with Graham Greene*. Edited by Henry J. Donaghy. Jackson: University Press of Mississippi, 1992.

———. *Graham Greene: A Life in Letters*. Edited by Richard Greene. New York: Norton, 2007.

———. "Graham Greene: The Art of Fiction, No. 3." Interviewed by Simon Raven and Martin Shuttleworth. *The Paris Review* 3 (1953). https://www.theparisreview.org/interviews/5180/the-art-of-fiction-no-3-graham-greene.

———. *The Heart of the Matter*. London: Vintage, 2004.

———. *The Last Word and Other Stories*. London: Reinhardt, 1990.

———. *The Living Room*. New York: Viking, 1954.

———. *The Power and the Glory*. New York: Penguin, 2015.

———. *A Sort of Life*. New York: Simon and Schuster, 1971.

Greene, Richard. *The Unquiet Englishman: A Life of Graham Greene*. New York: Norton, 2021.

Grob, Alan. "'The Power and the Glory:' Graham Greene's Argument from Design." *Criticism* 11:1 (1969) 1–30.

Gross, Neil, and Solon Simmons. "The Religiosity of American College and University Professors." *Sociology of Religion* 70:2 (2009) 101–29.

Gulledge, Jo. "The Reentry Option: An Interview with Walker Percy." In *Conversations with Walker Percy*, edited by Lewis A. Lawson and Victor A. Kramer, 284–308. Jackson: University of Mississippi Press, 1985.

Harris, Sam. *The Moral Landscape: How Science Can Determine Human Values.* New York: Free Press, 2010.

Hart, David Bentley. *Atheist Delusions: The Christian Revolution and Its Fashionable Enemies.* New Haven: Yale University Press, 2009.

Hedegaard, Holly, Sally Curtin, and Margaret Warner. "Increase in Suicide Mortality in the United States, 1999–2018." *NCHS Data Brief, no 362.* Hyattsville, MD: National Center for Health Statistics, 2020.

Hext, Kate, and Alex Murray, eds. *Decadence in the Age of Modernism.* Baltimore: Johns Hopkins University Press, 2019.

Holmes, John R. "'Like Heathen Kings': Religion as Palimpsest in Tolkien's Fiction." In *The Ring and the Cross: Christianity and the Lord of the Rings,* edited by Paul E. Kerry, 119–44. Madison, NJ: Fairleigh Dickinson University Press, 2010.

Hortmann, Wilhelm. "Graham Greene: The Burnt-Out Catholic." *Twentieth Century Literature* 10:2 (July 1964) 64–76.

Houellebecq, Michel. *The Elementary Particles.* Translated by Frank Wynne. New York: Vintage, 2000.

———. "Houellebecq, Tocqueville, Democracy." YouTube video, posted September 11, 2011, 7 min., 14 sec. https://www.youtube.com/watch?v=ZtiJQZTqu9M.

———. *Interventions: 2020.* Translated by Andrew Brown. Cambridge: Polity, 2020.

———. *The Map and the Territory.* Translated by Gavin Bowd. New York: Alfred A. Knopf, 2012.

———. *Serotonin.* Translated by Shaun Whiteside. New York: Farrar, Straus and Giroux, 2019.

———. *Submission.* Translated by Lorin Stein. New York: Picador, 2016.

Houellebecq, Michel, and Geoffroy Lejeune. "Restoration: An Exchange of Views on Religion." *First Things,* May 2019. https://www.firstthings.com/article/2019/05/restoration.

Huysmans, J. K. *Against Nature.* Translated by Robert Baldick. New York: Penguin, 2003.

———. "Preface, Written Twenty Years After the Novel." In *Against Nature,* translated by Robert Baldick, 205–17. New York: Penguin, 2003.

Hynes, Joseph. "The 'Facts' at The Heart of the Matter." *Texas Studies in Literature and Language* 13:4 (1972) 711–26.

John Paul II. *Evangelium Vitae: Encyclical Letter of Pope John Paul II.* Boston: Pauline, 1995.

———. *Tertio Millennio Adveniente* [Apostolic Letter to the Bishops, Clergy, and Lay Faithful on Preparation for the Jubilee of the Year 2000]. The Holy See, November 10, 1994. https://www.vatican.va/content/john-paul-ii/en/apost_letters/1994/documents/hf_jp-ii_apl_19941110_tertio-millennio-adveniente.html.

Kehl, Medard S. J. "Introduction: Hans Urs von Balthasar, A Portrait." In *The Von Balthasar Reader,* edited by Medard Kehl and Werner Löser, translated by Robert J. Daly and Fred Lawrence, 1–55. New York: Herder & Herder, 1997.

Kerry, Paul E. "A Historiography of Christian Approaches to Tolkien's *The Lord of the Rings.*" In *The Ring and the Cross Christianity and The Lord of the Rings,* edited by Paul E. Kerry, 17–56. Madison, NJ: Fairleigh Dickinson University Press, 2010.

Kreeft, Peter. *The Philosophy of Tolkien: The Worldview Behind The Lord of the Rings.* San Francisco: Ignatius, 2005.

Kierkegaard, Søren. *Fear and Trembling* and *The Sickness Unto Death*. Translated by Walter Lowrie. Princeton: Princeton University Press, 1974.

Leary, Robyn. "Surviving His Own Bad Habits: A Previously Unpublished Interview with Walker Percy.", *Doubletake Magazine* 19 (2000). https://www.doubletakemagazine.org/int/html/percy/.

Lewis, C. S. *The Abolition of Man or Reflections on Education with Special Reference to the Teaching of English in the Upper Forms of Schools*. San Francisco: Harper, 2000.
———. *Mere Christianity*. New York: Harper One, 2001.

Llewellyn, Mark. "Masculinity, Materialism, and the Introjected Self in George Moore's *Mike Fletcher*." *English Literature in Transition, 1880–1920* 48:2 (2005) 131–46.

MacIntyre, Alasdair. *After Virtue*. Notre Dame: University of Notre Dame Press, 2007.

MacLeod, Kirsten. *Fictions of British Decadence: High Art, Popular Writing and the Fin De Siécle*. London: Palgrave Macmillan, 2006.

Mahowald, M. W., C. H. Schneck, M. Goldner, V. Bachelder, and M. Cramer-Bornemann. "Parasomnia Pseudo-Suicide." *The Journal of Forensic Science* 48:5 (2003) 1158–62.

Marcel, Gabriel. "Existence and Human Freedom." In *The Philosophy of Existentialism*, 47–90. New York: Citadel, 2002.
———. "Introduction." In *The Philosophy of Existentialism*, 5–6. New York: Citadel, 2002
———. "On the Ontological Mystery." In *The Philosophy of Existentialism*, 9–46. New York: Citadel, 2002.
———. "Testimony and Existentialism." In *The Philosophy of Existentialism*, 91–103. New York: Citadel, 2002.

Martindale, Cyril Charlie. *The Life of Monsignor Robert Hugh Benson, Volume 2*. London: Longmans, Green, 1916.

McNamara, Fr. Edward. "Funeral Masses for a Suicide." *EWTN*, November 2005. https://www.ewtn.com/catholicism/library/funeral-masses-for-a-suicide-4296.

McQueen, Fraser. "Zombie Catholicism Meets Zombie Islam: Reading Michel Houellebecq's *Soumission* with Emmanuel Todd." *Forum for Modern Language Studies* 56:2 (2020) 155–76.

Miller, J. Michael. "Guidelines Regarding the Funeral Rites for Those Who Have Asked for Euthanasia or Physician-Assisted Suicide." Archdiocese of Vancouver, September 14, 2017. https://rcav.org/policies/661.

Miller, Walter M. *A Canticle for Leibowitz*. New York: Bantam, 1961.

Moncrieff, Joanna, et al. "The Serotonin Theory of Depression: A Systematic Umbrella Review of the Evidence." *Molecular Psychiatry* 28:8 (2023) 3243–56.

Moore, George. *Mike Fletcher: A Novel*. London: Ward and Downey, 1889.

Murphy, Michael P. "*Tantum Ergo*: Fury Destroys the World." In *Lord of the World*, xvii–xxiv. Notre Dame, IN: Ave Maria, 2016.

Murray, Alex, ed. *Decadence: A Literary History*. Cambridge: Cambridge University Press, 2019.

Murray, S. J. "Thanatopolitics." In *Bloomsbury Handbook to Literary and Cultural Theory*, edited by J. R. Di Leo, 718–19. London: Bloomsbury, 2018.

The New Criterion. "False Advertising." October 2000. https://newcriterion.com/issues/2000/10/false-advertising.

Nietzsche, Friedrich. *The Complete Works of Friedrich Nietzsche*. Vol. 8. Edited by Oscar Levy. New York: Macmillan, 1911.

Ohi, Kevin. *Innocence and Rapture: The Erotic Child in Pater, Wilde, James, and Nabokov.* London: Palgrave, 2005.

Omelianchuk, Adam. "*The Moral Landscape* (A Review)." *First Things,* July 16, 2011. https://www.firstthings.com/blogs/firstthoughts/2011/07/the-moral-landscape-a-review.

Orwell, George. *1984.* New York: Everyman's Library, 1992.

Panayotov, Stanimir. "Heart's Unreason: A Reading of Edelman's Anti-Futurism through Bataille." *Identities: Journal for Politics, Gender and Culture* 8:1 (2011) 129–38.

Percy, Walker. *Conversations with Walker Percy.* Edited by Lewis A. Lawson and Victoria A. Kramer. Jackson: University Press of Mississippi, 1985.

———. *Lost in the Cosmos.* New York: Picador, 1983.

———. *The Moviegoer.* New York: Vintage, 1998.

———. *The Second Coming.* New York: Picador, 1980.

———. "Stoicism in the South: Epictetus or the Psalms?" *Commonweal,* July 6, 1956. https://www.commonwealmagazine.org/stoicism-south.

Perry, Sarah. *Every Cradle Is a Grave: Rethinking the Ethics of Birth and Suicide.* Charleston, WV: Nine-Banded, 2014.

Pieper, Josef. *The Concept of Sin.* Translated by Edward T. Oakes. South Bend, IN: St. Augustine, 2001.

———. *Leisure the Basis of Culture.* Translated by Alexander Dru. Carmel, IN: Liberty Fund, 1999.

Preston, Alex. "Submission by Michel Houellebecq Review—Satire That's More Subtle than It Seems." *The Guardian,* September 8, 2015. https://www.theguardian.com/books/2015/sep/08/ submission-michel-houellebecq-review-satire-islamic-france.

R/antinatalism. "How Do You Feel About Blowing up the World?" Reddit, August 22, 2018. https://www.reddit.com/r/antinatalism/comments/99cyjh/how_do_you_feel_about_blowing_up_the_world/.

Ricoeur, Paul. *Freud and Philosophy: An Essay on Interpretation.* Translated by Denis Savage. New Haven: Yale University Press, 1970.

Rieff, Philip. *The Triumph of the Therapeutic: Uses of Faith after Freud.* Wilmington, DE: ISI, 2006.

Rosenberg, Randall S. "Walker Percy and the Racist Tragedy of Southern Stoicism." *Church Life Journal: A Journal of the McGrath Institute for Church Life,* June, 25, 2018. https://www.commonwealmagazine.org/stoicism-south.

Rosmarin, David H. "Psychiatry Needs to Get Right with God." *Scientific American,* June 15, 2021. https://www.scientificamerican.com/article/psychiatry-needs-to-get-right-with-god/.

Rothman, Joshua. "The Case for Not Being Born: The Anti-Natalist Philosopher David Benatar Argues That It Would Be Better If No One Had Children Ever Again." *The New Yorker,* November 27, 2017. https://www.newyorker.com/culture/persons-of-interest/the-case-for-not-being-born.

Sampson, Martyn. *Between Form and Faith: Graham Greene and the Catholic Novel.* New York: Fordham University Press, 2021.

Sartre, Jean-Paul. *Literary and Philosophical Essays of Jean-Paul Sartre.* Translated by Annette Michelson. New York: Criterion, 1955.

Schaffner, Anna Katharina. "On 'Cosmic Insignificance Therapy.'" *Psychology Today*, January 23, 2024. https://www.psychologytoday.com/us/blog/the-art-of-self-improvement/202401/on-cosmic-insignificance-therapy.

Schopenhauer, Arthur. *The World as Will and Idea*. Translated by R. B. Haldane and J. Kemp. London: Kegan Paul, Trench, Trubner & Co., 1910.

Sherry, Vincent. *Modernism and the Reinvention of Decadence*. Cambridge: Cambridge University Press, 2014.

Shneidman, Edwin S. "Letter to the Editor, Rational Suicide and Psychiatric Disorders." *The New England Journal of Medicine* 326:13 (1992) 888–89.

———. *The Suicidal Mind*. Oxford: Oxford University Press, 1996.

Spark, Muriel. *A Far Cry from Kensington*. London: Penguin, 1988.

———. *The Girls of Slender Means*. New York: Alfred A. Knopf, 1963.

———. *The Informal Air: Essays by Muriel Spark*. Edited by Penelope Jardine. New York: New Directions, 2014.

———. *The Public Image*. New York: Alfred A. Knopf, 1968.

Stannard, Martin. *Muriel Spark: The Biography*. New York: Norton, 2010.

Sterling, Grant C. "'The Gift of Death': Tolkien's Philosophy of Mortality." *Mythlore* 21:4 (1997) 16–18.

Steward, Samuel. "J. K. Huysmans and George Moore." *Romantic Review* 25 (1934) 197–206.

Taylor, Matthew A. "Life's Return: Hylozoism, Again." *PMLA* 135:3 (2020) 474–91.

Tocqueville, Alexis de. *Democracy in America Volume II*. New York: Alfred A. Knopf, 1956.

Tolkien, J. R. R. *The Letters of J. R. R. Tolkien*. Edited by Humphrey Carpenter and Christopher Tolkien. Boston: Houghton Mifflin, 2000.

———. *The Lord of the Rings*. 50th Anniversary ed. Boston: Houghton Mifflin, 2004.

———. "On Fairy-Stories." In *The Monsters and the Critics and Other Essays*, 109–161. London: Harper Collins, 2006.

———. *The Shaping of Middle-Earth: The Quenta, the Ambarkanta and the Annals (The History of Middle-Earth, Vol. 4)*. Edited by Christopher Tolkien. New York: Del Rey, 1995.

———. *The Silmarillion*. Edited by Christopher Tolkien. Boston: Houghton Mifflin, 1999.

Tolson, Jay. *Pilgrim in the Ruins: A Life of Walker Percy*. New York: Simon & Schuster, 1992.

Ward, Michael. *After Humanity: A Guide to C. S. Lewis's The Abolition of Man*. Park Ridge, IL: Word on Fire Academic, 2021.

Whitt, Richard J. "Germanic *Fate* and *Doom* in J. R. R. Tolkien's *The Silmarillion*." *Mythlore* 29:1 (2010) 115–29.

Wood, Ralph C. "Confronting the World's Weirdness: J. R. R. Tolkien's *The Children of Húrin*." In *The Ring and the Cross: Christianity and the Lord of the Rings*, edited by Paul E. Kerry, 145–51. Madison, NJ: Fairleigh Dickinson University Press, 2010.

———. "Lest the World's Amnesia Be Complete: A Reading of Walter Miller's *A Canticle for Leibowitz*." *Religion and Literature* 33:1 (2001) 23–41.

World Health Organization. "Psychiatrists Working in Mental Health Sector (per 100,000)." https://www.who.int/data/gho/data/indicators/indicator-details/GHO/psychiatrists-working-in-mental-health-sector-(per-100-000).

————. "Suicide Mortality Rate (per 100,000 Population)." https://data.who.int/indicators/i/16BBF41.

Yeats, W. B. "Introduction." In *The Oxford Book of Modern Verse 1892–1935*, edited by W. B. Yeats, v–xlii. Oxford: Clarendon, 1947.

Zeugner, John F. "Walker Percy and Gabriel Marcel: The Castaway and the Wayfarer." *The Mississippi Quarterly* 28:1 (1974–75) 21–53.

Zhang, Sarah. "The Last Children of Down Syndrome." *The Atlantic*, December, 2020. https://www.theatlantic.com/magazine/archive/2020/12/the-last-children-of-down-syndrome/616928/.

Zia-Ebrahimi, Reza. "There is No Islamophobic Elephant in This Room: A Reflection on Houellebecq's Submission and Its Reception." *ReOrient: The Journal of Critical Muslim Studies*. https://www.criticalmuslimstudies.co.uk/there-is-no-islamophobic-elephant-in-this-room-a-reflection-on-houellebecqs-submission-and-its-reception/.

Index